**He eyed the**

"Of course I'll hold him," he said, taking the boy. Again, the curious blue eyes latched onto Jesse's face, and he couldn't help but smile. Wyatt wouldn't look at him for so long and for so hard if he didn't like what he saw, right? That seemed like a plus.

*My son likes me.*

Wyatt suddenly reached up his arm and grabbed hold of Jesse's ear. The expression slightly changed to something of a smile.

"Whoa there, little guy," Jesse said. "That's some grip."

Lila laughed and slipped out of her jacket. She sat on the bench to take off her boots. "Forgot to mention that. He's a grabber. He likes ears, swatches of hair, earrings, necklaces and noses. Learned my lesson about the hair and jewelry, but nothing I can do about the nose."

As if on cue, Wyatt let go of Jesse's ear and grabbed hold of his nose, which made Jesse laugh.

"Okay, all set," Lila said, holding out her arms for the baby.

But Jesse suddenly didn't want to let him go.

Dear Reader,

For years, cowboy Jesse Dawson has moved from one ranch to the next, never committing to anyone or anything. Until he discovers he has a three-month-old son he never knew existed. The legal guardian is the twin sister of the baby's late mother. Lila Mack and her relatives are worried that Jesse will take little Wyatt away and leave them heartbroken.

But instead, Jesse makes a few promises. To commit to fatherhood and take good care of his son—alongside Lila. To help her with the fledgling goat farm that's the baby's legacy. And to give both her and his baby a merry Christmas. But putting down roots isn't easy for the drifting cowboy.

I hope you enjoy Jesse and Lila's love story. I love to hear from readers, so feel free to reach out to me with questions and comments. You can find my contact info and more information about me and my books at melissasenate.com.

Happy holidays!

*Melissa Senate*

# THE COWBOY'S
# CHRISTMAS
# REDEMPTION

## MELISSA SENATE

**Harlequin**

**SPECIAL EDITION**

Recycling programs for this product may not exist in your area.

ISBN-13: 978-1-335-40208-0

The Cowboy's Christmas Redemption

Copyright © 2024 by Melissa Senate

Harlequin Enterprises ULC
22 Adelaide St. West, 41st Floor
Toronto, Ontario M5H 4E3, Canada
www.Harlequin.com

**Printed in Lithuania**

MIX
Paper | Supporting responsible forestry
FSC® C021394

**Melissa Senate** has written many novels for Harlequin and other publishers, including her debut, *See Jane Date*, which was made into a TV movie. She also wrote seven books for Harlequin Special Edition under the pen name Meg Maxwell. Her novels have been published in over twenty-five countries. Melissa lives on the coast of Maine with her son; their rescue shepherd mix, Flash; and a lap cat named Cleo. For more information, please visit her website, melissasenate.com.

### Books by Melissa Senate

### Harlequin Special Edition

### *Dawson Family Ranch*

*For the Twins' Sake*
*Wyoming Special Delivery*
*A Family for a Week*
*The Long-Awaited Christmas Wish*
*Wyoming Cinderella*
*Wyoming Matchmaker*
*His Baby No Matter What*
*Heir to the Ranch*
*Santa's Twin Surprise*
*The Cowboy's Mistaken Identity*
*Seven Birthday Wishes*
*Snowbound with a Baby*
*Triplets Under the Tree*
*The Rancher Hits the Road*
*The Cowboy's Christmas Redemption*

Visit the Author Profile page
at Harlequin.com for more titles.

In memory of my mother.

# *Chapter One*

On this mild afternoon for Wyoming in December, Jesse Dawson sat on a bench outside Bear Ridge Park, sipping his take-out coffee and trying to rationalize what he was about to do.

Which was leave town.

He had everything he owned in the back of his pickup—a few duffel bags—and planned to head northwest toward Yellowstone. A large cattle ranch was hiring experienced cowboys, and that was Jesse. The job came with room and board—a small cabin and all the chili he could eat in the ranch cafeteria. He'd chosen this particular ranch because the foreman required employees to sign a Code of the West contract, a one-page document calling for integrity, honor and the golden rule, all of which Jesse tried to live by. No lazybones, work shirkers, liars or jerks-at-heart need apply. He figured he'd stay six months, the minimum, then move on again, as he'd been doing since he was eighteen.

But now there was a monkey wrench.

His father, who'd died last December, had summoned him back to Bear Ridge this morning—in the form of an actual lawyer—to receive an inheritance: a letter that had

Jesse tied up in knots and sitting on this bench instead of hitting the road.

> *Jesse,*
> *I have some last wishes for you.*
> *1. Put down roots—right here in your hometown.*
> *2. Welcome love into your life (marriage and family). It's out there, waiting for you.*
> *3. Adopt a dog. Truly man's best friend and a great listener.*
> *4. Don't make my mistakes. I wish I'd been more of a father.*
> *5.*

Jesse took a long slug of his coffee and looked around to distract himself from thinking about any of that. Or what his dad had planned to write for #5. Jesse would never know.

When around, Eddie Dawson had been a great father. More in the fun, adventurous way than in caring if Jesse went to bed at a reasonable hour or ate any vegetables, which had been fine with Jesse, of course. He'd pull Jesse out of school to go fishing for the day or camping right in the middle of the week, looming math tests and five-paragraph essays not a concern.

His dad would leave for months on end to earn money as a cowboy, then return with a small windfall and slip some cash and gifts to the half-resentful but loving aunt who'd taken Jesse in. When his dad was in town, they'd stay at a boarding house with bunk beds in the one-room efficiency, Eddie's stories about the cowboy life happily lulling Jesse to sleep with dreams of becoming a cowboy himself. There were plenty of ranches in Bear Ridge, Wyoming, but Eddie couldn't seem to stay in one place too long. He'd bring Jesse treasures from his travels, little things that had meant the world to Jesse as a kid.

He'd always known his father was thinking about him, that Eddie Dawson had loved him. Jesse had seen his dad as an adventurer.

His father's motto had been never make a promise you couldn't keep, then you'd never let anyone down. Jesse's aunt, who'd had it with her brother and his lack of dependability and refusal to grow up and raise his son "right," would shake her head at Eddie Dawson's supposed words of wisdom. His father *had* made one promise—his wedding vows, which he'd taken very seriously, to Jesse's mother, who had died young in an accident, their baby son barely three years old. According to his aunt, grief and shock over the loss had done a number on Eddie, and he'd figured his son was better off with her for months at a time. He always came back.

Sixty-year-old Eddie Dawson died of prostate cancer with little to his name. A black Stetson and a black leather jacket, which Jesse treasured and had worn for the past year. A plain gold wedding band, engraved with his and Jesse's mother's initials. Jesse had been surprised to find the ring in his father's wallet—also containing a small, dog-eared baby picture of Jesse and forty-two dollars and fifty-seven cents. And a backpack with a change of clothes, a bar of soap in a plastic case, a razor, shaving cream and lip balm.

Possessions, memories, thoughts that all brought a lump to Jesse's throat. And small-town Bear Ridge, decked out for Christmas with festive lights and garlands on every lamppost, every storefront, just like it had been when he'd last held his frail father's hand, had him itching to leave. Bah humbug.

Jesse drained his coffee and watched a family of three—mother, father, toddler bundled up in a pink snowsuit between them with a hand in each of theirs—heading into the park, the parents swinging the girl up with an "Upsy-daisy" and getting a delighted "Again!" in response.

Not any kind of a distraction from his thoughts.

*Sorry, Dad, but that wasn't you, and it's not going to be me, either*, he thought as the mom and dad swung the toddler up in the air again. Family life, commitment, promises—that was all good for other people. It just wasn't Jesse Dawson.

Roots, love, a dog. He shook his head. That wasn't him either.

He crumpled his coffee cup and let out a hard sigh.

Jesse would be thirty next month. He still couldn't see himself as someone's husband, someone's father. How could he regret avoiding commitment to anyone or anything when it wasn't in his blood, in his veins? Wasn't that part of the Code of the West—not to lie or make false promises? He was his father's son, wasn't he? His last girlfriend used to shake her head at him and remind him that Jesse's aunt had been plenty loving and responsible and had instilled good values in him, so why focus only on how his father lived his life? Jesse used to think about that late at night, when he couldn't sleep. It was a good question.

He'd worked hard to let that girlfriend in, to commit for the first time, but she'd ended up betraying him with a guy he'd considered a friend. Since then, two years ago now, he'd had no interest in commitment or even waking up beside a woman, no matter how much he'd enjoyed her company. He'd leave a warm bed just after pumpkin hour, making an excuse or just stealing away. *Never make a promise you can't keep, then you'll never let anyone down...*

"Again!" The little girl was shouting gleefully for another swing up. Jesse couldn't remember ever being with both his parents. He didn't remember his mom at all.

His gaze moved from the family to his silver pickup in the small lot. Time to go.

Not that he was getting up. His body felt like lead.

*Listen, Dad*, he said silently, looking heavenward at the bright blue sky, *I know you had regrets.* They'd talked a little about them that final day, which had been all they'd had together. *But I'm not ready for roots. Or love. Or even a dog.*

A bark from a Border collie with a red-and-green collar snared his attention. Even the dogs were decorated for the holidays in Bear Ridge. A reminder that he had to get going, leave his memories behind. The dog stood on the driver's seat of a black SUV in the lot of the feed store adjacent to the park. His tail swished back and forth at his owner coming, a woman in a Santa hat with a baby in a carrier strapped to her red jacket.

This town was just too family-oriented. With too many dogs. And way too much Christmas. He didn't belong here, couldn't stay here.

*Time to go*, he thought, standing up. *Sorry, Dad, but—*

As the woman with the baby got closer, he froze.

He knew her.

Or had.

She was approaching the black SUV, pulling a dolly behind her with a big bag of goat feed.

Kate.

The baby, a few months old, maybe, also wore a Santa hat. Even from where he sat, Jesse could see the dark wisps under the white furry brim, and startling blue eyes.

But it was the small round pin glinting in the bright sunshine on the baby's snowsuit that sent Jesse to his feet.

A bronze horse.

He also knew that pin. He knew it because he'd won it at a rodeo game years ago and had tucked it in his wallet as a lucky charm, a talisman of sorts. And when he'd met Kate a year ago and woke up naked beside her in her bed at close to 2:00 a.m., he'd been in his usual hurry to get away, but something had caused him to take that pin out of his wallet and leave it on the table. He'd never done something like that before. He'd certainly never left his name or phone number. But he'd left that pin and he'd never been entirely sure why.

He stared hard at the pin. Why would Kate have put it on the baby's—

Wait. Whoa.

No.

He dropped back down on the bench, then bolted up.

The baby. A few months old.

He knew exactly when he'd had that one-night stand with Kate. The night of his father's funeral last December—four people hastily in attendance, including the lawyer—when he'd been so unsettled. He'd driven around and noticed a bar and headed in. A pretty young woman was sitting by herself, eating a burger and fries and reading a book on animal husbandry. He'd nodded at her, not planning on even saying hello, but she'd offered him a french fry and they'd started talking about the book and ranching. Next thing he knew, an hour had passed. And they'd left together.

Now, she had a baby. Who looked to be a few months old.

Who had *his* coloring. The dark hair, the blue eyes when Kate's hair was auburn, her eyes green.

And the pin on his snowsuit.

The baby could be his. Twelve months ago. Minus nine months of pregnancy. Equaled a baby who'd be three months.

Now, Kate's gaze landed on his because he was staring at her, but in seconds she turned back to her task as if she didn't know him. Or recognize him in the slightest. He supposed he deserved that.

His heart hammering, Jesse started walking over to her, to them, staring at the baby the closer he got. The little guy not only had his coloring and his pin but he looked a lot like Jesse. The shape of the eyes. Something in the expression.

He swallowed hard past the new lump forming in his throat. "Kate," he said, and for a moment that was all he could manage.

She looked at him, the big feed bag in her arms now. There was something tired and weary in the green eyes. "I'm not Kate."

He hadn't expected that. Pretending she didn't know him, sure. But straight-out lying that she wasn't who he knew she was? Maybe she held a grudge over the way he'd left in the middle of the night.

He took the bag of feed from her and loaded it into the back of the SUV, then turned to her. "Kate, it's me—Jesse," he said, removing his Stetson and holding it against his chest.

Her eyes widened in surprise and she let out something of a gasp.

He looked at the baby in the stroller, his heart starting to pound. He tried to speak, to ask the question, but no words came out.

Lila Mack gaped at the man standing inches away from her. A carbon copy of her three-month-old nephew.

Lila didn't know much about Wyatt's father; she knew only what her sister had shared, which wasn't much other than his name.

Jesse.

Ooh, this cowboy, Kate had texted to her when he'd gone to the bar to order food for the table they'd moved to five minutes after meeting. Jesse. Six foot two. Built. Gorgeous. The warmest blue eyes. Strong, silent type, not interested in asking or answering questions, except about ranching. Gave me great tips on raising goats.

Have a good time but be careful! Lila, ever cautious, had texted back.

Turned out that Kate had had a *great* time but hadn't been careful. Her twin had been trying to let loose, do things she'd never normally do, like pick up a handsome cowboy in the bar she was working at part-time as a waitress—and take him home. Kate hadn't gotten his last name, likely because he hadn't offered it.

Lila had gotten a panicked call from her sister early the next morning because when she'd picked up her shirt off the floor where he'd tossed it, there was a *wrapped* condom packet under it. Apparently, when things had started heating up, the cowboy had taken a condom from his wallet and placed it beside the pillow. But between being very tipsy and very attracted to each other, the condom, likely knocked off the bed in the heat of passion, had been clearly forgotten.

If her sister hadn't seen the gold-foil-wrapped packet when she'd picked up her shirt, she would have thought they'd used a condom. Kate had figured the cowboy had thought so too. At least Kate had wanted to believe that, she'd told Lila later. Maybe he *had* noticed the wrapped condom there on the floor. Maybe that had been the reason he'd left in the middle of the night—no note, no number. Kate hadn't been sure.

All he'd left was the pin.

Six weeks after, her period, normally like clockwork, was *late*. Kate had stood with her nervous twin in the tiny bathroom of the studio apartment she rented above the Bear Ridge Bakery, Kate's eyes closed as the two-minute mark passed. *You look*, she'd said to Lila.

Lila had peered at the white stick of the home pregnancy test that was resting on the bathroom counter. The bright orange X was unmistakable.

*I don't even know his last name*, Kate had said, tears in her eyes. *I just have this*, she'd added, pulling the little pin of the bronze horse from her wallet. *That's all I have of my baby's father. That's all the baby will have of him.*

After a bracing hug and assuring her twin that everything would be all right, Lila had said, *The pin is* something, *though. And everything else aside, you told me your night with him was magical, that if you never did see him again, you'd remember it very fondly. That's something too.*

Kate *had* never seen her cowboy again. Her nerves and fears about being a single mother had given way to excitement as the months had gone by. Their mother and grandmother had been so supportive, Lila there every step of the way for her sister, sticky-noting what to expect in the pregnancy book, attending Lamaze classes, being Kate's birth partner and watching her dear nephew come into the world, squawking with every bit of his eight pounds, three ounces.

Kate had loved her baby boy so, so much. She'd attached the pin to his fleece bunting and had said: *That's your Daddy's. And now you'll always have a piece of him.* She'd never mentioned Jesse No-Last-Name or their one-night stand again. But Lila knew that pin gave her a measure of peace about the whole thing.

And then a rain-slicked road and a dark curve, and Kate was gone. Wyatt just one month old.

"I'm sorry about the way I just left," the man—Jesse—said, breaking into Lila's thoughts and the memory. "I'd just lost—" He seemed to catch himself offering up personal information and stopped talking, dropping back a little.

*You just lost what?* she wondered. *A bet? All your money gambling?* Or maybe someone close to him. She stared at him, oddly curious. Maybe not so oddly; her nephew, who she was raising now and had for the past two months, was *half* him.

Lila knew all about loss. Her grief over her sister's

death was still so raw—as though she'd gotten the news of the accident this morning. A hole in her heart that would never be filled. There were moments when she was so aware of how much she loved her baby nephew that the hole's edges felt less ragged. She was so blessed to have Wyatt. She knew it was the same for her parents and grandmother.

Lila's hands went protectively around the front of the carrier that secured the precious boy to her. "I'm not Kate," she said again, gently this time. "I'm her identical twin sister. My name is Lila."

His blue eyes narrowed as he peered at her. Closely.

And because this man was the last person on earth, the last person in Bear Ridge, anyway, not to know that her sister had died, for a second it was as if Kate was still alive. Still here, running errands on an ordinary Friday afternoon. Her twin was in the feed store, buying some last-minute goat treats before she and Lila would head back to the Double Sisters Farm. Lila wasn't guardian of her nephew; she was just doting Aunt Lila, who bought too many gifts for Wyatt, from cute teething rattles to fun onesies that said *Wyoming's Best Nephew* to a tiny chair in the shape of a panda. She had a stockpile of Christmas gifts ready for wrapping.

As quickly as the fantasy had taken over her heart and lifted it, sadness descended. Her twin wasn't in the feed store. Or at the farm. Kate wasn't in Wyatt's nursery, restocking diapers in the slate blue dresser.

And Lila wasn't just Aunt Lila anymore. She was Wyatt's legal guardian.

Before Jesse could say anything, Lila added, "Kate

died in a car accident two months ago. Wyatt was just four weeks old."

His eyes widened and then briefly closed. "I'm very sorry. Damn," he added after a few seconds. He gazed down at the baby. "The pin..." he began but then seemed at a loss for words.

"I know who you are. My sister and I were very close. She texted me the night she met you when you two had moved to a table and you went up to the bar to get another round and order the nachos supreme, I think it was."

"Yes, the nachos supreme," he said, as if lost in thought himself.

"Kate told me all about your night the next morning," Lila said. "About waking up to the unopened condom on the floor and the pin on the bedside table."

He looked confused. "Unopened?"

"Well, apparently, you set out a condom but both of you were too tipsy to realize you hadn't actually used it."

He closed his eyes again, then sucked in another breath and looked at her. "I have a baby," Jesse said with something in his voice she couldn't quite name.

"Yes. Of course, you'll need to take a DNA test. So we know for sure. But I'm hardly nervous you'll take off with him."

A man who didn't offer his last name in the six to seven hours he'd spent with Kate, who wasn't interested in swapping the most basic info about each other, like last names or where they lived, who'd sneaked out of Kate's apartment in the middle of the night with no note, inexplicably leaving behind a pin of a horse, wasn't going to demand to raise his motherless three-month-old baby.

In fact, she expected him to hightail it out of town in about two seconds now that she'd confirmed he was the father—as far as she knew, anyway.

"I suppose I deserve that," he said. "I left at two a.m. No idea she was pregnant. No idea she'd had my baby. No idea she...died." He shook his head.

Lila was absolutely fine that he was beating himself up. *Keep at it, Cowboy.* "She told me you'd said two minutes into meeting her: 'No last names, no stories, okay?' I suppose that's who you are."

He had the decency to wince. "I deserve *that* too. But it's not all I am," he added, putting the Stetson back on his head. "The baby looks just like me. He's wearing my pin. I'll take the paternity test, but I can see he's mine. And I'll take responsibility."

A chill ran up her spine. "Meaning? You're *not* going to take off with him, are you?" She stared at him, trying not to bite down on her lip too hard.

"Of course not," he said. "You've raised him since..." He trailed off again.

She nodded. "Wyatt. His name is Wyatt. And yes. I've raised him since we lost Kate. The past two months. With a lot of help from my parents and grandmother."

"Well, you're his family as much as I am then. Scratch that—you're his family and I'm just half his DNA right now. And I don't know the first thing about babies. Or being a father." He looked from Wyatt to Lila. "I mean, I'll learn. I'll work overtime at it."

"This is all a relief to hear," Lila said. She'd long harbored ill-will against the cowboy who up and left her sister in the middle of the night—and unknowingly pregnant. But here he was, looking and seeming sincere. Wanting to take responsibility.

"Can I hold him?" Jesse asked.

The chill was back, this time racing up her spine and along the nape of her neck. Once he held Wyatt, his baby son who he hadn't known existed until five minutes ago, Jesse would surely feel a powerful connection. And maybe he *would* take Wyatt away. Maybe Jesse had a big, loving family of his own who'd teach him the ropes of fatherhood. *Father* would trump guardian-aunt in a court of law.

"Sure you can hold him," she said warily. "But you should take a paternity test before you start handing out cigars."

Surprise lit his blue eyes. "Cigars? I'm hardly going to do that since anyone who knows me would be thinking: '*You're* someone's father?' I'm not exactly father material."

"That was before you knew you had a child, though. You said you'd take responsibility—that makes you father material."

He tilted his head as if considering that. "No, it means I try to live by the Code of the West. I will take responsibility. But my role model in the fatherhood department wasn't exactly traditional. I don't know the first thing about what fathers are *supposed* to do." He let out a hard sigh. "I should shut up. I'm just trying to assure you that I'm not going to run off with your nephew. That you can count on."

She stared at him for a second, air going back into her lungs, her shoulders relaxing.

Wyatt let out a fussy cry, and they both turned their attention to the baby.

Lila carefully lifted him from the carrier, her sweet nephew instantly quieting, enjoying the change of position and his aunt's arms.

Now she was about to hand him over to a man he'd never met.

His father. She was both very happy for Wyatt on that count and worried for herself. Things were going to change. She had no idea how, exactly, but the routine she'd tried to settle into, helped along because Wyatt was an easy baby, was about to blow up. She wasn't the only parent now. And Jesse held the power here. He'd have the rights. As Wyatt's father—once that paternity test proved it—Jesse would be able to supersede her.

The chill was back.

No wonder she was having trouble actually handing over her nephew. Except now the cowboy was awkwardly extending his arms to take him.

She inwardly sighed and carefully transferred Wyatt to him, her nerves now completely shot. "Just keep one arm underneath him and the other around him and hold him close to your body. It's more instinctive than you think to hold a baby."

She could see Jesse sucking in a breath.

"Okay," he said and cradled his son against his chest, the black leather jacket.

The cowboy went quiet, his expression so unexpectedly full of reverence and wonder that Lila's breath caught in her throat. "This is my son," he whispered as if testing the words on himself.

Wyatt let out another fussy wail—bad timing as Jesse's expression changed to worry and fear.

"Am I holding him wrong?" he asked.

"No. You're doing just fine. But it's a bit past his nap time and he's tired and ready for his crib."

"Ah," he said, giving Wyatt a little sway, which the baby seemed to like.

"During nap time, I need to tend to the goats and get some work done on the farm," she said, "but we can talk then."

"I *am* a cowboy," he said. "I can help at the farm. And yes, we definitely need to talk."

Huh. She did need help. Even if just with unloading the bag of feed into the barn.

"What's your last name, anyway?" she asked. "Wyatt's last name. He's Wyatt Mack now."

"Dawson," he said. "My name is Jesse Dawson."

"You're a Dawson? Related to the hundred or so in town?"

He nodded. "They're cousins."

Good. She knew plenty of Dawsons. Including three who were on the police force, just in case this drifter cowboy turned out to be less sincere than he seemed. She had no idea what she meant by any of that, but it was a comfort nonetheless.

A bark from her dog, Billy, had her moving over to the driver's side window, aware of Jesse following. She reached through the half-open window to give the pooch's furry head a pat.

"This is Billy," she said. "He's a Border collie mix. I found him as a stray puppy about a year ago. He loves being a farm dog now."

"Nice to meet you, Billy," he said to the dog, who

always looked like he was smiling. "What did he used to be?"

"An apartment dog." She'd only had the farm a couple of months, but her old apartment in town, her job as a vet tech for a large animal veterinarian's office, felt like a lifetime ago. "Follow me to my farm. It's just ten minutes from here. You can settle Wyatt into his seat if you want," she added, gesturing at the rear-facing seat in the back of her SUV. She opened the door for him.

He tilted his head and looked at Wyatt in his arms. "I don't want to let him go even for ten minutes."

Huh. She didn't know whether to be happy about that for Wyatt's sake—or nervous like she felt. She only knew she'd been right that everything was about to change.

# *Chapter Two*

A hand-painted signpost with four goats in each corner announced the Double Sisters Farm. Jesse turned left and followed Lila Mack's SUV down the evergreen-flanked road, snow still lingering on the ground and tree branches from a recent storm.

*My child is in that vehicle*, he thought, trying out the words, which didn't sound real to his ears. *My* and *child* applying to him? Jesse Dawson?

*I'm a dad.* That didn't sound real either. Or possible. In theory, sure. In practice? No way.

For the past ten minutes, one thought had echoed in his head, something his brain had latched on to to deal with the shock. *You said you'd take responsibility—that makes you father material.*

Did it? Jesse had no idea what taking responsibility for a baby actually meant, what was involved. He'd do whatever was required. He had a small fortune in the bank from ten years of working on prosperous ranches with room and board and little need for anything other than a truck, so financially, he was set.

A quarter mile down the road, a small white farm-house with a wraparound porch came into view, and a red barn across the path surrounded by a few fenced pastures and woods beyond them. This was a goat farm? He saw two goats in a small pasture beside the barn, one on a log, the other with its brown-and-white head poked out of what looked like a toddler's playhouse. No horses, no cattle. Just the two goats. Unless there was some livestock in the barn... But when he rolled down his window to breathe in the air, he could tell the barn was empty. The place smelled like a fresh December afternoon, like evergreens.

He'd pulled up beside Lila's SUV, but she was just sitting in the passenger seat, same as him. Giving herself a minute. Which he understood. He was doing the same. He could use many minutes.

But now she was coming out, Billy, the Border collie mix, leaping out as well. She opened the back door, a whirlwind of movement in her red down coat and faded jeans and brown leather boots. She had Wyatt in her arms in seconds, using her hip to close the car door.

He got out of his truck. Wyatt's blue gaze was locked on Jesse's face, no expression at all. The baby seemed to be saying: *I'm sizing you up and will withhold judgment till I see what you've got, Mister.* Jesse found himself swallowing past yet another lump in his throat.

Lila glanced down at Wyatt, still staring at Jesse. "He seems to like the looks of you." She smiled, her pretty face lighting up. "Let's get him settled for his nap, then we can talk while I clean out the goats' stall."

The baby let out quite a yawn. Lila headed up the three, wide porch steps and he followed her. The front door was red like the barn. The dog curled up on a cushion beside the little porch swing, clearly enjoying the bright sunshine and unusually warm temperatures for mid-December. It was almost fifty degrees, with little wind.

The farmhouse was one-story, with a bright entry-way featuring a red coatrack, a padded bench and a boot tray. He liked the place right away. There was something welcoming about it.

"Hold him for a sec while I take off my coat and boots?" Lila asked.

"Of course," he said, taking the baby. Again, the curious blue eyes latched onto Jesse's face, and he couldn't help but smile. Wyatt wouldn't look at him for so long if he didn't like what he saw, right? That seemed like a plus. *My son likes me.*

Wyatt suddenly reached up his arm and grabbed hold of Jesse's ear. The expression slightly changed to something of a smile.

"Whoa there, little guy," Jesse said. "That's some grip."

Lila laughed and slipped out of her jacket. She wore a fuzzy camel-colored V-necked sweater, her long auburn ponytail down one shoulder. She sat on the bench to take off her boots. "Forgot to mention that. He's a grabber. He likes ears, swatches of hair, earrings, necklaces and noses. Learned my lesson about the hair and jewelry but nothing I can do about the nose."

As if on cue, Wyatt let go of Jesse's ear and grabbed onto his nose, which made Jesse laugh.

"Okay, all set," Lila said, holding out her arms for the baby.

But Jesse suddenly didn't want to let him go. He liked the feel of the baby's sturdy little weight in his arms. He even liked that Wyatt still had his nose in his little grip.

Jesse couldn't say he felt a connection, exactly, but surely that would come. They'd just been introduced, after all.

"Oh, wait, forgot this," she said, reaching up and grabbing off her Santa hat, which she frowned at as she hung it next to her coat. She eyed the matching mini one on Wyatt's head and took that off, barely looking at it as she draped it atop hers.

Interesting. What was that frown about? Maybe nothing. Maybe something.

He had nothing but frowns himself for anything to do with Christmas. Maybe she was a kindred spirit in that regard. But if that were the case, she wouldn't have been wearing a Santa hat in the first place. Or given her dog a Christmassy collar.

He had a few extra seconds with the baby staring up at him. Wyatt really did look like him. He had Jesse's eyes, for sure. Same as Jesse's dad—Wyatt's grandfather. And again, something in the face, the expression. Dawson all the way.

Lila stood and held out her arms again. "Okay, all set."

He did have to take off his own jacket, so he reluctantly handed over the baby, who finally let go of his nose.

He hung up his leather jacket beside Lila's and set his boots next to hers on the tray, which had little bits of snow clinging. Lila was unzipping Wyatt's snowsuit and shrugging him out of it. She hung it next to their coats, then hoisted the baby in her arms and planted a kiss on top of his head. Wyatt wore a long-sleeved navy T-shirt with a dog on it—a chihuahua in a cowboy hat—and blue sweatpants with white socks.

"We've lived here just a month," Lila said on something of a deep breath. "Kate and I were supposed to buy the farm together, but then..." She bit her lip, and he could see the fine mist of tears in her eyes. "We had this crazy dream of starting our own small dairy farm and selling goat milk, butter and cheese and one day having a petting zoo, which would likely also attract visitors to our shop."

"Doesn't sound crazy at all," he said. When he was young, he remembered that his grandparents had wanted to start a dairy farm but they never could make it a reality.

"I sank all my money into buying this place," she said. "I've gotten as far as purchasing the two goats and putting up the Double Sisters Farm sign, but things are kind of at a standstill financially, which is fine. I can care for the two goats and when I'm ready, I'll add to the herd and slowly build up the place. Kate would understand that I have to go slow. I closed a month after the accident, and just knowing that I did make good on our dream—the start of it, anyway—was a comfort." She stopped at the window in the living room that overlooked the front yard and the barn, the goats now both on the log in the pasture. "She would have loved those two funny little girls. Dolly and Lulu are their names. Dolly's the one with the white mark on her ear."

The man who usually didn't want to know too much about anyone suddenly wanted to know everything about Lila. About how things had been the past two months. About her life before she'd lost Kate and had become a single mother. About her life now.

Lila was his son's aunt. Of course he wanted to know

her story. It was Wyatt's story, really. That had to be why he was so interested. He waited a beat to see if she'd keep talking, but she seemed lost in thought and had stopped walking as if to collect herself. The emotion plain on her face, the sorrow in her voice just a few seconds ago, had him wanting to give her a hug, but he didn't know Lila Mack at all and besides, he'd smush Wyatt between them.

"I'm very sorry about Kate," he said. "She had a great laugh."

She looked up at him in surprise, a wobbly smile forming. "She did. She was a laugher." She sucked in a breath and gave Wyatt another kiss, this time on his cheek, then started walking.

He'd surprised himself with that comment about Kate. Jesse didn't feel like he had the right to talk about her— out of respect for Kate and for her twin. He hadn't known *Kate* at all, either. The mother of his child. He hung his head as a sudden shame descended. Just several hours in her company—and suddenly there was a baby. The notion itself took his breath. He thought he'd been all about keeping things light. No strings. And then he'd brought a life into the world.

They passed through the living room with the bay window facing the front and sliding glass doors to the wraparound porch along the backyard. There was a stone fireplace, many photos on the mantel. He noticed one of Kate beaming as she held Wyatt as a newborn; he was so tiny in the photo. He could see, even from a few feet away and passing by quickly, that although Kate and Lila were identical twins, there were differences in their faces. Lila's features were softer. They looked so much alike, enough that he'd mistaken Lila for Kate, but if they'd been side by side, he'd have been able to tell which twin was Kate.

He turned to take another look at the other photos on the mantel. Wyatt over the past few months. Jesse was suddenly aware of how much he'd missed since Wyatt had been born. Three months of his son being in this world with Jesse having no idea of that fact.

His gut twisted over that. If he'd been a different sort of person, he'd have known about Wyatt. A different kind of man wouldn't have sneaked out on a woman at two in the morning. He would have given his last name, asked hers. He would have known she was an identical twin. Instead, he only knew she was interested in buying a farm to raise goats, to start a dairy business. He hadn't asked her what she'd name the farm or what properties she was looking at. He hadn't asked her anything, in keeping with Jesse Dawson tradition.

He shook his head at himself, that shame deepening. He wasn't used to letting someone down.

He trailed Lila past two bedrooms, then into the nursery. It had the basics—crib, round rug with the alphabet on the border, a dresser, two rocking chairs and a bookcase near the window. A little chair in the shape of a panda. *Wyatt* was stenciled on the edge of the white spindle crib.

She carried Wyatt over to the dresser with a terry-cloth-covered pad atop it, shifted him in her arms to open a drawer and grab a diaper, then laid the baby down. He watched closely as she changed his diaper, then dropped the old one in a white trash can beside the dresser. A little ointment dabbed, cornstarch sprinkled and Wyatt was ready for his nap.

"I could try putting him in the crib," Jesse said, surprising himself again. He'd never put a baby to bed before.

Wyatt let out another yawn, a small hand reaching up to rub his eyes.

"Sure," Lila said, handing him over.

Wyatt went to him so easily. Jesse carefully held the baby, whose sleepy blue eyes were half on him, half closing. *Well, I guess this is how you can tell a baby is tired and ready for a nap*, he realized. He now knew two things: How to change a diaper. How to assess crib-readiness.

But the feeling coming over him, settling in his chest as he gazed down at this little being, his senses on red alert—*that* he couldn't quite name. Maybe it was protectiveness? Wyatt *was* his, after all. He didn't need a paternity test to tell him so. He'd take the test but he knew what the results would be.

He walked over to the crib, Wyatt's eyes getting droopier and droopier, but every few seconds opening halfway. "So I just lay him down?" he asked Lila.

She nodded. "Hopefully he'll fall right asleep. He usually does but sometimes he needs a few minutes to settle."

Here goes, he thought as he gently set Wyatt onto the crib mattress, the sheet covered in silver-and-blue moons and stars. Wyatt's face scrunched and turned a bit red and he let out a wail and started kicking his legs.

Uh-oh.

He expected Lila to shove him out of the way and

tend to the fussy baby, but she stayed where she was, at the foot of the crib.

"Why don't you try caressing his forehead up toward his head," she said. "He likes that. With just a smidge of pressure."

Jesse put his hand on the baby's tiny forehead and gently rubbed upward. In a few seconds, the wailing stopped, the scrunched face softened. The eyes were drooping again, then opening halfway. Jesse continued to caress upward toward the soft dark hair, and Wyatt's eyes closed. An arm shot up along the side of his face, the bow lips quirked upward, and then a sigh came out of Wyatt that had Jesse's shoulders relaxing. He watched the baby's chest rise and fall, rise and fall.

"He's asleep!" Jesse whispered, half triumphantly, half exhausted.

Lila laughed. "Good job, Dad."

He stared at her, feeling his smile fade out of pure astonishment. "I'm a dad," he said, testing out the words again. They still didn't feel real. None of this felt real.

"He usually sleeps for an hour and a half to two hours. I want to get the stalls mucked. We can talk in the barn. I keep a baby monitor in there so we can hear if he cries out."

Jesse could stand here and watch Wyatt sleep for hours. He couldn't seem to look away from his beautiful face, the rising and falling little chest in the onesie with the chihuahua, the sudden quirks of movement. *You're my son*, he thought in a state of absolute wonder.

The doorbell rang and they both started.

"It's us," a woman's voice called in a raised voice

through the door. "You have company? We'll wait for you on the porch."

Was it his imagination or did Lila pale a bit? She poked her head out of the nursery and called out, "Be right there."

With a nervous tinge to her voice.

Who was at the door?

"Us?" he asked.

"My mom and grandmother, maybe my aunt too," Lila said. "They stop by on their lunch break every day to see Wyatt."

"Really? Every day?"

She nodded. "My grandmother is an amazing cook and whips up lunch and we sit around and talk and marvel over Wyatt or sometimes we just cry over Kate. Depends on the day. You have a huge family, I figure. You know how it is."

He shook his head. "It's just me and my aunt Bess. Used to be three of us, but my dad died last December."

"Oh—I'm so sorry. But what about all the Dawsons in town?"

"They're second or third cousins. And I haven't lived in Bear Ridge in ten years. My dad moved around a lot the last years of his life and spent most of the previous year traveling the southwest in an old RV with a girlfriend. My aunt had her issues with her brother, but she also enjoys the RV life and is often on the road too, so there wasn't much reason to visit Bear Ridge."

"Why'd you come today?" she asked.

"Long story," he said. "Well, not that long but your family's waiting for you."

She looked at him, tilting her head, her auburn ponytail sliding. "Ready to meet three of the most important people in Wyatt's life besides us?"

He swallowed.

The look on Jesse's face as she led the way toward the front door. Half deer-caught-in-headlights, half get-me-out-of-here. All *I'm not ready for this.*

She wasn't either. She could barely believe Wyatt's father had suddenly walked into her life. Their lives. Her mom, aunt and grandmother were going to be stunned.

"My family is great," she said. "Very warm, never met a stranger and they say what's on their minds so you always know where you stand. My dad won a weeklong fishing boat cruise in a fundraising raffle, and since my granddad was the only one who wanted to go, they're away for a few more days."

Lila and her mother, aunt and grandmother all thought the two very stoic Mack men, who'd spent the first two weeks after losing Kate breaking down in tears, could use a getaway. They weren't talkers like the women in the family were, and talking, in their daily get-togethers, was a huge help.

Jesse just nodded. Lila pulled open the door. Her mother and aunt were on the swing, her grandmother on the padded rocking chair, Billy's furry chin on her gram's knee. They turned and stopped chatting as the door opened.

"Well, who is this?" her mother asked with a delighted lilt, eyes on Jesse. Deandra Mack, fifty-five and petite with an ash-blond bob and the Mack family green eyes, was obsessed with getting Lila married or at least dating a "wonderful guy," so her face was all lit up.

"Handsome," she heard her grandmother whisper to

her daughters. Her gram, Eleanora Landry, looked remarkably like her two daughters, down to the five-foot-two height and ash-blond hair, but Gram wore her hair in a chignon every day because it "made her feel fancy." Her grandmother owned a hair salon called Hair Royale that had been in business for almost fifty years now, and Lila's mother had long worked there as stylist. Growing up, Lila and Kate had been sweepers and then shampooers, and when neither was interested in going to beauty school, Gram was fully supportive of them going after their own dreams just as she had been about Aunt Raina becoming a nurse.

"Mom, Aunt Raina, Gram, this is Jesse Dawson." She paused, about to add the bombshell, but her grandmother was too quick.

"Dawson?" her gram repeated. "Any relation to that wonderful Reed Dawson on the Bear Ridge PD? He helped me get my cat down from a tree outside the salon just yesterday. Whiskers comes to work with me every day," she added.

"Reed is a cousin," Jesse said, and Lila recalled that Reed had recently become a father to a baby left in his and his social worker wife's care. "Second or third, I'm not sure. There are a few branches of the Dawson family in Bear Ridge."

"And thank God for that," Aunt Raina said on a laugh. "The Dawsons' rate of marriage has pretty much kept Hair Royale in the black. Bridal party updos and makeup practically every weekend. There's always a Dawson getting hitched or celebrating something. Are you one of the branch who own the Dawson Family Guest Ranch?"

Jesse shook his head. "They're second cousins," he

said. "I've been to the guest ranch only once since it was rebuilt a few years ago. Beautiful property."

Lila had been to three weddings over the past two years at the Dawson Family Guest Ranch. Both she and Kate had talked about having their "someday" weddings there if they never did make their goat farm a reality and couldn't have their weddings on their own property. She sucked in a quick breath, that constantly lurking reminder of losing her sister settling in her chest. Kate didn't even get to see their long-held dream come true. And they'd both been unlucky in the romance department. Anyway, with a baby to raise, Lila had given up dating and saying yes to fix-ups. She had enough on her plate and she wasn't sure the man existed who could step into her life and love her child and her farm with every bit of his heart the way she did.

Her mother nodded. "My husband surprised me with a weekend there for our last anniversary. VIP cabin and everything." She peered at Jesse, then looked at Lila, then back at Jesse.

Lila could see she was trying to assess their chemistry, to get a sense of what they were to each other. *Who* they were to each other. She could tell her mother was trying to figure out if they were dating or if Jesse was perhaps a potential ranch hand or a goat consultant.

Lila figured their chemistry, if such a word could be applied to them, had to read as *highly awkward.*

"So how do you two know each other?" her mother finally came out and asked, as was the Mack women's way. "Are we interrupting a date? We can come back later. We brought over pecan pie from the bakery." She held up a pale blue box with a logo of cake and a steaming cup of coffee on the white label.

Lila felt her cheeks burn. Oh God. She couldn't just blurt out the truth, that Jesse was Wyatt's father, that he'd appeared suddenly in the parking lot of the feed store. She just couldn't put them all on the spot, Jesse included. Who Jesse was would shock her family. She'd tell them when they were alone.

"I'll, uh, explain in a minute," Lila said, biting her lip.

Jesse seemed to read her mind, to understand. "Why don't I go grab the goat feed from your SUV and bring it into the barn. I could fill the trough and call in Dolly and Lulu to eat."

"That would be great," Lila said, relief sagging her shoulders. She liked that he remembered the goats' names. So far, he was earning her trust, and trust could sometimes be built on the little things too. The man *listened*, paid attention—that much was clear from the way he'd tended to Wyatt for his nap to how he was handling meeting her family. Wyatt's family.

He shot a fast smile at the four of them, then hurried off the porch and headed for Lila's vehicle. They all watched him cart the feed bag into the barn, closing the door behind him.

"Ooh, hire him for sure," Aunt Raina said, wriggling her eyebrows. "He lifted that huge bag of feed like it was a feather."

"And so handsome," her gram added. "Like a movie star with that thick tousled hair and those blue eyes."

"Dating?" her mother asked, hope in her eyes.

Lila let out the breath she'd been holding. Then she sucked in another one.

Her mother peered at her. "Honey? What's wrong? What's going on?"

Now her aunt and grandmother were stepping closer, staring at her with concern.

"He's..." Lila began. But the words wouldn't come.

*Because you're afraid what it means. That things are going to change. You don't know what to expect, what Jesse Dawson is going to want once the shock that he's a father wears off.*

Maybe the shock was why he was so...nice and forthcoming and accommodating. Could be that the news—that he was a father—hadn't sunk in fully. When it did...

"He's...?" her aunt Raina prompted.

"Wyatt's *father*," Lila finally said.

Three mouths dropped open.

"Wyatt's father?" her mother repeated, her hand flying to her heart. *"What?"*

Lila gave her mom's hand a quick squeeze. "Let's talk inside."

The three women practically ran into the kitchen and sat down at the table by the window, but they were uncharacteristically quiet since they were waiting for Lila to explain herself. Lila's gram got up to brew a pot of coffee, which was probably a good idea; no one would have an appetite for pie, but they'd need the caffeine boost.

Lila dropped down in a chair between her mother and aunt. "I was in the feed store about an hour ago. I came out, Wyatt in the carrier on my chest, and a stranger came up to me—the man you just met—and thought I was Kate."

Three gasps.

"He thought you were Kate?" Aunt Raina asked. She

glanced at her sister and mother, who looked as confused as she did. "Ooh," she added. "He didn't know."

The room got very quiet for a moment.

Lila nodded. "I had the same reaction as all of you to that. He has to be the only person in town who didn't."

"And he didn't know he had a baby either," her mother said. "Or did he?"

Lila shook her head. She told them everything, catching them up from the conversation in the parking lot to Jesse putting down Wyatt for his nap. She tried to remember everything he'd said about not running off with his son, but Lila herself was still overwhelmed by Jesse's entrance in her life. All that had happened, all they'd both said, was jumbling together.

Her grandmother poured four cups of coffee. Lila got up to bring the cream and sugar over to the table and she and her gram sat down.

For a few seconds, they all just sat there, the hands wrapped around the hot mugs, the pecan pie ignored in its box on the counter.

"I agree that Wyatt looks just like him," her mother said. "But I want proof of paternity."

Lila nodded. "Me too. I'm sure he'll get that taken care of today or tomorrow."

"What's he like?" her mother asked. "He really seems sincere? Like a good person?"

Lila took a sip of her coffee. "Well, I've known him all of an hour. But he seems honest. And yes, sincere."

"He's a cowboy?" Gram asked. "I remember when Kate sat us down to tell us she was pregnant that the father was a traveling cowboy. Nice way of saying a drifter?"

"I don't know much about him," Lila admitted. "I

did notice he had a few duffel bags in the back of his truck. Like he was leaving town until he noticed me in the parking lot."

"If you'd been five minutes later, he might have been gone," her mother said. "You'd never have crossed paths. He wouldn't know about Wyatt." She shook her head. "That's wild."

"It's good that he knows," her gram said, taking a sip of her coffee. "Yes, he's a mystery. But he is Wyatt's father, and now our beloved little boy has gone from not having a daddy to having one. That is a blessing. Even if things get…messy."

Lila felt that chill sneak up her spine at the word *messy*. She didn't want things to get messy. But how could they not? *Was* Jesse Dawson leaving town? Was that what the duffel bags were about? He didn't live in Bear Ridge; he might live hours away. He might be expected somewhere. And he might insist on taking his son to wherever that was.

He'd assured her he wouldn't take Wyatt from her— from the only family the baby had known the past two months.

Still. She didn't know Jesse Dawson. *Seemed* this or that didn't mean he *was* this or that.

She bit her lip. She could not lose her nephew. None of them could. Her father had just started seeming like his old self, looking up when walking in town arm in arm with Lila's mother instead of eyes glued to the ground, sad frown marring his kind face. Finding comfort in the town square's holiday tree, all lit up. Lila could barely look at it. Kate had loved Christmas. And though Lila tried to put some holiday spirit in her and Wyatt's lives for his sake, buying Billy that red-and-green collar with the tiny embroidered Christmas trees, wearing the Santa hats today, she'd just been reminded her of loss, not of any kind of joy of the season. She couldn't dare be a Scrooge when it was Wyatt's first Christmas. But she couldn't bear Christmas at all.

"At least he's a Dawson," Raina put in. "He doesn't seem like such a stranger."

"I've never met a Dawson who wasn't a good person," Gram added.

Raina's eyes widened. "Oh. My. God. I just realized why Jesse looks familiar. He was at the clinic last year—last December. His father died from cancer just a day after he was admitted."

All eyes turned to Lila's aunt, who worked at the county hospital in the ER and did a twice-weekly rotation at the Bear Ridge Clinic.

"He did mention he lost his father," Lila said.

Aunt Raina sipped her coffee, then put the cup down, her expression compassionate. "A girlfriend—an *ex*-girlfriend, I remember her saying—brought him in and said the poor man had just been diagnosed the day before. He'd refused to go to a doctor for the longest time. She said he had prostate cancer and wanted to see his son. He didn't have a cell phone, but we found a folded-up piece of paper in his wallet with his son's name and at least twenty numbers crossed out. A nurse called the last number and he answered. Jesse Dawson. He drove four hours to get to the clinic. His father died the next day."

"That's so sad," Lila said. She thought about what Jesse had said about not having a role model in the fatherhood department. She wondered what their relationship had been like, what his childhood had been like.

"We should go and let you two talk," her mother said, standing up. She collected the coffee mugs. "Call me later so I won't worry, okay?"

"I will," Lila promised. "We do have a lot to talk about. If he's going to take responsibility for Wyatt, we'll have to work out some kind of schedule. We'll have to go from strangers to co-parents pretty quickly."

Three sets of eyes were staring at her.

"Lila, I'm just going to say this outright," Aunt Raina said. "If the paternity test says he's the father, are you still co-parents? Or is he…"

The *messy* that Gram had mentioned. "I'm Wyatt's legal guardian," Lila said, that chill back and running up and down her spine. "That has to mean something—in court."

"You're the legal guardian because Kate didn't know how to find the baby's father," her grandmother pointed out. "Now that he's here, that may change things."

Lila bolted up. "Well, that's not fair. I've been raising Wyatt for two months. I'm his legal guardian." Tears filled her eyes. "He's ours."

"I shouldn't have opened my big fat mouth," her aunt said, putting her arm around Lila. "You said that Jesse seems sincere, that he said he's not going to run off with Wyatt. Let's take him at his word, give him the benefit of the doubt. While being careful and watching his every move."

Lila bit her lip. How would she take care of Wyatt, get the farm up and running and watch Jesse Dawson's every move?

"There he is," her mother said, upping her chin out the kitchen window.

They all looked out. Jesse was in the goats' pasture, leading them into the barn.

"We'll let you two make that schedule," her mother said, eyeing her own mother and sister, and the three headed for the door, stopping to put on their coats and boots.

Lila didn't want them to leave but she did want to talk to Jesse and find out what his intentions were.

And how worried she had to be.

# Chapter Three

Jesse had mucked out the goats' stall, an easy job since there were only two goats, refreshed the straw bedding, filled the trough with the feed, changed the water and led Dolly and Lulu in. They were beauties, Nubian goats with long silky ears like bloodhounds and a white patch down their furry cinnamon-colored bodies.

They were now chowing down and acting up, like goats did. Dolly seemed to like to jump on her log, then jump back down to eat a few bites of her feed, then jump back up. Lulu ate her fill, then sneezed up a storm, something young goats did often, and then poked at her new bedding and curled up. Jesse could see that Lila had done her research on goats—they had everything they needed and creature comforts, like a couple of bean bags to act as pillows since goats liked to keep their heads elevated while they slept.

He heard the barn door open and looked forward to seeing Lila again, to talking more. He was out of his element, out of his depth, out of his comfort zone, and her calm, kind nature was a help. But when he left the stall, his heart speeding up a bit at the thought of seeing Lila's pretty face and long auburn ponytail, he was surprised to find her grandmother heading his way instead. Her eyes were narrowed and she kind of charged forward. He had a foot of height on her and she was somewhere in her midseventies, but she loomed large.

"Let me tell you something, young man," she said, pointing a finger, which always meant business. "You start as you mean to continue. You hear me?"

"I do hear you," he said. "That phrase was a favorite of my aunt's."

Her green eyes flashed. "Good, then you understand that you shouldn't start something if you're leaving town in a day or two. If that's your plan, you make sure Lila knows it. You make sure she knows your intentions for being Wyatt's father. This family has been through hell and I won't stand for you adding to it."

He liked this protective, tough woman. He could see so many emotions on her face. From heartache to joy to hope to fear to determination. He would not let her down.

"I'm Wyatt's father and I intend to live up to the title," he said.

The grandmother lifted her chin as if surprised and taking his measure. Trying to get a sense of him, if she could believe a word he said.

"I will not take Wyatt from his maternal family," he added. "I promise you that. He lives here. At this farm in Bear Ridge. That won't change."

She visibly relaxed. "Well, I'm glad to hear that. I'll expect to see the paternity results."

"Not five minutes ago I made an appointment at the county hospital's lab," he said. "Tomorrow at nine thirty. I should have the results within forty-eight hours."

The chin lifted slightly again. "You might not be his

father, you know. Maybe in these next two days, you shouldn't get too attached. Just in case."

"I'm not one to get attached at all," he said before he could stop himself. He supposed he'd blurted it out because it was the main thing on his mind, the thing worrying him about himself. About being a father.

"Well, just like Lila's life is going to change now, so will yours. If you are the father. Taking responsibility is about more than buying a box of Pampers."

He nodded.

"I have my eye on you, Jesse Dawson," she said, wagging her finger between her eyes and him.

He almost smiled. But he didn't want her to think he wasn't taking her very seriously. He was. To the point that he needed to sit down.

"Bye now," she said.

"Bye," he said as she turned and headed back up the walkway and pushed open the door.

He let out a long breath. Dolly and Lulu were both on their logs on the far side of their pen, eyeing him.

"I wouldn't want to be on her bad side," he said to them.

"No, you wouldn't," a voice called.

He whirled around and there was Lila, standing on the other side of the feed trough. He hadn't heard her enter the barn.

"I didn't mean to eavesdrop. I was checking on how much the goats ate and overheard. Anyway, I'll get started on my chores and we can talk. Wyatt's still asleep." She patted her jacket pocket. "I have the baby monitor."

He nodded and waited while she walked over to the pen.

"Wow," she said, looking surprised. "You took care of everything."

"I'm a cowboy between ranches. I'd been planning on joining a big spread near Yellowstone but—" He clamped his lips together, not wanting to talk about his dad. Or maybe he did because he found himself opening up. "Turned out my dad left me a letter. To be delivered a year after his death during the month of December. A list of his last wishes."

Her eyes widened. "Why did he want to wait a year?"

"I guess he thought I'd be too raw for a while to do anything on the list. And he was right about that. I was numb for a good six months. I was used to not seeing my dad for very long stretches, but I always knew he was in this world, you know?"

Her face fell. Of course she knew. She'd just lost her sister two months ago.

"I know," she almost whispered. "Unless it's too personal, what was the gist of the wishes? Things you can do?"

"I didn't think so," he admitted. "Until I saw you coming out of that feed store, I'd been sitting on a bench at the park entrance, nursing a lukewarm coffee, and trying to figure out why I wasn't hitting the road for Yellowstone when that was the plan."

"You didn't want to skip out on your dad's last wishes," she said.

He nodded. "Doing that didn't feel right, of course. But actually checking off anything on the list? Also didn't feel right."

"Like what?" she asked.

"Putting down roots in Bear Ridge. Adopting a dog,

man's best friend. And—" He shut up fast again. He wasn't about to look for or find love, so no need to mention that. His dad would get his wish with number one and maybe that was enough. Jesse would have to put down roots here in Bear Ridge. His child was here.

Granted, that hadn't stopped his father from leaving town for months at a time. But Jesse couldn't even imagine doing that. He wondered how his father had been able to. And he didn't like thinking about that— those old criticisms his aunt had leveled against his dad, which he always tried to defend. *He's an adventurer...*

"Thanks for getting all my chores done," she said. "Usually I can't nap when Wyatt does because I'm too busy with the farm. But I could probably sneak in a good twenty minutes."

"Why don't you go take your nap, and I'll take the baby monitor. I'd like to walk around the farm and see what might need to be done or bought."

"Hey, I'll take you up on that nap," she said, handing over the monitor. "But you don't need to do anything on the farm."

"I want to. It's Wyatt's legacy and future. And I'd like to do it for Kate too. And for you. You've raised my son on your own for the past two months."

The chin lifted like her grandmother's had. "Well, I can't say that's not nice. Okay, have a look around. I'll be snoozing."

He smiled. "Oh, about this thing," he said, the smile faltering. He took the monitor out of his pocket. "It's on, right? I'll hear Wyatt if he wakes up?" He'd used monitors plenty in his job as a cowboy, bunking in barns outside a sick animal's stall, the monitor beside his head turned way up high to ensure he heard the slightest whine.

"Yup. Wyatt wakes up noisily, trust me. You'll hear him. And the farm is tiny, as you can see."

He nodded and put the monitor back in his pocket.

She took one last look at the goats, then at him and then turned and hurried out of the barn. Once again, he was aware of wanting her back with him.

*Start as you mean to continue.* Her grandmother's sage words echoed in his head.

Problem was, he had no idea how he planned to continue anything. He only knew he wasn't heading to Yellowstone any time soon. If ever.

Ahhh, Lila could get used to this. She was under the covers in her comfortable bed and could feel herself drifting off. She'd set her alarm for a half hour, not wanting to sleep for as long as the baby might and wake up all groggy. A thirty-minute power nap, and she'd be refreshed.

From the shocking news too, she hoped. She figured she'd sleep on that too and wake a little more accustomed to Wyatt having a father—in their lives.

She turned onto her stomach, let out a satisfied sigh and felt herself drifting...

"Yo, yo, yo, I'm here to hang with Wyatt and see the goofballs," came a booming voice and a slamming front door a second later. Lila then heard the refrigerator door shut and the pop of a can of soda opening.

So much for the power nap. Lila's seventeen-year-old brother, Micah, was here. And given that he was in trouble at school and at home, she was glad he was here and as interested in his nephew and the goats—the goofballs, as he called them—as ever. Micah had been a surprise baby, an eleven-year age difference between him and his older siblings. He was doted on by his parents and twin sisters, but last year, he'd started changing, hanging out with a rougher crowd than his old group of friends, ditching classes. He'd been brought home by police three times the past two years for being caught drinking by the river with his friends. Their parents had tried a bunch of different tactics to reach him. The only thing that had was a farm camp for teens offered this past summer by a large dairy in town. Dinner conversation—when he'd actually show up—about how cows had four stomachs and how he might want to be a rancher when he graduated made them all feel so relieved.

And when she and Kate started talking about making their dream of a goat farm and dairy business a reality, his eyes had lit up. He could apprentice at the Double Sisters when he couldn't at other ranches since he'd developed a reputation in town as a young troublemaker. The whole family was so excited about the new venture. Micah started turning around his attitude and life, especially when she and Kate found the property and put in the offer. The three of them had always been close, and he adored baby Wyatt, coming over every day to play with his nephew.

But then the accident changed everything. They'd all been grieving messes, but Micah's pain was coated with anger, and instead of finding comfort from his family, he turned inward and away. He'd refused to have anything to do with Wyatt or the farm or the family for that matter. He started skipping school again, getting suspended for being caught drinking and vaping on school grounds. He was in danger of not graduating from high school in June.

When Lila had bought Dolly and Lulu two weeks ago, the news had reached Micah and he'd stopped by to see them, a light in his eyes that had Lila so hopeful. She taught her brother everything she knew about raising goats and let him know that when she had some more money saved up to add two more goats, he could come with her to pick them out. His eyes had really lit up then.

He came by every other day or so, and he always stopped in the house to see Wyatt. Not for long. But he was there, reading him a story or making one up. Walking around the house with him in the chest carrier and teaching his nephew random facts about the trees outside or why he preferred sausage over bacon in his breakfast sandwiches. He'd been invited on the cruise with the Mack men and had said he liked the idea but didn't want to leave the goats or Wyatt for even a few days, and the whole family was thrilled. Micah was on his way back to them. They all felt it.

So she'd gladly give up her much-needed nap to spend some time with her brother.

She was on her way to find him when she saw him out the side window in the pasture, talking to Jesse. Micah looked so young beside Jesse, lanky where the older cowboy was so muscular. She was reminded that her brother was just seventeen—a kid. She grabbed her coat, slipped on her boots and headed outside.

"I didn't know you hired someone for the farm," Micah said to her—warily. He slid an uneasy gaze toward Jesse.

"I didn't. Jesse's a cowboy and just helping me out. He's taking a look around and seeing what might need to be done or ordered."

Micah nodded. "That's what he said. But I don't get why he'd be doing that for free. Oh, wait—so you guys are a couple?"

Lila felt her cheeks burn. "We're not dating." Oh God. This again. "Micah," she said, in a voice her brother seemed to know meant something important was coming. He stared at her hard, taking a step back like he was going to hear something upsetting. "Jesse is actually Wyatt's father. He'd left town after he and Kate...met, and he didn't know she was pregnant."

Micah gaped at her, then turned an angry green stare on Jesse. "And?"

"And this all just happened today," Lila said. "Mom, Aunt Raina and Gram happened to stop by a little while ago and they just learned the news themselves."

"So you're gonna take Wyatt away?" Micah asked, his face turning red. "This sucks!" Then he ran and was gone in the woods before they could even blink.

"Oh, dammit," Lila said. She grabbed her phone from her pocket and called her brother. Voicemail. She texted him. He's not taking Wyatt away. He said so.

Micah texted back right away. Oh, he said so. People say a ton of crap they don't mean.

Micah, come on back. You can talk to Jesse yourself and get assured.

Bullcrap, he texted.

She held up the phone for Jesse to read.

"Sorry," Jesse said. "I would definitely assure him."

Lila put her phone away when it was clear her brother was done communicating. "He's going through a hard time." She explained the past couple years to Jesse and the past couple of months in particular.

"I have an idea," Jesse said. "It has to do with the big talk we should have about Wyatt and the farm."

"The farm? Um, Wyatt is half yours. The farm is all mine."

"I know. I just mean that I can help with both and maybe with your brother, too."

She tilted her head, trying to get a read on him. Help with her brother? How? "That sounds promising."

Jesse pulled out the monitor and put it to his ear. "You sure this thing is working? Not a peep."

"Wyatt naps for at least an hour and a half, sometimes two and a half."

"I guess you didn't get your nap in?"

She shook her head. "That's okay. It was just nice knowing I *could* take to my bed." She took one last look toward the woods, hoping to see her brother coming back. But all she saw was trees. She sent a quick text to her mom about what had happened. A few seconds later, her mother responded with a sad-face emoji and assured her he'd just need a little time and space for the news to sink in.

Lila put her phone away and headed for the porch. "Let's go talk. I can prep dinner. Yesterday, my grandmother gave me a pot of her amazing meatballs in marinara sauce. Up for linguini and meatballs?"

"Always," he said, following her into the house. "And thanks for the invitation."

They hung up their coats and took off their boots. Still not a sound from Wyatt. She hoped the baby would give them another half hour. She did want to hear what Jesse had to say about his intentions and plans.

Suddenly her mind was echoing with her grandmother's warning about things getting messy. Her brother's *People say things they don't mean all the time.*

And the chill was back.

She had to keep her guard up with Jesse Dawson. No matter how nice he seemed.

# *Chapter Four*

The moment Jesse followed Lila into the kitchen, fussy wails started coming from the monitor, which he heard loud and clear. Lila had been right—Wyatt was very vocal that he was now awake. Their talk—and dinner prep—would have to wait a bit.

"I could show you the routine," Lila said.

"I feel like I should take notes, have something to refer to."

Lila laughed. "Trust me, most of it is instinctive and common sense. And anything you need to know is one search bar away on your phone. You can watch a video of anything. How to move a baby's legs to help them expel gas from their tummies. How to burp a baby. What various cries might mean. Hungry? Tired? Achy?"

"What's Wyatt's cry saying right now?" he asked as they headed down the hall to the nursery.

"It's saying—I'm lonely in here. Change me and feed me and cuddle me pronto."

Jesse smiled. "I guess that does seem like common sense."

"Yup. You'll get the hang of it in no time."

He appreciated her confidence. He still felt like a total novice at even holding a baby, but he'd already semi-mastered putting Wyatt down for a nap. That was something, even if it had taken a while for Wyatt to actually fall asleep.

In the nursery, Wyatt was on his back, moving his arms and legs, letting out more fussy cries.

"Here goes," he said, reaching into the crib. He carefully put his arms under Wyatt and lifted him up, but the crying didn't stop, the sweet face scrunching up as if he hated Jesse's guts.

"Uh-oh, what happened?" Jesse asked. "Did I pick him up wrong?"

"Not at all," Lila said, coming over to give the baby's back a soothing rub. Wyatt stopped crying, his big blue eyes latching onto her face. "You're new to him, is all. He'll get used to you fast."

"I hope so," Jesse said and realized how much he meant it.

He gave Wyatt a little bounce, and his son's attention turned to him with curiosity. The baby stared at him hard, and when Jesse bounced him again and rubbed his back the way Lila had, Wyatt seemed to settle down. Then a little arm shot out and grabbed his nose, letting go in a few seconds.

A new feeling came over Jesse, gathering in his chest and pulsating. *Connection*, he thought. This baby against his chest was his own child.

A bit more confident, he brought Wyatt over to the changing table and laid him down. "I might put the diaper on backward," he said to Lila, who moved over to one of the rockers and sat down.

"The front has little monkeys on it and is slightly lower than the back, so you can't miss," she assured him.

"Make sure you keep a hand on him while you grab a diaper from the drawer. He's little but he just started rocking side to side, a precursor to being able to roll over."

Jesse snapped to even greater attention. He put a hand on Wyatt's belly and slightly bent to get a diaper. He took off the old one and tried to remember the order of the ointment and powder. He figured ointment first, then cornstarch, and Lila didn't correct him, so he must have gotten that right.

"You're doing great," she said.

"You hear that?" he said to Wyatt, gently tapping the baby's nose. "I'm going to do right by you, little guy. That's a promise—"

He froze, stunned by what had just come out of his mouth.

"You okay?" Lila asked, looking at him curiously.

"My father's motto was: don't make promises you can't keep so you won't let anyone down. I narrowed that to not making promises at all because sometimes the best of intentions..."

"Is this the first promise you've made to someone?" she asked.

He frowned, trying not to let a face, a memory get in his head, but it did anyway. "I let my guard down with the last woman I dated. I promised her she could count on me, that we were exclusive, that I'd be faithful." Once again, he froze, shocked all that had come out of him. "You're too easy to talk to, Lila."

"And you broke your promise to this woman?" she asked, wariness in her eyes.

"Nope. She broke hers. I didn't see it coming and it did a number on me. That was two years ago."

"So now you just leave in the middle of the night," she said.

He glanced at her, and her eyes widened as if she hadn't meant to say that aloud.

"Sorry," she said, her expression so contrite he had the urge to take her hand and let her know it was okay. But he didn't. "That was uncalled for—and mean. You just shared something with me and I used it against you. That was wrong."

"It's okay. And true. I do leave in the middle of the night. But I have new priorities now," he said. "This guy," he added, scooping up Wyatt and holding him horizontally against his chest.

Except Wyatt cried out again and seemed out of sorts. Jesse frowned, not sure what to do.

"It's all right," Lila said, stepping over to smile at Wyatt and run a finger down his cheek as if to assure him Jesse was a good guy.

Jesse looked down at the bundle in his arms. "You'll get to know me because I'm not going anywhere." A warmth settled in his chest. He wouldn't let this little guy down.

The baby grabbed his ear this time and let out a hearty giggle. That was promising. "Whoa, I didn't even know babies could laugh, let alone that loud."

"It's the best sound in the world," Lila said.

He looked at her and nodded. That baby laugh had gone right inside him, warming him up. Unexpected. Like everything that had happened today. "So what's next? His dinner?"

"You can feed him," she said. "And burp him. And then play with him."

"What's play like?"

"He likes to lie on his playmat and grab for dangly toys. And chew his toes." She laughed.

He liked Lila's laugh too. It also seemed to get inside him. Make him feel like he was part of something here, not an outsider. He'd never cared about that before.

She was eyeing him as if she'd caught him in deep thought. He wasn't used to that, either. Thinking too hard *or* someone paying close attention.

"That does sound like fun," he said to Wyatt. "Chewing your own toes." He smiled at the baby in his arms, again that feeling of...wonder coming over him.

Lila got up and headed out and he followed. In the kitchen, she showed him how to make a bottle and explained how often Wyatt ate, that he was sleeping longer stretches overnight but still woke up twice to eat. Jesse said he'd handle those feedings and that Lila should get her rest.

"Okay, you are too good to be true," she said. "I'm supposed to not like you at all."

*I deserved that zinger too*, he thought, trying to keep the frown off his face. "I'm a different person since I saw you, Lila. The moment I found out I was a dad, Wyatt became everything."

He wouldn't have thought that was possible, but it was how he felt. He looked down at his son cradled in his arms. *Yes, you are everything*, he said silently.

She tilted her head. "I really think you mean that."

"I do." He did. Again, Jesse wasn't sure how it could be, given his background, how he was raised. To do right by his child was his priority. "I'm not at the point where I can carry him *and* the bottle," he said.

Lila smiled—a warm smile that soothed something in him. "I'll carry the bottle."

Wyatt seemed fine as Jesse carried him over to the sofa and sat down. Lila set the bottle on the coffee table, then sat across from him on the love seat. She explained how to hold Wyatt and how to angle the bottle. Jesse focused on his son drinking away, amazed that it could be this simple to do something as extraordinary as feeding a baby.

He heard a gentle click and glanced up, catching Lila taking his picture with her cell phone.

"Sorry, but I had to," she said. "The look on your face while you were feeding him." She pressed a hand to her heart. "I'll send it to you."

He felt his face burning a bit. God, was he actually blushing? That she'd caught him in an emotional moment? Then again, he'd been having those moments ever since he'd run into Lila Mack and discovered he had a child in this world. He'd have to get used to all these new...*feelings*.

He gave her something of a smile and a nod and then realized the bottle was nearly empty. Good, something more concrete to focus on. Wyatt was turning away. "Does that mean he's done?"

"Yup. Now you can hold him against you vertically and pat his back until he burps. But take one of these," she said, getting up and pulling a white cloth from a stack of them in a basket under the coffee table. "Set it on your shoulder so if he spits up, he gets the burp cloth and not your nice shirt."

He set down the bottle and shifted Wyatt, giving him three good pats on his upper back. The baby let out a giant burp, which made both him and Lila laugh. And was surprisingly deeply satisfying to this new father.

*Well, what do you know*, Jesse thought, cuddling Wyatt against him. *I'm actually doing this. Taking care of you. Learning the ropes.*

"You're really doing a great job," Lila said, and he appreciated the praise.

For the next hour, they talked about all things baby, Wyatt specifically, all about his routine and habits and milestones and the upcoming ones. They'd moved to the playmat, Wyatt enjoying trying to grab the springy stuffed toy dangling down.

By six thirty, Wyatt was yawning again, and this time Jesse handled bedtime on his own. The baby was fussy again, but Jesse discovered Wyatt liked to be rocked and sung to. Jesse would have to learn lullabies, but so far his son enjoyed The Beatles. He was definitely figuring out what worked and what didn't.

After changing him, including into pj's, Jesse sat down with him on a rocker and realized he was too exhausted to get up again and pick a book, so he told his son a little about himself, that he'd missed his first three months, but he wouldn't miss a day from here on in.

"And that's another promise," he whispered.

The big blue eyes drooped, then opened, a tiny fist wrapping around his pinky. And that was it. Wyatt slipped right inside his heart.

Okay, this man in the nursery with her nephew kept making Lila's heart ping in her chest. She hadn't meant to eavesdrop on his conversation with Wyatt. But she'd been about to go into the nursery to ask if he needed any help and he was telling Wyatt that he was sorry he'd missed his first three months but he wouldn't miss a day from now on.

Tears had come to her eyes. She wanted to march into the room and throw her arms around Jesse Dawson. He cared about Wyatt. That was plain to see. He would honor his word to take responsibility. She was so sure of that.

What she wasn't sure of was whether he'd take the baby he was falling in love with and leave town. He'd said he wouldn't. And he might have meant it at the time. But things could and would change. The more comfortable he felt around Wyatt, about being a father, maybe he would decide he could handle parenthood on his own. And take Wyatt away.

It was time to have that talk.

She waited until it was clear Wyatt was asleep in his crib before walking into the nursery. Jesse stood at the crib, watching his son sleep. If she had her phone on her, she'd sneak another photo.

"How'd it go?" she asked, though she knew full well how it had gone. "From the looks of things, I'd say it went great."

"I think he's getting more used to me. And you were right about it being mostly instinctive. I know I have a lot to learn. But he kind of tells you what he wants and needs without saying a word—just a little squirm or fussy whine."

She smiled. "I was the same two months ago. I was a doting auntie, yes, but I wasn't Mommy. I had a lot to learn too."

He looked at her then as if he hadn't considered that. "There's been so much to process, to take in and think about that I didn't even get as far as that—what you went through when Kate died, becoming his legal guardian. Your whole life changed."

"It did. The worst pain I've ever felt and then the greatest joy of taking care of my nephew. Every time I wanted to cry my eyes out, I'd look at Wyatt, who needed me for every little thing, and he'd get me through." She sucked in a breath. "Stop being so easy to talk to, to confide in. I don't know you yet, Jesse Dawson."

"I'm only here to make things easier. That I can promise you."

Coming from someone else, that might be a throwaway line, something someone just said without thought. But from Jesse, it was big.

"Then you'll help me make dinner? Great." She laughed, needing to break this too-close connection between them.

"I sure will," he said.

"And we'll talk. Hammer out a plan for going forward."

*Yes*, she thought, taking a breath. Sound business-y instead of personal. She had to remember that Jesse Dawson could turn her life upside down. She couldn't trust him, not until she knew him better.

But something told her that knowing him better would only make her like him more.

Five minutes later, Jesse stood at the kitchen counter slicing a red bell pepper for the salad while Lila added the linguini to the big pot of boiling water on the stove. Her grandmother's meatballs and sauce were heating up beside it and smelled amazing. Jesse wasn't sure of the last time he'd had a home-cooked meal. And slicing tomatoes? A cucumber and a green bell pepper waiting on deck? He never cooked—or sliced. If he wasn't eating in a ranch cafeteria, he'd be getting a burger at a bar and grill or a turkey club at a diner.

He glanced over at Lila, stirring the pasta, stirring the meatballs. "How are these looking?" he asked, showing her his peppers.

"Perfect," she said. "Any way you cut them would be perfect. Anything goes when it comes to salad, in my opinion."

He laughed. "So my peppers are terrible but it's fine?"

She laughed too. "Exactly."

He added the peppers to the bowl of romaine lettuce and tomatoes and got to work on the cucumber. He barely recognized himself. Chopping vegetables in a kitchen, a baby monitor on the counter nearby. A woman sliding garlic bread into the oven.

A dog lying on the rug by the fireplace, chomping on a dental treat in the shape of a bone.

Couldn't get more domestic than this.

Actually, it could. Because his ideas for how they might go about co-parenting Wyatt involved serious domesticity. The plan he'd come up with in the barn when she'd been talking to her relatives made absolute sense to him and would benefit both of them—and of course Wyatt. And after meeting her brother and hearing about his issues, Jesse was even more sure. But actually bringing it up, proposing it—that he wasn't quite ready for.

"I noticed you don't have a Christmas tree yet," he said instead. "On the drive over here, I saw a sign for a tree farm a few miles away."

What the hell was he doing? Now he was adding to the domestication of Jesse Dawson by talking about Christmas trees? The last thing he wanted was to be up close and personal with the holiday. It would just remind him of his last day with his dad, the big decorated tree in the clinic that had been in his face every time he entered or left.

"More like I can't bear it," she said, closing the oven door and setting the timer. "Kate loved Christmas. She'd wear those ugly Christmas sweaters and Santa hats and volunteer as Mrs. Claus in the Santa hut in the town square. Every time I see twinkling lights or someone wishes me a Merry Christmas, my heart actually aches. Every day this week, I've forced myself to put on the Santa hat and the mini one she'd bought right before she—"

He could see her eyes well, and he reached for her hand and held it. "I know just how you feel. My dad died close to Christmas. It was everywhere that day."

The shared understanding was another surprise. He'd known Lila Mack for one day and already felt unexpectedly close to her—a rare occurrence in his life.

She squeezed his hand back and then let go to turn off the pot with the linguini. "I have to get over it, though. For Wyatt. This is his first Christmas."

"I'll have to also, then. One year when my aunt was going through a bad breakup after her divorce and feeling very Scrooge-y, she realized not having any Christmas spirit made her feel worse. So she got a big robust tree and made ornaments out of things she hoped for, like a better man—who was represented by a celebrity magazine photo of Colin Firth on the tree. A trip to Disneyland, so lots of Mickey Mouse ornaments. A new car to replace her beater. Instead of a star at the top, there was a little toy Tonka truck that always made her laugh when she walked into the living room. She said it reminded her of me as a little kid."

"That's great," Lila said, her face brightening. "I should do something like that. Who says the tree has to be traditional?"

"Right. We can go to a tree farm tomorrow."

"Sure is nice having you around," she said, and he caught her wince and her cheeks redden a bit.

They definitely both seemed to say things they didn't intend to around each other.

She cleared her throat. "My gram is a little worried about your intentions, though, as you know. As is my brother. So we should talk about that. Wyatt, I mean. What your plans are. How you want to go about things, a schedule. That'll help set our minds at ease."

"Understood," he said, adding the cucumbers to the salad. "I had a chance to think when I was in the barn and out walking the farm earlier. If you're open to it, I'd like to stay here—in the empty guest room."

He glanced at her, and he caught her freeze for a moment, her hand stilling on the wooden spoon in the pot of meatballs. But she didn't look at him or say anything.

"I can help with Wyatt and the farm," he rushed to add. "And I have my appointment for the DNA test at the hospital lab tomorrow morning. Once I have the results and it's a sure thing, we can sit down with your family—Micah included—and I can assure them that I won't take Wyatt away. Staying here, right under your nose, will likely make you all feel better about that."

He figured so, anyway.

She was quiet, stirring the meatballs and still not looking at him. He could see she was thinking. Hard.

"I want to be there for my son, Lila. I want to wake up where he wakes up, sleep where he sleeps. I don't want to miss another moment. I mean, of course, I'll miss moments when I'm working on the farm. But I'll be right here. I'll pay rent, of course."

The more he talked, the more he realized how much he wanted this. To be under the same roof as his child—and the woman who cared about Wyatt the same way he did.

She *had* to say yes.

"So you're talking about moving in…indefinitely."

"Yes," he said. That word worked fine. He had no idea about anything else, including a time frame.

She stared at him hard for a moment. "The guest room is yours. But I'll tell you right now, Jesse Dawson. I won't expect anything from you. You're here—great. You're helping care for Wyatt and learning the ropes of fatherhood—great. Helping me with the farm—great. But I won't count on you. I won't have expectations. If you're gone in a few days—and I don't mean *with* Wyatt…"

He bristled. "I'm not going anywhere. And I could be a big help with getting the farm going. You need a bigger herd. You need more equipment. Some of the fencing and barn posts need repair. I can help with all that."

"I have no money for three-quarters of what you just listed," she said, her expression tight.

"Ten years of working on prosperous ranches with good pay and room and board included means I have a small fortune in the bank, Lila. Let me do this. The Double Sisters Farm is my son's legacy. And I want to do it for you, for the woman who's taken care of my child for the past two months without any help from me."

She was staring at him, her hand stilled once again around the wooden spoon. Her eyes were a little misty, but she seemed overwhelmed. He got it—this was a lot. All of it. "Well, you didn't know about Wyatt," she said.

"That's my own fault."

"Yeah, it is," she said, resuming stirring with just the hint of a smile. But the smile faded and he saw tears welling in her eyes.

Now he felt like hell. "I didn't mean to upset you."

She shook her head. "You didn't. Far from it. I've been putting on this brave front for the past two months but between raising Wyatt and trying to get the farm going and worry about my parents and worrying double about Micah, I've been kind of a fragile wreck inside. And suddenly you turn up and it's like I have a partner even if for just a little while." Her green eyes glistened. "I'm relieved, Jesse. You have no idea."

He was relieved too right now. "Well, now I think I do."

She smiled. "Thank you. For everything. And yes. I like everything you said. And while I'd like to wait for those DNA results, it's obvious you're Wyatt's dad—from your name, which Kate mentioned, to the horse pin you instantly recognized, to the fact that Wyatt is your mini-me. The test will just confirm what we both already know."

He nodded and held her gaze for a moment.

"I won't take a penny in rent from you," Lila added. "I'll have my own experienced cowboy. I'll have a live-in co-parent. I can take a bubble bath again." She gave a wobbly smile, and he understood. It was *a lot*.

"Tell you what," he said. "Why don't I take the money I'd pay in rent and instead put it into the farm?"

She stared at him. "You'd do that?"

"Like I said, this is my son's legacy. One day, this will be his."

He could see her eyes mist again.

But she turned and extended a hand. "We'll take it day by day."

He shook her hand, which was both soft and calloused at the same time.

The little jolt he felt at the physical contact with this woman didn't escape him.

# *Chapter Five*

"This feels so weird and not in a good way," Lila said the next morning to her mother and grandmother. She sat in one of the hairstyling chairs at the Hair Royale salon, staring at herself in the huge oval mirror. "Wyatt isn't with me, he's not with you two, and he's not at Aunt Raina's house. I don't like it."

This morning, Jesse had confirmed his appointment at the hospital lab, then had actually called his cousin Reed Dawson at the Bear Ridge police department to ask if he'd go with him and Wyatt. As moral support for himself and assurance for the Mack family since they knew and liked Reed, cat-rescuing detective. Apparently, when Reed had gotten over the shock of the news that Wyatt's dad was not only suddenly in the picture but a Dawson cousin, he'd said absolutely.

And now the three were at the lab, Jesse and Wyatt getting swabbed. Lila, anxious, hadn't been able to stay home after they'd left. The house was too quiet. And it did feel weird that Wyatt was with someone other than her or one of her relatives.

She'd have to get used to that.

She had no idea how she'd get used to Jesse living in

her home, though. After dinner last night, they'd cleaned up the kitchen together, Jesse insisting on helping even though she'd told him to go relax. He'd asked her to write out Wyatt's schedule and tips and tricks about caring for him, and so they'd brought coffee into the living room and the pecan pie her grandmother had left earlier in the day. He'd said he'd take the night wakings, that she should just turn over and go back to sleep if she heard Wyatt crying, and he'd been good to his word. She had woken up, heard Wyatt cry and had instinctively thrown off her down comforter, then remembered. Wyatt had another parent in the house. Who'd actually offered to get up in the middle of the night.

She kept picturing him in the nursery, sitting on the rocker with Wyatt in his arms, or in the living room on the sofa, giving him his bottle. She'd wanted to go find him and check in but that hadn't felt right. He'd want that private time with his baby and she needed to let him feel comfortable with caring for Wyatt instead of running to the rescue, not that she'd had to do much of that at all.

She hadn't been able to go back to sleep easily; she'd been too aware of Jesse Dawson being in her house, in her guest room—*his* room now. At five fifteen, she'd heard Wyatt cry and realized the shower was running too, so she'd slipped out of bed only to catch Jesse, towel wrapped around his hips, dashing into the nursery, monitor in hand.

Her heart had sped up a little in that moment. At both how seriously he was taking his new role in life. And how damned sexy Jesse Dawson was. He was at least six-one, maybe six-two, and leanly muscular. And that thick, tousled dark hair, wet from the shower? She'd seen him only from the back, but his damp muscles... Ooh.

She wasn't supposed to have that reaction to him. And it had left her unsettled.

"Want a little trim?" her mother asked, standing behind her white leather stylist's chair and shaking Lila from her thoughts. The salon would open at 10:00 a.m. and would be full of clients all day. "Or I could shampoo you and give you my premium scalp massage."

Those scalp massages were heavenly. "Nah, but thanks," Lila said. "I'm so anxious to hear from Jesse and see Wyatt that I wouldn't be able to enjoy it."

Her grandmother came over with her mug of tea and sat in the chair next to Lila's. "I have to say, everything you've told me about Jesse has impressed me. He's thoughtful, polite, hardworking, caring, and the way he's taken to fatherhood with Wyatt—that's something. He went from never holding a baby to doing both nightly feedings?"

"And he not only made the salad for dinner last night, he helped clean up after when I told him to go relax."

Her mother nodded. "He has a good heart, that's for sure. And this plan of his, to move in so he can be there round the clock for Wyatt and help with the farm? That's something. He's like your own personal Prince Charming."

*You should see him in just a towel, his tall, strong body damp from the shower...*

She gave her head a mental shake. She had to stop thinking about that.

"I'm not sure he's anyone's Prince Charming," Lila said. "He's never settled down. He's moved from ranch to ranch. He doesn't have a home. And he said his father was the same way—even though he had a child, one who also lost his mother young. He just left Jesse with his aunt and would come back months later with gifts and money." She couldn't imagine that, but Jesse clearly loved his father. "What if in a few days, a few weeks or worse, a few years, when Wyatt has a deep bond with his dad, he gets the itch to leave? That's all Jesse knows—*leaving.*"

"Micah talked about nothing else last night," her mom said. "About the fact that Jesse might take Wyatt away. I did my best to assure him."

Lila nodded. "I'll call Micah after school and invite him over. He didn't give Jesse much of a chance to talk— he just took off. Now that Micah's had some time to calm down, he can hear it straight from Jesse himself."

"Sounds like a plan," her gram said. "And now that Jesse's someone's daddy, a tiny baby's daddy, I think Jesse Dawson is going to discover just who he is."

"Agreed," her mom said, resting her hands on Lila's shoulders. "Just because his father shirked his responsibilities doesn't mean Jesse will. I wonder if he's worried he's his father's son, that his ways are hardwired into him."

Lila definitely thought he did worry about that. "He's made it crystal clear that he's not going anywhere, that he's Wyatt's father and is stepping up. So I guess we'll see."

She caught her mother eye her grandmother in the mirror.

"Just be careful," her mother said.

Lila nodded. "I know. No expectations. He could

leave tomorrow or in a week or a month. And Wyatt could have a part-time father. Or an absentee father."

"No," her grandmother said. "I do think Jesse will honor his word. I have a very good feeling about that. But I think your mother is talking about being careful with your heart."

Lila almost gasped. "What? Why would you even say something like that? There won't be anything happening between me and Jesse Dawson."

Then why would she have been so affected by seeing him half-naked in that towel?

Her mother raised an eyebrow. "Living under the same roof? Sharing parenting responsibilities? Working the farm together? You two are going to get close fast. And like your grandmother has pointed out quite a few times, he's very handsome."

"I guess," Lila said, trying for nonchalance. But inwardly, she absolutely agreed. And was a little worried for her heart. She already felt close to Jesse. And a connection she hadn't expected.

"And he *is* making a commitment to fatherhood and to Wyatt," her gram said. "That's big. Something huge that the two of you have in common: a baby to raise."

"Committing to taking care of your own child is different than committing to a relationship with a woman. This is a man who's taken off at whim every few months, right?"

Lila thought about what he'd told her, how he'd been betrayed by the woman he'd worked hard to commit to. Between his natural bent to leave and that, she *would* have to be very careful with herself.

She couldn't let herself fall for him. Because any issues between them would become issues in the house and cause a problem with raising Wyatt together.

*No matter how wonderful he is, no matter how helpful, no matter how hot in that towel with his tousled hair and muscles—you will not fall for Jesse Dawson. Repeat, repeat, repeat.*

She closed her eyes and chanted it in her head.

But all she saw was Jesse with his bare torso glistening.

"I have to agree with you *and* the Macks," Detective Reed Dawson said as he and Jesse settled into a back table at the coffee shop. "The DNA results will confirm what's visible on both your and Wyatt's faces. He's your mini-me."

Jesse's mini-me was at this moment taking a snooze in his stroller, which was parked right beside Jesse's chair. He hadn't been sure how the baby would respond to having a giant Q-tip poked into his mouth and swabbing his cheek, but he'd handled it like the curious champ he was, then had promptly fallen asleep while Jesse was getting swabbed.

The two samples had been placed in a big, official-looking envelope by the lab tech at the hospital and that was that.

"I really appreciate that you came with us," Jesse said as the waitress set down water and menus. "Yesterday at this time, I didn't know I *had* a child. Suddenly, I'm taking a paternity test just for the record and moving into Lila Mack's guest room so I can be right there with my son."

"I've known the Macks a long time. Great family."

"They're all wary of me, though, and my intentions. If I'll take Jesse away. If I'll stay in town—which was one of my father's last wishes for me. He wanted me to put down roots. Get a dog. Be open to love." Jesse shook his head. "I don't know how I can undo my childhood and the last twelve years of how I've lived just like that. My father couldn't do it, but he wants me to?"

Reed nodded. "It's called regrets. At the eleventh hour. When you can't change what you've done but you can want more for those you love. Your dad wanted better for you. He wants you to have the stability, the permanence, the *dog* he never did."

The waitress came by to take their orders—pancakes and bacon for Reed and the western omelet for Jesse—which gave Jesse a minute to let Reed's words sit.

"He did seem to have regrets," Jesse said. "He wrote in the letter that he wished he'd been more of a father. But I thought the world of him. I was crazy about my dad."

"Because he loved you and you knew it, despite his absences. He made you feel it, Jesse. I'm not sure how he pulled that off, but he did. I barely knew your father—just met him a couple times years ago. But I remember him as warm and friendly."

Jesse smiled. "Yeah. He was. Drove my aunt crazy. She wanted to be mad at him for the way he'd say he'd be back in a few weeks and then return in a few *months* with money and gifts. He charmed his sister every time into forgiving him."

"And your aunt probably liked having you live with her," Reed said. "She was probably relieved knowing you'd consume more than hot dogs and soda and she'd make sure you did your homework."

He laughed. "Yeah, between her and my dad, I turned out fine. My aunt instilled a sense of responsibility and my dad instilled the adventurer in me."

"Well, there's no greater adventure than being a dad," Reed said. "I'm speaking from very personal experience." He pulled out his phone and showed Jesse at least ten photos of his baby daughter, Summer, who'd recently turned a year old. When she was just a newborn, someone had left her in an infant car seat on his desk at the PD when no one had been around. An anonymous note asked Reed to take care of her for a few days. He and a social worker, Aimee Gallagher, had gotten snowed-in during a blizzard and ended up caring for the baby together—and falling in love. They married and adopted Summer. This all despite Reed's very complicated past that had made being around babies hard. But Aimee and Summer had changed his life.

"I also have photos," Jesse said. "Well, *a* photo." He pulled out his phone and looked at the one Lila had sent of him feeding Wyatt. He held it up for his cousin to see.

"Oh yeah, you have *nothing* to worry about, Jesse. How you feel about fatherhood, about that baby, is stamped on your face. Being a good dad is about wanting to be one. But the way you're looking at your son while feeding him his bottle? That's all you need to know about how you're gonna do as a father."

Jesse looked at the photo. Reed's conviction and the fact that Lila had seen something that had made her take the picture did wonders for his confidence.

"I still worry that I'm hardwired to be bad at this," Jesse admitted. "The commitment part. I want to be there for my son. I intend to be there. But what if I *am* my father's son? What if I walk away for months at a time and think that's okay? Wyatt lost his mother young like I did—and I know he has a loving aunt just like my father knew I did." His shoulders tensed at the similarities.

"Look, Jesse, I can't claim to know you too well. But I'm a detective and you're no mystery. You're committed. I can see it. Just don't hurt Lila. That woman has been through enough."

Jesse stared at his cousin in a kind of shock. "Hurt her? Ah—wait." He shook his head. Vehemently. "There's nothing going on between me and Lila. And I need to keep it that way. No matter how beautiful she is."

"You only need to keep it that way if your intentions with her are the same as they are with Wyatt. If you can commit. If you can't, don't start what you can't finish."

"Lila's grandmother said that same thing yesterday. With her finger pointed at me."

Reed laughed. "Oh yeah, I know her nana. I can see that."

The waitress set down their steaming plates. Jesse glanced over at Wyatt to make sure he was still asleep—he was—and then he and Reed dug in.

He'd rather eat than talk—that was for sure.

Or think about how he had to somehow keep his mind in the strictly platonic zone when it came to Lila.

He wouldn't hurt her. And the only way to not hurt her was to not touch her. Kiss her. Or even think about it.

Problem was, he'd thought about kissing her and more when he'd been in bed last night after caring for Wyatt. He'd pictured her in her bed, wearing a slinky nightie—or more realistically, a T-shirt and yoga pants, which was equally sexy.

*She's beautiful, she's kind, she's your lifeline to this new existence. Of course you're drawn to her. Just leave it there. That she's this important new person to you. You could do a lot of damage in a lot of ways by giving in to the attraction.*

He couldn't and wouldn't touch her.

If he could turn into some kind of good father, he could force himself to keep his hands and lips to himself with Lila. That was for the best, and he knew it.

Just wouldn't be easy.

# *Chapter Six*

Lila heard Jesse's pickup pulling in, and she ran outside, dying to see Wyatt. They'd been gone close to three hours. As Jesse hopped out, she pulled open the back door and there was her dear boy, napping without a care. "I missed you so much!" she whispered to Wyatt, carefully unbuckling him and cuddling him close. "I'm not used to him being away."

Billy gave a woof as if he too was relieved that the baby of the house was back, then padded over to Jesse, sniffing his boots.

Jesse gave the dog's head a rub and a scratch under the chin. "Wyatt did great out there—a champ getting swabbed, and he let Reed hold him without grabbing his ear or nose. Oh, and he slept through breakfast at the diner."

He took out his phone and Lila saw him press the Notes app. Wyatt's schedule popped up. She smiled as she realized that he'd entered the long list and the tips and tricks and had likely referred to it while he was out.

"Let's see," Jesse said. "Wyatt should be waking up soon, then I'll change him and give him a bottle. In the meantime, why don't we go over what the farm needs?"

"Sounds good," she said, excited to talk all things Double Sisters. Her family liked the idea of the ranch, but none were all that interested in goats or a dairy business, except her brother.

They went inside the house. Lila got the baby out of his snowsuit without him waking up, then lowered him into his baby rocker in the living room, which gently swayed and played soft lullabies. Jesse headed into the kitchen to make coffee, and then they both sat down on the sofa, mugs of coffee in front of them.

For the next hour, they devised a new business plan for the farm, decided to add four more goats to start, including a buck. The farm would be a licensed dairy, and they'd have to have the inspector out to approve the milking area and their processes, from the bucket assembly to the chilling station and bottling system to the cleaning equipment. Lila hoped that local grocery stores and takeouts across the county would carry Double Sisters Farm goat milk and cheeses. And maybe they could even grow bigger from there. Jesse had worked on the dairy side of many ranches, and he knew the goat business well, which was an enormous help. Lila had done her research, but Jesse had the actual experience. With him around, getting the farm and dairy business going could actually become a reality.

"So tell me," Jesse said, taking a long sip of his coffee. "Why goats? How and when did that become a dream? Though, granted, goats are awesome, and Dolly and Lulu are beauties."

Lila grinned. "They really are. The goat love started when Kate and I were eight years old. We joined a 4H club, and we both fell madly in love with goats—particularly the

Nubians. Something about their long droopy ears. They look regal and like Eeyore at the same time."

He laughed. "They definitely do. And I was a 4H kid too. Each kid in my group was assigned a calf to monitor, and between wanting to be a cowboy like my dad and loving everything about cattle, I found my calling by the time I was seven."

"Aww, I love that. Same here. Except Kate and I were both too unsure about actually starting our own farm and making a success out of it. So we just worked for other farms and the past couple of years as vet techs for the steady paycheck and experience and kept talking about someday."

"What got you both to finally start the Double Sisters?" he asked, sipping his coffee.

Her heart gave a little ping at the question. It meant a lot to her that he asked, that he was interested in this topic. Most men she met were not. Even ranchers and cowboys and hands. Last year, when she and Kate decided to try online dating, Lila had thought narrowing her matches to cowboys and ranchers meant she and her dates would start out having a lot in common, a shared passion. But her last three first dates involved the guy talking her head off about himself and not asking her a single question that didn't somehow revolve around himself. Kate had had the same luck or lack thereof and decided to forget dating and pick up a second job waitressing on weekends to boost their Our Someday Farm joint savings account.

Lila's extra shifts at the big farm she worked for only brought her into contact with more self-absorbed or I'm-not-the-settling-down-sort cowboys. So she'd finally

agreed to be set up by her aunt Raina, who'd been wax-
ing on about her many good-looking and interesting single colleagues at the hospital. Six months ago, her aunt
had arranged a blind date—Lila's last—with a radiolo-
gist who was incredibly handsome. He'd wrinkled his
nose when she mentioned her dream to start a goat dairy
farm and business and told her she'd stink of goat 24/7,
and added that in fact, she did kind of give off a farm
smell. He'd chuckled as though that was remotely funny,
then asked if she'd showered before the date or had she
come right from her job. She'd gotten up and told him
she wouldn't be staying for the shared chocolate rasp-
berry tart they'd ordered for dessert. She'd apologized to
her aunt Raina for walking out on the fix-up, but Raina
had clapped and said she would have approved waiting for the tart only if Lila had upended it on his head.

"What made Kate and I finally decide to go for it is
a little silly," she said. "I'm not sure I want to tell you."

Jesse smiled and raised an eyebrow. "Well, now you
have to tell me because I have to know."

There it was again. The real interest. It was like an
aphrodisiac—just with the wrong guy. "Well," she said,
draining her coffee to procrastinate telling this particular
story. "We were at the county rodeo last summer, and we
passed a booth with a sign that said 'Psychic Readings
by Alina. Your future foretold for only $25!'"

Jesse didn't laugh in her face and say, *No way did you
actually pay some crackpot to tell you anything about
yourself.* He just looked very curious.

"We had the choice of having our readings together
or separately," Lila added. "We chose together. Alina
said: 'Each of you may ask me one question. Sometimes,

I won't have the answer. Sometimes I will. But rest assured that I will be honest.'"

Jesse leaned forward, waiting for her to continue.

"Kate went first. She asked, 'Should we quit our jobs and start our own goat dairy farm?' Alina looked at her—hard. Then took Kate's hands in both of hers and closed her eyes for like two minutes, which is a long time when you're sitting across from someone."

Jesse smiled. "It is."

"Finally, Alina opened her eyes, staring straight at Kate, and she nodded firmly. She said, 'The answer is yes. You should quit your jobs and start your own dairy farm.' Kate and I both gasped. We started to ask her a million questions—'Would the farm succeed and grow? How many goats should we start with?' And she held up a hand and said 'I've told you my answer.'"

Lila smiled at the memory of sitting with her twin across from Alina in the little booth, the silver curtain drawn for privacy. Maybe she should stop at this point and not mention her *own* question to the psychic. That was a little embarrassing.

"And what was your burning question?" Jesse asked. He sipped his coffee, his gaze never leaving hers.

Drat. Of course he asked. She could make something up. Something about the farm.

"I did have a burning question," Lila said. "But since we got a positive response about the farm, I was afraid to hope for good news again. I wasn't even going to ask. But then Alina looked at me and said, 'Your question, please.' And so I just blurted it out. 'Will we find true love?'"

He smiled. "That was brave."

"Right? I mean, if we were going to take her *yes* about

the farm and jump in whole hog, we wouldn't be able to dismiss her 'No, sorry,' about love."

"Well, what did she say?" he asked.

Lila sighed. "She said, 'Yes, you both will.' And I figured that would be that since she didn't seem open to elaboration. But she looked at us and added, 'You may not know it at the time. But you will each find your true love.' She gave us a little too much to think about there. But you know what?"

"What?" he asked.

"I have this beautiful picture of Kate holding Wyatt when he was an infant. We were at the duck pond in the park with the whole family—my parents and grandparents and my aunt Raina. The look on Kate's face as she gazed down at her son. It stopped me in my tracks. Like this morning when you were feeding Wyatt. I almost didn't get the shot of the two of them because I was so struck by the pure love on her face. She was *glowing* with it."

"That's really beautiful," he said.

"And you know what I realized? That the psychic was talking about *Wyatt* being Kate's true love. I recalled how Alina said, 'You might not know it at the time.' I think she meant that true love is what fulfills you, what lights up your heart. And for Kate, that was Wyatt more than anything."

Jesse put down his coffee cup, his gaze intent on hers. "And what about you?"

She bit her lip. "I've had a lot of blah first dates, a bunch of short-term romances, and nothing's worked out. I pretty much gave up on dating, but Alina's fortune always made me feel like it's possible. That's enough."

He regarded her for a moment, then picked up his coffee. She wondered what he was thinking. She wanted to ask him if he'd been involved with anyone beyond a few hours, but she could see on his face that he was hoping she wouldn't.

Billy came over to the sofa and sniffed Jesse's leg, then rested his chin on Jesse's thigh.

"Aww, Billy likes you," Lila said.

*And God help me, so do I.*

Jesse stroked the dog's soft, furry head, Billy letting out a happy sigh.

Everyone seemed to respond well to Jesse Dawson. Even her discriminating dog.

She cleared her throat. She had to stop thinking of Jesse as a man. And start thinking of him as her partner—in raising Wyatt, in getting the farm going.

"Oh, and another thing," Lila said to shift her thoughts. "As we were leaving Alina's booth, she said she'd stop by the farm someday to try our goat cheese and that she liked to have Wheat Thins crackers with her sample so I should keep a box around."

He smiled. "Wheat Thins. I love them."

"I do too. I did buy a box. Just in case she ever does show up. Of course, it'll be a while before I'm ready to make cheese."

"So you left the psychic's booth and quit your jobs?" he asked.

"We did wait a few days. We talked for hours, hovered over our laptops, making a business plan, talking money, crunching numbers. And we both said, *We're doing this. We'll never be ready-ready. So let's just do it. Let's believe in ourselves.*"

"Good," he said with a firm nod.

Just about everyone else thought she and her twin were crazy to embark on something so risky, to give up their solid jobs and part-time work for *goats*. Jesse's *good* went straight into her heart and fluttered there.

She remembered how excited they both had been. She'd always have these beautiful memories. "We decided to start by finding our location. It was actually Micah who told us about this property being for sale. He'd stopped by to ask the owner if she needed a ranch hand and she said she was actually putting the place on the market, that she was turning eighty and it was time to pack it in. So Kate and I went over to see the farm and it was perfect. She was a widow the last few years but kept up the house so well. Though like you said, the barn and fencing needs some work."

Jesse drank the last of his coffee. "Well, I love that whole story, from the rodeo psychic to the fact that it was Micah who found the location for the farm. He already has a connection to the land. You know, getting him on board with working for the farm after school or even just on weekends could change his attitude and entire future. He'd see that I'm not taking Wyatt away too."

She could hug him. She wouldn't of course, but she wanted to. "I'll talk to him about that. I feel so hopeful about everything—the plan for the farm, for taking Micah under our wing. And I know Kate is watching. She was watching when I signed all the closing documents and handed over all that money to the bank. She was watching when I hung the Double Sisters Farm signs at the turnoff and on the barn. She's watching now."

"You think so?" he said and seemed a little uncomfortable.

"She clearly approved of you, Jesse. Let's just face facts. And Wyatt has his daddy. She cried about that a few times. That she wanted to give Wyatt the world, everything, but couldn't give him one of the most fundamental things—his own father. And here you are."

A warm, thoughtful smile lit up his handsome face.

She finished her coffee, content and feeling positive.

A fussy cry came from the nursery and Lila popped up. "You sit. You deserve a break. Maybe after his bottle we can go to the Christmas tree farm just down the road and get that tree you were telling me about."

"Sounds like a plan."

She knew her twin was definitely watching and smiling.

Jesse figured Lila would pick a small tree, but she went for a seven-and-a-half-foot balsam fir that she said smelled like the season. He had a feeling that would be the case. The holiday with all its reminders of what they'd both lost—closest of family—was now about Wyatt. The baby's first Christmas.

Looking at it that way helped when they'd arrived at the tree farm and he was suddenly in tree overload, samples decked out with all the lights and decorations. His heart had given a lurch; for a second he was back at the Bear Ridge Clinic last December, all that festivity greeting him coming and going when he felt his lowest. Lila, too, seemed to have her own moment of grief when they'd pulled into the lot. She'd looked down at her lap, and he knew she was thinking of her sister. But then Wyatt let out a happy sound, a *ba*, and she'd immediately brightened and said that was a sign they were supposed to do Christmas right.

He'd secured the fir to the top of her SUV, while Lila got Wyatt into his car seat in the rear. Then they went to the Bear Ridge General Store, which Lila said had a back section devoted to the holidays. Jesse attached the baby carrier to his chest and Lila slid Wyatt in. He liked having his son so close to his heart.

And maybe because *Lila* was so close that he could smell her shampoo, he had a blast of awareness of her. He'd been trying not to pay attention to how pretty she was, how sexy in her faded jeans and fuzzy sweater and red down jacket. The Santa hat on her head, which he found touching, especially knowing the full story. That combo was doing him in, he realized. Too sexy and too able to somehow sneak inside him. He'd thought that would be impossible. Wyatt had managed it, but he was a three-month-old baby. Jesse's baby.

Lila, he had to be very careful about.

"Ready?" she asked with a bright smile, her green eyes happy.

He sucked in a breath. "Ready."

The strange thing was that he was. He wasn't dreading this, as he'd expected. Maybe because they were calling this mission the UnScrooge, UnGrinch Christmas Shopping Expedition and would use his aunt's "hope" tree as their model. What they hoped for instead of what were they missing.

Inside the semi-crowded shop, they found an entire wall of ornaments, every possible style from the more traditional to the whimsical, with several local craftspeople offering their handiwork. Because this was a ranching town, there were plenty of range-focused ornaments.

"Ooh, look at those goats!" Lila said with a big smile, beelining for them. She held one up and laughed. It was a little painted wooden cut-out of a baby goat, black and white, with a textile tail, and he looked like he was smiling. Lila grabbed a bunch of them. "I'll get six since I plan to add four goats to our little herd."

He smiled and glanced down at his baby's head. "What do you think, Wyatt. Perfect, right?"

Lila beamed. "And you pick out some too, Jesse. Ornaments that represent what you hope for."

Uh, that *wasn't* part of the plan. He'd thought this would just be about her—and wanted it that way. But as he looked at the rows and rows of various ornaments, his gaze landed on a red pickup, also wooden and cut-out, and it looked exactly like the truck his father had had when he was a kid. Eddie Dawson would pull into his aunt's drive in that sputtering old pickup and Jesse would come running out, so happy he'd thought he'd burst. His dad would drive him into town for pizza or burgers, and everything was all right with the world. He put the ornament in their basket.

"That's for your grandfather on my side," he told Wyatt, giving his hair a caress.

"Perfect," Lila said, her gaze soft on him.

Jesse had that feeling that someone was staring at him, and indeed someone was—a man in the next row who looked vaguely familiar. His arms were full of strings of lights and red garland.

The guy smiled and nodded. "At first I thought you

were Jesse Dawson," he said, "but no way is Jesse Dawson married with a baby!" He let out a loud snorting
laugh. "But dang, it *is* you."

Ah. Jesse placed him. He'd worked with the guy,
Hank Something, at his last ranch and remembered that
they were both originally from Bear Ridge. Jesse was
a few years younger and had barely been able to stand
him. The guy thought vulgar jokes and talking about
everyone behind their backs was funny.

Jesse glanced at Lila, who continued to look at the
ornaments, but he could tell she was listening. He gave
Hank a quick nod in acknowledgment and hoped he'd
just continue on his way.

"Jesse Dawson with a baby," Hank added, letting out a
low whistle of disbelief. "How'd *that* happen?" he added
on a guffaw, jabbing an elbow toward Lila. "Man, the
kid looks just like you so he must be yours. Just don't
take after your old man, and you'll do fine, am I right?"
he added with a grin and a slap on Jesse's upper arm,
then sauntered off to a woman waiting for him by the
checkout.

*Jerk*, Jesse thought, narrowing his eyes after the guy.
He hated that someone he didn't give a whit about had
managed to actually piss him off.

Maybe because what he'd said had merit.

Great. Now Jesse felt like hell.

"Ignore, ignore, ignore," Lila said, stepping over. "My
new motto since getting very busy with a baby to raise
and a farm to figure out. I don't have time for nonsense,
especially from people like that. Same for you, right?"
she asked, peering at him.

His shoulders unstiffened a bit. "You're absolutely

right. But it's not like he was wrong. I was the last guy anyone would expect to have a kid."

"Well, aren't you full of surprises, then," she said with a smile.

Jesse looked at Lila and felt a smile of his own tugging unexpectedly at his mouth. He appreciated her take on the situation, that she didn't even feel it warranted talking about. A blowhard former coworker. But anyone who knew Jesse, even his aunt, would be shocked to discover that he was someone's father. That he had it in him to take care of a tiny, helpless being, that he was in it for the long haul, which was forever, actually.

Jesse's aunt Bess was away for the next couple of days on an RV tour of the south with her second husband, Bill, a guy Jesse liked fine. She didn't even know she was a great-aunt. But he'd stop over with the baby when she was back home. He had no doubt she'd lecture him on not being like his father. He wasn't looking forward to that.

"What if I am like my dad?" he asked, almost on a whisper. He hadn't meant to say it aloud.

Lila put her hands on either side of his face. "Jesse Dawson, you're your own man. You'll be the father *you* want to be. It's up to you, nothing else, no one else."

She always knew what to say to make him feel okay, to make him feel better. Hopeful.

"I want to believe that," he said, recalling that his cousin Reed had said something similar at the diner.

A little foot poked out and gave a kick, followed by a brief cry.

Jesse looked down. "Someone's fussy," he said, trailing a finger down the baby's cheek. He walked the length of the ornament wall so that Wyatt had some move-ment. "Hey, that worked," he noted to Lila. "He seems content."

"Exactly my point," she said with a smile. "You moved around because you care that Jesse was bored or uncom-fortable. And because in a very short period of time, you already know quite a bit about taking care of your son."

"Okay, fine, that makes me feel a lot better."

"Good, because it should." She looked in the basket hanging on his forearm. "One mere ornament? It's a *big* tree, Jesse."

He stared hard at the little red pickup truck on the silver hook. Suddenly, his memories turned on him, though. Now he wondered how his father *had* left a motherless three-year-old for months at a time. There were a few Christmases Eddie Dawson hadn't come home at all because of girlfriends, none of whom lasted by February. He'd always defended his father's adven-turous, cowboy spirit. But maybe his dad had just been a neglectful parent.

Great. Now Jesse felt like hell again.

"Pick just one more," she said. "And we'll get this guy home for his nap."

He wasn't really up for this anymore. But he didn't want to call attention to his mood. He looked at the rows of ornaments and noticed one of a small, white house with a black cat sitting on the brick roof beside the chimney. He recalled his dad saying his mother had loved black cats. Because of his father's lack of senti-mentality, he didn't have any of his mother's things and she didn't have family of her own, so he had little to con-nect himself to her. His parents had eloped to Las Vegas, and there was one wedding photo from the insta-venue. His aunt had some photos of Jesse as a baby and toddler, but his mother was in very few. Apparently, she'd been camera-shy, preferring to be behind the lens.

His cousin Reed's words came to him again. *Being a good dad is about wanting to be one.* He wished he could remember his mom, but he'd been only three when she'd died. He didn't recall a thing about her, something that bothered him.

He reached for the ornament and stared at it, at the black cat. *This is for you, Mom*, he sent heavenward. Silly as it was, just a tiny house with the cat on the roof, a red loop to hang it, the ornament meant something to him anyway, and he put it in his basket.

"Is it the cat or the house that represents something for you?" Lila asked, her green eyes full of curiosity.

"Both. My dad told me my mother loved black cats because they were so sleek and spooky. She was allergic, though, so she never had one of her own. My aunt showed me a photo of her, me and my dad when I was a baby in front of a small white house kind of like this one," he said, tapping the ornament. "She said it's where we lived when my mom was still alive. I don't remember it, though."

"Your mom must have taken the photo," Lila pointed out.

He nodded. That was likely. Maybe he'd ask his aunt for that picture.

"That ornament counts as two, then," Lila said with a soft smile.

He sucked in a fast breath and nodded. How'd this outing to the general store turn so...emotional? Jeez.

They headed toward the checkout, Wyatt kicking out another foot in a telltale gesture that meant: *I'm tired.* How Jesse knew that with such certainty he wasn't sure after just a day and a half, but he did.

Every time he thought he was kidding himself about being a dad, that he could do this and be good at it, he surprised himself.

*It's been a day and a half,* he reminded himself. *Let's revisit in a few weeks when fatherhood isn't a novelty but a daily routine.*

"Ba!" Wyatt said in a high voice, a little foot kicking again.

Lila laughed. "I love that he's starting to make sounds. I can't wait until he can talk. I know that's months and months away. But we have a lot of exciting milestones coming."

Jesse leaned down to press a kiss on his baby son's head. Wyatt *had* just talked. He'd cut right into Jesse's gloomy thoughts and seemed to be saying: *Hey, one day at a time, Daddy.*

*Daddy.* It was the first time Jesse had attributed that to himself.

He almost laughed at his ability to read that much into one *ba.*

He smiled and put a protective hand on Wyatt in the carrier. All Jesse knew for sure was that he was changing right before his own eyes.

# Chapter Seven

The tree was coming along. Jesse had brought it in and they'd set it up in the corner near the sliding doors to the backyard. Lila stepped back to look at it in all its trimmed glory—wrapped with white lights and red garland, her new ornaments—and felt her heart give a little leap. She loved the tree. And it was thanks to Jesse that it was here since she'd probably have procrastinated getting a tree till Christmas Eve if at all. Now she had this beautiful, festive fir in Kate's memory and for Wyatt's first Christmas.

And atop it was something very special to her.

A few days after Kate learned she was pregnant, she'd bought Wyatt a squishy stuffed black billy goat with striped horns and buck teeth. When Lila and Jesse got home from the general store, Lila took it from the bookshelf in the nursery and told Jesse she wanted the cute goat to be like his aunt's Tonka truck. He'd smiled and pulled over a step stool to wedge it on top of the tree like a star.

Lila felt her heart expand every time she came into the living room, the tree making her happy with a tinge of bittersweet instead of downright sad.

"Where are your two ornaments?" Lila asked him, looking all around the tree. They'd been decorating it for the past hour and a half while Wyatt napped in his crib. She didn't see either the cat on the house or the red pickup truck.

"I stuck them in the back," he said. "Honestly, I'm not sure I want to see them. Some things are one day at a time, like my entry into fatherhood. The ornaments and what they represent—that might be a one-*minute*-at-a-time thing."

She took his hand and gave it a squeeze. She was about to say *Hey, I get it* and leave it at that, to give him some privacy with something that was clearly emotional for him. But at the same time, she already felt close to him and maybe getting him to open up a little would be a good thing. To the point that he'd soon move the ornaments a little closer to the front of the tree. "I figured that might be the case when you said that you *used* to like seeing pictures of your family, when it was you, your mom and your dad."

"Did I say that aloud?" he asked with a rueful smile. "You're too easy to talk to, Lila Mack."

"That goes ditto for me."

His smile turned warmer, but then it faded. "I guess it got kind of…hard to look at the very few photos I have of when my mom was still alive. It just felt like a life I couldn't lay claim to, let alone remember. Once I left Bear Ridge at eighteen and would only come back on holidays or for my aunt's birthday, I suddenly couldn't bear to look at them anymore."

She put a hand on his arm, the soft comfort sending a jolt through his entire body. "Oh, Jesse. I'm so sorry."

She put her arms around him and she felt him stiffen for a second, but then he wrapped his arms around her.

And kissed her.

She should gently step back. Pull away. Let him know that this was a *bad* idea. Dangerous, really.

But she couldn't move. She wanted more. She deepened the kiss and he backwalked her against the wall. She could feel all the hard planes of his tall, strong body.

Jesse Dawson was kissing her passionately. His hands were in her hair. Hers on his broad shoulders and around his back.

His phone pinged with a text.

"You should go read that," she said fast and stepped back, trying to catch her breath. "We needed an interruption." It was like a gift from the universe.

"You okay?" he asked, ignoring his phone, which was on the coffee table. "That I kissed you?"

"I did kiss you back."

"Yes, you did," he said with that warm smile that made her want to get right back in his arms. "But you're relieved we were interrupted by a text."

She nodded. "Very, actually. Because you and me, Jesse—not a good idea."

"I know. For a few complicated reasons."

"Right," she said, not surprised he understood. Of course he understood. He always seemed to get what she meant.

Because they *were* getting close.

And the most important thing in his life was the most important thing in hers. The baby they would now raise together.

He walked over to the coffee table and picked up his phone. "Whoa."

"What?" she asked, going over to him. "What's wrong?"

"It's the hospital administrator. The DNA results are in but won't be available for pickup until first thing in the morning."

They stared at each other for a moment.

"I'd like to go with you," she said. "With Wyatt. I mean, it's just going to confirm what we already know, but it feels monumental."

"It sure does," he agreed, sucking in a breath.

She wondered if he was hoping the results would say he wasn't the father. That he could go back to the life he was used to, the life that got interrupted by seeing her in the parking lot of the feed store with a baby that looked just like him, a baby with the telltale pin on his snowsuit.

She didn't *really* know Jesse—deep down. The heart and soul of him, the life experiences that made him tick. He'd opened up some, but she had to be sensible. Given their situation, how delicate and complicated it all was, getting romantically involved was out of the question.

The kiss—the very passionate kiss—said there was attraction on both sides. And even though they both said it couldn't happen again, they were living in the same house.

She had to be very careful.

At nine o'clock the next morning, Jesse had the manila envelope in his hands and was having trouble opening it. He and Lila and Wyatt in his stroller were in the lobby of the hospital, in an alcove with a few chairs.

Lila was sitting down, and Jesse had sat, then stood up, about three times.

Now, he was standing again, staring at the envelope with his name on it. The piece of paper inside would confirm that he was Wyatt's father. Between the baby being his mini-me and the pin, there was no doubt.

But he was avoiding ripping open the envelope and finding out for double, triple sure. Because he was scared of the black and white of it all?

Lila was staring at him with slightly narrowed eyes, which told him she knew exactly why he was standing there, clutching the envelope and looking like he might pass out.

She looked disappointed. And he understood.

"It's not that I don't want to be his father—officially," he said. "It's that I'm afraid I'm not going to live up to the title."

Her expression softened. "Hey, remember what I said. It's up to you, Jesse."

Was it that simple, though? When you were raised a certain way, had a certain way of thinking stamped in your DNA, when nurture and nature were the same, what would make him any different from his dad?

He glanced at Lila, who got up and pushed Wyatt's stroller over to the window. To give him a little privacy, he figured.

But she was staring at him.

So was the baby.

His son was watching.

Jesse walked over to the stroller and knelt down. "Hey, Wyatt, inside this envelope is our entire future. It's going to say that I'm your father. And I'm going to promise you right here and now that I'm going to do right by you. And if I ever don't, Lila will tell me so and I'll fix it."

She burst into tears.

He stood up, reaching a hand to her face, and she threw herself into his arms.

"I had that right, right?" he said to her.

She pulled back and wiped under her eyes. "Yes. You did. I'll tell you. Oh, will I tell you. So will my mother and aunt and grandmother. You can count on that."

He smiled. "Well, I'll hold myself to account, but I'm glad you and yours will be my backup."

She smiled too.

"Okay, I'm ready," he said and slit open the envelope. He pulled out the top sheet of paper and scanned it, his heart starting to beat a little faster.

Holy...

In a good way.

"Where are those cigars I'm supposed to hand out?" he asked with a grin. He put the paper and envelope on a chair and bent down to unbuckle Wyatt's harness. He lifted the baby up and snuggled him close against his chest. "Guess what? I'm your daddy. You're my son. We're a family. Officially."

Lila was happy-crying now. He could tell the happy part because she was smiling and laughing while tears were streaming down her cheeks. "I'm overjoyed for him," she said. "He has his father. He even has Christmas." She put her arms around them both.

He stiffened for a second, and so Lila did too. She stepped back as though she'd intruded on a moment when she was actually part of it. A huge part. But he didn't know how to say that or what exactly he meant.

Still, it was probably for the best that she'd stepped away. Just like she had in the farmhouse last night. Getting involved—getting too involved—could be a bad idea. He would end up hurting her or disappointing her or end up not being who she thought he *could* be. And problems between him and Lila would mean problems for raising Wyatt together.

They'd gone to their separate bedrooms last night, Jesse unable to stop thinking of that kiss. Wondering if she was thinking the same. He'd reminded her that he'd take care of Wyatt's night wakings, and he had. Jesse had actually been grateful when the baby had been a little fussy at being stuck with the new guy again, the still unfamiliar arms and face looming, because he'd hoped that Lila would come in to see if everything was okay. He'd wanted to just *be* with her. But she'd stayed put. A good thing, he knew.

"When we get home, we should work out some kind of schedule for sharing parenting," he said. "Like one of us will take the morning with Wyatt, and one will take the afternoon, and we'll alternate evenings and middle of the nights."

*Yes*, he thought. More structured and less like they were *living together*. Like they were a family. They were co-parenting, and that was completely different.

There was no kissing in co-parenting.

She nodded. "Yes, I think we should, something we can both follow and count on."

"Let's go home, then," he said.

Was it his imagination or had she winced at the word

*home*? Maybe because they hadn't talked about how long he'd be staying in her guest room.

For the next eighteen years?

He had no idea. If he was moving in so they could raise Wyatt together, what did that mean, exactly? Would they just be platonic for those eighteen years?

Co-parenting, he reminded himself.

They had *a lot* to talk about. But he didn't have any answers himself.

As they were leaving the hospital, Lila got a text from her mother asking if the DNA test results were in.

Lila turned to Jesse. "My mom asked about the results. Can I tell her? Or is there anyone you want to tell first?" Perhaps he'd wanted it official before telling anyone.

"My aunt is the only close family I have besides Wyatt. But she's away till the day after tomorrow. So of course tell your mom. I'll let my cousins know later."

Lila took a deep breath and texted her mom that Jesse was indeed Wyatt's father. And that they were headed to the farmhouse to figure out how to co-parent Wyatt.

Wow, her mom texted back. Good for Wyatt. One day at a time, honey, okay?

One minute at a time, Lila texted back, stealing Jesse's line. It absolutely applied.

Will you stop by the salon? I want to welcome Jesse to the family and give my grandbaby a big kiss.

The family. Lila supposed Jesse *was* family now. No matter what, they'd always be connected through Wyatt.

Unless Jesse did end up taking after his dad. Lila had a very good feeling about Jesse—on instinct and what she'd seen so far. The man had integrity. She couldn't see him just walking away, not even for a few days, let alone months like his own father had.

"My mom wants to welcome you to the family," Lila said. "Her exact words. And give her grandson a kiss. Mind if we stop at the salon? Hair Royale, just off Main Street by the used bookstore."

He tilted his head and she realized he wasn't familiar with Bear Ridge anymore and hadn't been for a long time. Hair Royale had been around forever but it wasn't the only hair salon, and the used bookstore, which had a complimentary coffee station and a few overstuffed chairs and couches, had just opened last summer. "I appreciate the welcome," he said. "She could be giving me the evil eye."

Lila smiled and shook her head. "They're thrilled that Wyatt has his father. I am too."

"You're good people," he said.

Good people who'd be watching and listening closely. If he took off on Wyatt, particularly once familiarity was built up? There'd be hell to pay. From all the Macks.

They headed to Lila's SUV, got Wyatt settled, then make their way to the center of town.

"I'll park in the town green's lot," she said. "We can show Wyatt the Santa hut on the way to the salon and since it's another nice day, maybe Santa will be outside and will wave."

The lot was crowded because of the weather and the timing—Santa and Mrs. Claus were in the hut, and a line of families and a ton of little kids were waiting, while someone dressed in an elf costume handed out take-out cups of hot cocoa.

They might not get a wave from the Clauses but at least Wyatt got to see the adorable hut, which was painted red with a green faux chimney, a little window decorated with multicolored lights.

"Ooh, Lila!" a voice trilled.

Lila turned to see the town mayor walking toward her. "Hi, Audrey. Long line for the Santa hut." The town collected five dollars per family, which went straight to Bear Ridge's holiday fund to provide those in need with Christmas turkeys or gifts.

The mayor, who was a warm, friendly but harried woman in her late forties, type A and incredibly organized, was looking curiously at Jesse. Then at Wyatt, whose same-blue eyes were wide open and alert. "I would not be surprised to hear that these two are related," Audrey said. "Same eyes!"

Oh, why not. Lila might as well let the entire town know, and the mayor was a talker. "This is Jesse Dawson. He grew up in Bear Ridge but has been away mostly the last decade. He's Wyatt's father."

Audrey's eyes widened just slightly in surprise at the news. People had whispered about who Wyatt's dad was, but since one hadn't presented himself in the past three months, the gossip died down since as one busybody put it, "these things happen." There had been lots of chatter, and Lila had even heard some gossip about Kate Mack going to a sperm bank. Whatever.

Jesse extended his hand and they shook. "Nice to meet you."

"And you!" Audrey said warmly. She looked from

Jesse to the baby again. "Yup," she added, nodding. "Same eyes. Well, maybe you can *both* help me out with a big favor. I'm in a bit of a holiday pickle. Tomorrow, both Santa and Mrs. Claus can't make it. I have a two-hour shift I need to fill and unfortunately it's at the early-bird hour of eight to ten. Any chance you two can take it?"

Lila remembered Kate telling her she signed up to dress up as Mrs. Claus once a week. Wyatt had been a newborn then, and Kate had her hands very full, but she never turned down an opportunity to be part of a holiday. "Kate signed up to be Mrs. Claus. Of course I'll help out."

"Me too," Jesse said, surprising Lila. She knew Christmas was rough on him. But he was putting his painful associations aside for Wyatt's sake. And maybe even hers. "Wyatt can be our house elf," he added.

Lila laughed. "The cutest elf in Bear Ridge." She turned to Audrey. "Sign us both right up. One of my relatives will babysit Wyatt, for sure."

Audrey's entire face lit up. "Splendid. Tomorrow eight to ten!" With that, she hurried off toward the town hall.

"You really are full of surprises, Jesse Dawson," Lila said.

"Right? Half the things I say just fly right out of my mouth. Don't get me wrong—I mean what I say. But no one will be more shocked than I am to see me dressed up as Santa, hearing what little kids want and making sure they haven't been too naughty."

She laughed and they started walking toward the crosswalk. "Were you a naughty kid?"

"No way. If I acted up on my aunt Bess, she'd take 4H Club away that week."

"Ah, she knew your currency," Lila said as they headed across the street. "I look forward to meeting her."

"In the coming days, for sure. I'm excited about telling her the big news."

Lila liked the idea of meeting Jesse's family—his only close relative, well, aside from his son, of course. Having his own family connection, by introducing his baby son to the aunt who'd been such an important part of childhood, would surely help him feel connected to both the word *family* and to Bear Ridge. His aunt was Wyatt's great-aunt. And that mattered.

Lila pointed a few doors down on West Elm Street. "There's the hair salon. Your aunt must go to the competition, or my mother and grandmother would have mentioned her. They know every client's life story. It's the hair salon way."

He smiled as they approached the shop, which was dolled up with white lights, a big sprig of mistletoe hanging from the doorframe.

"We have to avoid that," she said, pointing up. But she immediately thought of their kiss. How it had felt to be in his arms. Warm. Safe.

Wait—*safe*? Last night she'd thought their attraction was *dangerous*. And it was. One big blow-out fight where they both retreated to their separate corners would only hurt Wyatt in the long run—and short run. Miscommunication, hurt feelings, unmet expectations, bad moods, flat-out animosity... Wyatt wouldn't thrive with that kind of negative energy around him. He'd *feel* it.

So how could she possibly feel safe with Jesse Dawson passionately kissing her?

They had to be platonic while they lived together.

"Yes, we do," he agreed, wrinkling his nose at the mistletoe.

Okay, as long as they were both on the same page, they could move along and make their co-parenting schedule and figure out how to do this.

While being attracted to each other.

Without acting on it.

Inside the hair salon, Johnny Mathis was singing a Christmas ballad. Lila tried to just listen, let the song she'd loved forever lift her up. She was back on her own turf—with her family. Now that her farm and the small house were shared, they weren't quite the same sanctuary they had been for the past two months.

"They're here, Mom," her mother called, and all eyes swung to Lila, Jesse and Wyatt in his stroller.

Her grandmother came from the back room with foil all over her head and her treatment apron on. Lowlights today. She patted one side of her hair. "Hey, we're family, right, Jesse?" she asked, giving him a big hug.

Lila laughed. Her gram was always coiffed. If she was willing to show her "before" to Jesse, then she really did accept him as family.

Jesse hugged her grandmother right back. "That's right. My aunt, who mostly raised me, was always in some kind of green facial mask with potions and lotions and whatnot in her hair at night. I'm used to it."

Her mom laughed. "We're a hair salon family, so I'm glad to hear it." She grinned at Jesse and also pulled him into a hug. "Congratulations on having the world's greatest baby," she said as she stood back.

Jesse smiled. "Wyatt *is* pretty awesome. Excellent nose-grabber."

"Yup, he got me the other day," her mom said. "Rookie mistake on my part despite being with him from day one."

Lila caught Jesse's smile fading. She hoped he knew that wasn't any kind of dig.

Or maybe it was. Maybe it was Deandra Mack's way of saying: *You're new here, buster. And we're watching you. We'll reserve judgment, but we're watching.*

"Well, I want you all to rest assured that I'll be the best father I can be to Wyatt," Jesse said. He lifted the baby from the stroller and cuddled him.

"We think you're doing a great job so far," her grandmother said with a warm nod.

Her gram was nobody's fool. If she had this good feeling about Jesse, then maybe Lila could lighten up a little. Stop being so on guard.

His immediate devotion to Wyatt, the way he tried so hard, how…nice he was to be around—all made it easy to *not* be on guard around him so she had to constantly remember to be wary.

Her mom's phone rang. "Uh-oh," Deandra said, looking at the screen. She answered and listened, her face falling. She shook her head. "We'll be right there. Thanks for calling."

"What's wrong?" Lila asked.

"That was Reed Dawson at the PD," her mom said. "Micah's been detained for both truancy and trespassing on private property."

Lila's heart sank. "Oh no. Where was he?"

Her mom let out a long, tired sigh. "Skateboarding down the long paved drive at the Piedmont Ranch. Reed said it was the third time the owners had to tell him to leave—the driveway is still slick from the last storm and they're afraid of liability. So they called the police."

"I don't blame them for worrying," Gram said, shaking her head. "I wish he'd open up to us instead of taking off by himself all the time and getting himself into trouble."

And worrying about whether the interloper was going to make off with his nephew had sent her brother backward just when things had been looking up.

Her mom checked her phone. "Oh, darn. We're booked this morning. Mariel Montrose is due in ten minutes for a double process and cut and Dani Gomez is getting highlights."

"We'll go get Micah," Lila said. "Don't worry. Jesse and I have been talking about him working at the farm after school and on weekends. It might help turn him around."

*We'll* go get Micah. That she'd said that without hesitation wasn't lost on her.

Her mother pulled her into a hug. "I appreciate that. And I think it's good for you two to be handling this instead of boring old mom who probably lectures too much when I should be listening more. It's just so hard."

"I have a good feeling about Micah's immediate future," Jesse said, giving her mother's hand a quick squeeze. "I was the same kid at seventeen. Different reasons, but going down a bad path until I got some sense knocked into me. I think I can do some good here."

Her mother and grandmother both brightened.

"Oh, I'm so relieved to hear that," Deandra said. "I know he loves the farm. You just have to *reach* him. That's the hard part. Hard for us but maybe easier for you, Jesse."

"I'll do my best," he assured her.

Lila put a hand on her mother's arm and then they hurried out. They wheeled the stroller back to Lila's SUV and quickly got Wyatt re-settled, then drove over to the police station, which was just a few minutes down the road.

Jesse was opening his door when Lila suddenly burst into tears.

"Hey," he said, getting back in. "It'll be okay." He put his arm around her and she sagged against him. She tried to sit up, back in her seat, to avoid the warm comfort of his arm and strong shoulder. But she just couldn't move. "Everything's going to be okay, Lila. I promise you."

Now she did sit up. "I thought you didn't make promises you couldn't keep. So no one got disappointed." She caught the edge in her voice. "You can't know everything will be okay. It might not be."

"Like I said, for a while there, when I was seventeen, I *was* Micah. Let me help, okay?"

She looked at him, at his sincere, handsome face, his concerned, intelligent eyes. *I can't do this alone*, she thought. *I want the help. I need the help.*

"Okay," she whispered, worried nonetheless. Because it seemed she was relying on Jesse Dawson a little too much for the most important things in her life. Her nephew. The farm. Now her brother.

One day, one minute at a time, she reminded herself.

# *Chapter Eight*

**W**hile Lila went to speak with her brother in the interrogation room where Micah had been sent to wait for a family member to pick him up, Jesse sat down at his cousin Reed's desk to find out what he could about the situation. Wyatt was wide awake in his stroller, but hopefully not listening.

Reed assured Jesse that Micah hadn't been arrested but he was headed in that direction. The Piedmonts hadn't wanted to press charges, but they never wanted to see Micah skateboarding down their drive again. According to Reed, Micah had shrugged to every question Reed had asked. Including if he intended to stay away from the Piedmonts' driveway.

"I was telling Lila—I used to be Micah," Jesse said. "I went through a hard patch at seventeen. A bad breakup, my father disappointed me by not coming home for my birthday when he said he'd be taking me on a camping trip. I started hanging around with some rougher guys. Maybe I can help turn Micah around by offering him a job on Lila's farm. Apparently he's shown a real interest in goat farming but he was deeply affected by the loss of his sister. And finding out that Wyatt's dad is in the picture after all got him worried that I'll take Wyatt and leave town."

"Will you?" Reed asked. "Can you make that promise? If you can't, don't say you're not going anywhere."

He liked that his cousin gave it to him straight. "I *can* make that promise. I've said that—to Lila and her family. That I wouldn't take Wyatt from the Macks. I think they're all having a tough time believing in that."

"I can see you mean it," Reed said. "About not taking Wyatt away. But it doesn't mean *you* won't leave."

"All I know is that right now, I'm here to be a father to my son. I can't imagine leaving him, Reed. I don't know how my dad did it. My entire childhood."

"Same," he said. "I get itchy being away from Summer for just a *workday*."

Jesse nodded. He could completely understand that now. "Well, that's how I assume I'll be when I'm out working the Double Sisters Farm."

"I think it's a good plan to get Micah involved with the farm. Go talk to him. I don't think Lila's having much luck," he added, upping his chin toward the interrogation room, which had a one-way mirror on the door.

Jesse turned and saw Lila looking very tense, Micah pacing. They seemed to be arguing.

Uh-oh.

Jesse stood, his hands on the stroller. "Thanks, Reed. For everything. And by the way, I got the results from the DNA test. It's official."

Reed grinned and extended his hand for a shake, then gave Wyatt a gentle tap on his nose. "I had no doubt. But congrats. And I mean that in every sense of the word."

Jesse figured there was a lot packed into that line, but

he had no time to think about it. He wanted to get in that room with Micah and see what he could do.

He walked across the bullpen to the interrogation room. He tapped on the door, and Micah didn't even bother looking to see who it was. But Lila did and she looked so relieved.

He walked in and parked the stroller, then sat down, sending Lila a quick glance of *it's gonna be okay.* "Hey, Micah. We met yesterday. Jesse Dawson."

Micah eyed him with a scowl, then fixed his gaze on his baby nephew before turning away. For a moment Jesse was struck by how much he and Lila looked alike. Same green eyes. Micah's mop of thick straight hair, gelled to stick up in a swoosh, was darker than Lila's auburn. He was lanky, but Jesse could see he was strong and he had a vibration to him that told Jesse he had energy to burn. "Right. Wyatt's dad who's gonna take him away from us."

"I won't do that," Jesse said, looking intently at Micah. "All I can give you is my word."

Micah rolled his eyes. "Oh, that means a lot."

"Look," Jesse said. "I know you don't know me, have no reason to believe anything I say. So I'm asking you to give me a chance. I'm going to help Lila get the Double Sisters Farm going. We've worked out a great plan. To add four more goats, to acquire the necessary equipment and machinery, and upgrade the farm itself—"

Micah looked at him like he'd grown another head. "There's no money for that."

"There is. Because I'm investing in the Double Sisters. For my son's future and his family. That includes you."

He saw Micah glance at Lila as if looking for confirmation that Jesse had money, that any of this was true. Lila gave a slight nod.

"We need good help, though," Jesse continued. "Someone emotionally invested in the place, someone who's passionate about goat farming and breeding, someone we can count on. That's you, Micah. If you could work from four to six p.m. a few times a week after school and a few hours either Saturday or Sunday, that would be ideal. But if you don't go to school, if you're not passing your classes, there's no job."

Micah didn't say anything, but he didn't say no or get up and try to leave.

"I really need you at the farm, Micah," Lila said.

"I'll teach you everything I know," Jesse added. "All aspects of being a ranch hand. And it would be a great way to get to know me. You'll see who I am. I try to live by the Code of the West. Do you know what that's about? Basically, doing the right thing."

"Is it for real?" Micah asked, glancing at him.

"The rules are unwritten, but respected in ranch country."

Micah glanced at Lila and she nodded again. It was clear that Lila had his respect. That would be a big help.

"When can I start?" Micah asked.

Jesse saw Lila's shoulders sag with relief. "How about tomorrow after school? But remember, if you don't attend every class, there's no job. If you're not passing, you have to get your grades up before you can work. If we have a deal on that, you're hired."

"Fine," Micah said as if he was trying hard to scowl but was actually happy.

Jesse stood and extended his hand. Micah shook it. "Handshake is big in the Code of the West. It's a gentleman's agreement."

"Got it," Micah said. "Maybe tomorrow you can tell me more about what's involved in the Code of the West."

Jesse smiled. Excellent sign. "I definitely will."

Micah nodded. His demeanor had definitely changed—for the better.

"We'll drop you home," Lila said. "I'm really glad you're on board, Micah. Kate would be very, very happy."

Micah bit his lip and and they all headed out. Lila slung an arm around her brother's shoulder and started telling him something funny that Dolly and Lulu did that morning. Micah laughed and asked if he could bring treats for them after school tomorrow.

The look Lila shot Jesse went straight to his heart.

He had his work cut out for him at the Double Sisters on all fronts. And it would be worth every minute.

"I can't thank you enough for how you handled things with Micah," Lila said for maybe the fifth time since they dropped her brother off at her parents' house.

Micah had been full of questions on the way, asking everything from if he would focus on a certain area of the goat farm, like mucking out the stalls and spreading straw, or if he'd learn all aspects, such as milking and the dairy business process. He looked very excited to hear that both she and Jesse thought he should learn everything involved in the Double Sisters Farm. He'd given Wyatt a big kiss on the head before getting out of the SUV in their parents' driveway, and there had been a skip to his step when he walked into the house.

"Really, my pleasure," Jesse said. "It feels good to help."

She had a great feeling about this.

Now, at the farm again, as they walked toward the porch she slid a glance at Jesse, touched at how sweetly he was holding his son, cuddling him, kissing the top of his head, pointing out that Dolly and Lulu were on their logs. She opened the front door, Billy coming to greet them. They took off their coats and boots, Jesse getting Wyatt out of his snowsuit.

"Like I said, I was him at seventeen. Local ranches heard about my reputation and wouldn't hire me, but a farmer took a chance on me. Crops, chickens, some sheep. He said he himself was me when he was my age and a rancher took a chance on him. I guess there are a lot of us."

"You're paying it forward and maybe one day Micah will too," Lila said. That had her feeling so hopeful for her brother.

Wyatt let out a big yawn, and Lila laughed. "Someone's ready for a nap," she said.

Jesse glanced at the baby in his arms. "Perfect timing since we can work on the co-parenting and farm duties schedule. And set up the plan for Micah so he always knows what he's doing when he comes to the farm."

"Good idea." She gave Wyatt a kiss, taking an inhale of his baby-shampoo-scented head. "I'll make coffee," she said as Jesse took a yawning, eye-rubbing Wyatt to the nursery.

Fifteen minutes later, Jesse was back and sat beside Lila on the sofa in the living room, two mugs of coffee in front of them, and the last slice of pecan pie to share. Two forks. Which suddenly seemed a little intimate, now that she looked at the plate. She could have cut the slice in half.

Jesse took a fork and cut a piece. "Thanks for sharing. I'd never pass up pecan pie."

"Me either," she said.

He had his iPad on the coffee table and tapped a few buttons until a spreadsheet appeared.

"Wow, you're organized," she said, taking a bite of the pie.

"More like I really want to do right by the farm and you. I created the spreadsheet last night and worked on it between feedings."

He was doing it again. Being so forthright. Honest. Coming at her from a real place. "So what are you thinking?"

"Between the two of us full time, and Micah part time, we can get by. We can always bring on an experienced hand too, if we need to. But if we're going to start with six goats, that seems manageable for three of us. I was thinking that you and I could split the morning, then the afternoon, then each take on evening chores as needed."

"So, you'll work three hours, then I'll relieve you, that kind of thing?"

He nodded, and took another bite of pie. "I'm used to getting up with the roosters. So I can take the first shift."

Her heart gave a little leap. "I'll have Wyatt for three hours in the morning without worrying about the farm or the goats or cleaning up the breakfast dishes. I have to say, having a partner is nice. Necessary, even."

"I guess we need to talk about that too," he said.

Her heart stopped soaring and fell back to place with a thud. "*That* being…"

"The kiss. The one I want to repeat more than you will ever know, Lila."

There was that forthrightness again. One of her favorite things about him.

She bit her lip on saying *Me too*. That would just make her vulnerable. *More* vulnerable. "I think we need to remember what my wise gram said. 'Start as you mean to go on.'"

"Agreed," he said, taking another bite of pie.

"Getting romantically involved because we're attracted to each other when we're both in a very intense situation as co-parents and co-farmers and living in the same house…" she said. "I think everything feels like a novelty and exciting right now. Scary too. But we're there for each other, which adds to the attraction side. I just think that might burn out fast when reality and routine become the norm, you know?"

She had no doubt. Right now, of course they wanted to rip each other's clothes off. Things were hot and passionate and they truly needed each other—she with his help on the ranch, he with her help with learning to be a dad.

They could develop a true friendship instead, a true partnership. Building that and preserving it had to be the focus. Not a hot night in bed together.

Though she would love that.

He nodded slowly, then more firmly. "I know you're right. We have to protect our relationship. And nothing kills a relationship more than romance—with all its potential of stomped-on expectations."

Well, maybe she wouldn't go *that* far. "Protecting our partnership for Wyatt is paramount. It's everything."

"So we're...friends," he said. "Housemates."

"Co-parents and co-farmers," she said.

"Let's shake on it." He extended his hand. And of course, the moment she slipped hers into his, that lightning bolt of attraction lit up all her nerve endings. "Okay, then."

"Okay."

"I'll work up a schedule for Micah and email it to you. You can make changes or approve it. And we'll be set for him to start tomorrow after school."

"Sounds good," she said. "I think we're handling this the only way we can. Nothing is more important than Wyatt. For both of us. If we got involved romantically and it went bad and we're suddenly throwing plates at each other's heads in six months, he's the one who gets hurt the worst."

"Well, when you put it like that," he said with a shaky smile that faded fast. "I guess it *is* good you put it like that. Because it's easy to see why we need to keep our hands and lips off each other."

"Right."

"So—friends" he said. "*VIP* friends."

She laughed. "VIP friends," she repeated.

She supposed it was fine that she wanted to kiss him senseless right then. That they wanted each other wasn't in question. That they should be platonic had been agreed upon for very good reasons.

This wasn't going to be easy.

# *Chapter Nine*

"And I want a blue bike and the next book in the killer robots series," said the boy sitting in the chair in front of Jesse—Santa—in the holiday hut the next morning.

Jesse and Lila, Mr. and Mrs. Claus, were all dressed up in their red suits and white wigs and Santa hats, provided by the mayor. They had their own sleighlike chairs, which crafty volunteers from town had made. A red chair with a green cushion was across from each of them with a sign reading *Nice All Year*. No naughty kids in town apparently.

There was a holiday-decorated cardboard partition between him and Lila to give the kids a little privacy while sharing their lists with Santa and Mrs. Claus. Every time a kid came in, which was every ten minutes, sent by the Santa hut elf who was monitoring the line outside, Lila said a cheery *Ho-ho-ho, hello* and their name. She knew them all, which was life in a very small town.

Jesse had to ask names. And the next kid, a mini-Scrooge, wasn't having it.

"If you're Santa," said the boy, around eight years old, shoving his mop of blond hair off his forehead, "then why don't you know my name? It's because you're *fake*. You're just some man in a costume."

True. But still. Christmas was about believing, about good cheer, about the joy of the season. Or it was supposed to be, even if last year and the lead-up to this Christmas had been really rough on Jesse. *So think fast*, he told himself, *and turn this kid's frown the ole upside down*. "Santa can't know *gazillions* of names of good boys and girls," Jesse told him. "His head would explode."

"Aha! Busted!" the boy gleefully shouted. "You didn't say *I* can't know or *my* head would explode."

Jeez, tough customer. "Well, my name is Santa," Jesse said. For the next hour and a half, anyway. "And *I* would like to know your name."

The boy scowled. "Scotty Ames. Okay, *Santa*?"

Yup, just fine. "So, Scotty, what's on your list? What do you want for Christmas?"

"What's the point of even telling you?" Scotty asked, crossing his arms over his scrawny chest. "I'm not getting anything. I haven't been good this year. I haven't even tried. I only came because my dad brought me."

"Well, your dad must think you've been good enough to get Christmas presents," Jesse pointed out.

His own dad had been great with Christmas presents, whether he'd been home for the holiday or not, and more often it was not. He'd make sure gifts were under the tree each year—one from him, one from Santa and one with a card that read: *What your mom would probably have gotten you*.

The thought, the memory, took away any negativity that had been knocking around his head and heart the past couple of days as he'd ruminated on his childhood. That one gesture—the gift from his mother—told Jesse everything he'd needed to know about Eddie Dawson.

No matter what, the man was gold.

Even his aunt had had to admit that it was "very nice," as she'd put it.

And yeah, the gifts from his mother would be stuff he needed, like a warm down jacket or snow boots. He'd wear the black down jacket and red plaid scarf from his mom and feel her with him. Feel comforted. Feel *warm* in the dead of a Wyoming February.

His father's and Santa's gifts were fun stuff, like the model airplane kit he'd desperately wanted one year. Jesse had been twelve and though his father hadn't come home for the holiday, he'd made sure the gift at the top of his son's list was under the tree. Santa had gotten him a twenty-five dollar gift certificate to his favorite pizzeria, which was always appreciated. Aunt Bess, however, would get furious when a girlfriend or an ice-fishing trip with "the boys," his cowboy buddies, took precedence over coming home for his son at Christmas. *Presents can't make up for presence*, he'd once heard her snap to someone on the phone while complaining about her absentee brother. It took him a while to understand that one. But it had always stayed with him.

*You can't do the most important things halfway*, was another thing he'd overhear her mutter often when she was spitting mad at her brother. She'd try hard not to bad-mouth his dad to Jesse, but he'd overhear her venting to others about how a responsible father didn't leave a motherless child, whether three or sixteen, for months on end.

Jesse had never wanted to think too hard about any of that, so he'd chosen to keep true to himself and his childhood belief that his father was like Santa. Eddie was busy, he was out there, working hard. And a few times a year, he'd come home with gifts that made Jesse feel like he was special to his father. Now Jesse realized it was all he'd had to cling to.

He hated this dawning awareness that he himself had rationalized his father's behavior. It made him question himself *now*, made him wonder if he knew himself as well as he thought.

Made him worry that the promises he'd made—to Lila, to Wyatt—were in jeopardy. He'd heard his father say *But I meant it at the time... But my intentions were good* plenty as a kid and as an adult.

Dammit.

*Focus on the here and now,* he told himself. Another favorite phrase of his aunt's.

Still, he found himself wondering what Scotty's dad was like. He had the feeling the kid was on the naughty list at home and school but that his dad clearly cared about Scotty's psyche, and no matter what, Christmas was for *everyone*. Even those sent to the principal's office three times a week. No lumps of coal in the stocking.

"My dad only took me here to get me to say I'd do a better job on my homework and study for my spelling tests," Scotty said. "But I hate school so who cares." The scowl was back.

*Your dad is trying,* he thought. Jesse knew that everything was relative, but the kid's father was present and actively trying to help his son.

Again, he thought of his father waving goodbye from the old red pickup, not coming back to Bear Ridge for months at a time.

Jesse just couldn't see it. How had Eddie Dawson been able to do it? How had he not turned right back around, scooped up his young son in his arms and stayed *home*?

*I thought you were focusing on now*, Jesse reminded himself.

He supposed he really was, though. The past *did* have a bearing on the present. There was no way around that.

He looked at the boy in front of him, all the stuff that made Scotty act up radiating from him. Not that Jesse thought bad behavior should be excused, just that sometimes, oftentimes, if the reasons, if the real *why* was dealt with, the problem could be more easily solved.

"Yeah, I didn't like school, either," he told Scotty.

The boy gaped at Jesse. "I didn't know Santa had to go to school as a kid."

Huh. Scotty had said that without a hint of sarcasm. On some level, the boy did believe in Santa. And Jesse was going to run with it.

"Oh, definitely. And it's a good thing I decided to make the best of school since I *had* to be there anyway. Because learning about geography and math and science and working on my reading helped me plan my routes for flying my reindeers and sleigh to kids all across the world. And spelling tests made writing kids' names correctly on their gifts a lot easier."

Scotty brightened some. "Yeah, I guess. But I'm gonna be a rodeo star and you don't need school to ride a horse or learn how to lasso. You just have to practice."

"You know, even champion rodeo riders need to try

hard in school," Jesse said. "To be a champ, you need to learn all kinds of important things. Math will help a rider calculate times. Science teaches you about horses and bulls and getting that lasso just right. Reading and writing are important for signing deals and contracts. And going to school—that's about taking ownership of your life and your goals."

"I didn't think of it that way," Scotty said. "But I sorta see what you mean."

Jesse almost fell out of his sleigh that he'd actually helped this boy look at things a different way. And this wasn't a seventeen-year-old like Micah who Jesse recognized from his own past and knew how to connect with. It was a little kid who needed to hear the right words at the right time. Somehow, Jesse had gotten through.

A knock came on the door and the Santa hut elf poked his head in and tapped his wrist, which meant Jesse was running over the ten-minute-per-child allotment.

Jesse nodded at the elf and turned back to Scotty. "So Scotty, you never did tell me what you want for Christmas," Jesse said.

"I want tickets to the rodeo next month. But whatever," he added before getting up and walking toward the arched door. Hand on the knob, he turned back. "Thank you," he added in a low voice, then left.

The *thank you* got Jesse. Squeezed his chest. He'd get Scotty those tickets with a tag from Santa.

"I might cry," Lila said, peering over the partition, her green eyes a little misty. "You handled that so beautifully, Jesse."

He'd almost forgotten Mrs. Claus was on the other side of that partition.

"I appreciate that," he told her. "I think you're the one who said life is full of surprises. It definitely is."

The big warm smile on her beautiful face also got him. Also squeezed his chest.

Man, he could use a hug. Another surprise since he couldn't remember the last time *that* was the case. Or maybe he could: a year ago, the day he'd lost his father. He'd gone looking for that hug in those three beers.

And he ended up a daddy.

Yes, life was full of surprises.

He might have leaped over the partition to get that hug from Lila, but the elf was already sending in another two kids.

*Maybe later*, he thought. *Back at the farm.*

Hugs could be platonic, right?

"You should have heard Jesse with this boy in the Santa hut, Micah," Lila said to her brother as they each raked the straw in the goats' pen that afternoon. "Surly little kid and Jesse turned it around. He surprises me constantly."

"I'm giving Jesse the benefit of the doubt," Micah said. "Since he is Wyatt's dad. And I am really happy that Wyatt has his dad in his life."

Lila put down her rake and grabbed her brother into a hug. "*I'm* so happy to hear you say that—you have no idea!"

"Uh, you're squishing me," Micah said but she could see he was pleased that he'd said something that had touched her so deeply.

She laughed and picked her rake back up.

When she and Jesse had gotten home from their shift at

the Santa hut, they'd each filled up their coffee thermoses, then had gone their separate ways per their co-parenting schedule—Lila to take care of Wyatt for the rest of the morning, and Jesse to the outermost fences with his tool kit. They'd met up for lunch and both played with Wyatt and put him down for a nap together. Then they switched, and Lila headed for the barn while Jesse was on baby duty.

So far, co-parenting, sharing the day, was working well.

Now it was just after three, and her brother was beside her in the barn. He'd been a few minutes early, she'd been both relieved and happy to see. And she'd checked in with the school—Jesse had gone to all his classes that day.

"So what did Jesse say to the kid that was so great?" Micah asked, scooping the dirty straw into the big dustpan and emptying it in the trash can just outside the pen.

"He really listened—to what the kid said and *didn't* say. This boy seemed kind of angry when he came in. And he left different. I think what Jesse said really got through."

"So you think he'll really stick around?" Micah asked. "He'll live here in Bear Ridge while Wyatt grows up?"

*I think so. I hope so. I don't know so.*

"It looks that way," Lila said. "He has said many times that he won't take Wyatt away. If he leaves Bear Ridge to go back to his old life, he'll leave alone. Not with Wyatt. He's promised. And he's also said many times that he doesn't make promises he can't keep."

"He'd better not, or he'll deal with *me*," Micah said on a laugh, flexing his lack of muscles. Micah was tall and very lanky.

"It really means a lot to me that you're here, Micah." She reached over and topped his hand with hers for a moment. "And it would mean a lot to Kate too."

"Yeah, cuz if I'm here I'm not skateboarding down the Piedmonts' excellent driveway."

She faux-socked him in the arm. "I really mean it. I need you here. You're really good at ranch work, you *care* about this place and you're family."

"Meaning you thought you could make me work for free," he said on another laugh. "Jesse's really the one paying me?"

"That's what he said. Apparently he has a big bank account from twelve years of working hard without having to pay rent or buy his own meals. He always had room and board at the ranches where he worked as a cowboy."

"And he's putting it into the Double Sisters?" Micah asked, pausing in his raking. "Why would he do that?"

"He said it's Wyatt's legacy. His son's family farm."

Micah seemed to be taking that in. "I don't get this Jesse Dawson. But hey, I'll take it."

"Exactly. So far, he's been very kind and has done nothing to break my trust. He's so good with Wyatt, Micah."

"So I have to be nice?" Micah asked, resuming raking.

"Yes. Or at least respectful. But the thing is, you can learn a lot from Jesse. No one else in the family knows anything about goat farming besides us, and we're not experienced. Jesse's a true expert."

Her brother was staring at her. "Plus I guess *he's* family too. He's my nephew's dad."

Lila nodded. "Yup."

Micah seemed lost in thought, *good* thought, she had a feeling.

She emptied her dustpan and put the rake away, wondering what Jesse was doing right now. He was with Wyatt, who'd be awake from his nap. They were probably in the living room, the baby on the playmat. Or maybe he was giving him a bottle. Or telling him a story.

Lila had such an urge to suddenly *need* something from the house, like her car keys or a refill of her coffee thermos so she could go see.

It took everything to stay here in the barn.

Until her own words came back to her. *If he leaves Bear Ridge to go back to his old life, it'll be alone. Not with Wyatt.*

Her heart clenched and her stomach felt funny, and that awful chill ran up her spine again. Just at the thought that he would leave. Not be the man she hoped he was without even realizing it.

The man she was falling for against all her better judgment.

# *Chapter Ten*

While Wyatt napped, Jesse had been busy. He'd made plans to see his aunt tomorrow night for dinner, only telling her he had big news and a surprise for her. She'd tried to get him to spill the beans, but he insisted on *showing* her. Aunt Bess would be stunned in a good way, he was sure. And she'd be a wonderful great-aunt, doting on Wyatt. It was just him and Bess as close relatives on Jesse's side, and he was grateful his son would have another great-aunt in his life.

His phone pinged. An email. Something from the Brewer Adult Education Center.

Co-parenting for non-couples. Never married? Separated? Divorced? Need co-parenting skills and tips for raising your newborn to three-year-old? Class is tonight at the Brewer Adult Education Recreation Center, 7-8:30. Note: This class is for parents only.

What the heck was this?

Now his phone pinged with a text. From his cousin Reed.

Thought you might find this useful. Gifted one to Lila

too. Last minute, I know, but just heard about it now. Aimee and I are happy to babysit.

Useful, maybe. But...

He heard the front door open and then Lila's and Micah's voices as they went back and forth with goat puns. *What do you call a backwoods goat? A hillbilly. Why was the student goat sent to detention? He was butting heads with the teacher.*

A sharp cry came from Wyatt's room—the baby making it clear he wanted to be with the people trading the goat puns, Jesse thought with a smile as he headed into the nursery. He'd get Wyatt from his crib and then head back to chat with Lila and her brother, find out how his first hour of work at the farm had gone.

"Hey, there, little cowboy," he cooed to his son as he picked him up from his crib. The sight of Wyatt, those blue eyes, alert and curious and locked on his, rendered him speechless for a moment. "Look at you," he whispered. "Fourteen pounds of the best thing in the world." He cuddled the baby close against his chest and kissed his forehead, the scent of his baby bath lotion and soft brown hair tickling his senses.

"Jeez," came a voice from behind him. "Lila wasn't kidding when she said you already loved Wyatt."

Jesse turned. Micah and Lila were in the doorway, Lila grinning, and Micah nodding with a *maybe you're all right* kind of approval.

"You caught me getting all ooey-gooey," Jesse said. "How's your first day on the farm going, Micah?"

Jesse liked the way Micah's eyes instantly lit up at the question. Clearly it was going great.

Micah shoved a mopful of auburn-brown bangs out of his eyes. "Lulu and Dolly are hilarious. And Lila showed me the website for ordering the milking equipment. I want to help with the dairy business too. Did you know you need ten pounds of goat milk to make just one pound of cheese?"

Jesse smiled. "Yup. One of the dairies I worked at years ago made the new hands go to dairy school. The classes were just a half hour a day and taught by an experienced farmer, but man, did I grumble about it. Turned out to be very helpful."

"Yeah, I think seven hours of high school a day is enough," Micah said with a frown.

"Hey, no worries," Jesse assured him. "Here you'll learn by doing. And with me jabbering in your ear about everything. Like this," he added, whispering into Wyatt's tiny ear about how to place the thumb on the goat's teat to hand-milk.

Lila laughed. "Wyatt, you'll be milking goats at eighteen months." She took her phone out of her pocket and held it up to Jesse. "I almost forgot the reason we came to see you. Did you send me this?"

The gifted co-parenting class at the rec center. He explained about the text he himself had just gotten from Reed and his offer for him and Aimee to babysit.

"You two should definitely go," Micah said. "Whoever had the idea for the class is a total genius. Co-parenting for people who can't stand each other." He grinned.

"I can stand Jesse just fine," Lila said.

Jesse smiled at her. "And you're all right yourself."

"Yeah, *now*," Micah said. "All this is brand-new. We'll see in a month."

Jesse's smile faded. "We'll be fine in a month and a month from then. We have a co-parenting plan already in place."

And having shaken on being platonic and not letting romance and its inevitable burnout come between them and create the problems Micah was talking about, they would be fine in a year too.

"Yes, we do," Lila said, turning to Micah. "A solid plan we can both count on. The class is a good idea in itself but we *are* just fine and we'll continue to be fine. We're putting the baby first."

Micah nodded. "Sounds good."

"And how are you so cynical at seventeen?" Lila asked, giving her brother a playful punch on the shoulder. "Your parents have been happily married for thirty-one years. Your grandparents for fifty-two years."

"I notice you didn't mention Aunt Raina," Micah said with a grin.

Lila mock-narrowed her eyes. "Hey, she tried hard. She put up with way too much from that jerk."

Micah held up his hands. "Okay, okay."

"Fifty-two years," Jesse said. "Thirty-one years. That's really amazing." He didn't know anyone whose marriage had lasted longer than five years, except maybe a few of the rancher-owner bosses he'd had. One couple had been married over forty years but word was that the husband had a long-standing affair. Another had an open marriage, which struck Jesse as bizarre. It all added up to marriage being something to avoid.

"So are you guys gonna go to the class?" Micah asked.

"I think we should," Lila said, looking at Jesse. "We even have a babysitter team covered."

He nodded. Maybe the class wasn't a bad idea. They could get some good pointers and tips, he was sure. And it was just a couple of hours and then they'd be sprung.

Plus, he liked the idea of him and Lila doing this together. They were *Wyatt's* team.

"Remember to raise your hand and not wear your cowboy hat in class," Micah said with a chuckle, "or you'll get sent to detention like me."

Lila shot her brother a mock-scolding look. The more Jesse got to know Micah Mack, the more he liked the kid.

Same went for his sister too.

Lila and Jesse had dropped off Wyatt—along with a chocolate pecan pie and a bottle of wine as a thanks for both babysitting and the class—at Reed and Aimee Dawson's house, then had driven the half hour to Brewer. A more bustling town than Bear Ridge, Brewer was where everyone went for the big box stores off the highway. The downtown still managed to be quaint and had every possible shop, from one of a kinds to the usual. Lila tried to do all her Christmas shopping in Bear Ridge to buy local but she did love taking a trip to Brewer when she needed something specific that she couldn't get in her sleepy hometown, like the particular ice-fishing rod her father was hoping to find under the tree.

"Would you want to live in Brewer?" Jesse asked as he pulled into a parking spot in the recreation center's lot.

"I'm more a very small-town gal," she said. "But I do like coming here. When Kate and I were teenagers we always wanted to go to Brewer but now I appreciate how quiet Bear Ridge is, the slower, sleepier pace. How about you?"

"You're talking to a guy who prefers thousand-acre cattle ranches with nothing but pastures, barns and a cafeteria," he said with a smile. "Give me open spaces, the sky above, and I'm set."

"My parents' neighbor's daughter graduated from high school and moved to L.A. to seek her fortune," Lila said. "They're a quarter excited for her, three-quarters miserable for themselves that she went so far away. Maybe Wyatt will be a small-town boy and want to stay in Bear Ridge."

Or a small-town boy who'd be like his dad and grandfather and live on faraway ranches... She frowned at the thought.

Jesse squeezed her hand. "Well, we've got a good eighteen years to worry about him leaving us."

Lila brightened. "I'm getting *way* ahead of myself."

"Definitely goes with the territory of being a parent," he said.

She wrapped her arm around his and rested her head against his shoulder; that was how close she felt to him right then. Here they were, about to go to a class on co-parenting for those who weren't couples and she couldn't feel more connected to him.

*Yeah, now,* she could hear her brother saying.

"You okay?" he asked, peering at her.

"I just get overwhelmed by what a big job we're doing," she said. "We're responsible for a tiny, helpless baby who's relying on us to give him everything he needs. *Be* everything he needs."

He nodded. "I'm not as scared as I was."

Again she was struck by his honesty. That he didn't have to sound like a he-man.

"I go back and forth," she said. "One day I feel like I've got this parenthood thing down, and the next, I worry I'm not spending enough time with Wyatt, that I'm working too much. Maybe the class will cover stuff like balance."

"I'm sure it'll be helpful," Jesse said. "Just the subject alone of how to co-parent is important for us."

She nodded. *Because we'll never be a couple.* And even if romance's ups and downs didn't make them argue or poke at each other, being different people would anyway. They'd have disagreements, of course. They wouldn't see eye to eye on everything.

*Ha, we might as well rip each other's clothes off, then,* she thought suddenly. If they were going to disagree and argue and have the occasional cold wars *anyway.*

She slid a glance at him as he took the keys from the ignition.

Damn, he was handsome. Sexy.

"Ready?" he asked.

She pictured herself in bed with Jesse Dawson. Naked. And the chill that ran along the nape of her neck was both exhilarating and scary. She hoped she wasn't about to rationalize starting something with this man—they both knew that was risky beyond the basic disagreements they'd have as platonic co-parents.

She glanced out the window at the people walking into the rec center. A couple stood at the door, arguing so loudly she could hear them even though the windows of Jesse's truck were closed.

"If you didn't show up forty minutes late to pick up

Dylan I wouldn't *have* to yell at you," the woman said, finger pointed.

"I told you I got a flat tire," the man said. "What the hell do you want from me?"

The woman threw up her hands and went inside, the man shaking his head and staying put for a few seconds, then going in himself.

"Wow, do they need this class," Jesse said.

*That could be us in a month*, she thought, *different argument, same awful feeling.*

The mental picture of her in bed with Jesse immediately poofed from her head. Good.

A couple who'd been divorced for five years—previously married for ten—was teaching the co-parenting class. Jackie and Jim had two teenagers in high school. They looked alike in that they had the same coloring—both tall with dark brown hair and eyeglasses and both wearing fleece vests. Jesse figured that was part of their co-parenting class uniform—a strategy to appear *unified* and friendly. They sat on a desk facing the U-shaped arrangement of students' desks. Jesse had counted twenty-three students, and that was when it had occurred to him that not everyone here had come with their co-parent; some had likely come on their own.

One nosy class participant wanted to know why Jackie and Jim had gotten divorced.

"I'm not saying it doesn't matter why we got divorced," Jackie said, "because everything matters when you're trying to forge a relationship to allow for good co-parenting. But I can sum up this course in one line: what you want for your children, whether you have a baby or a teenager, should dictate everything you do and say and think. If you can let your goals and hopes for them be the focus, everything else will fall into place."

"What if you can't get along with your ex, though?" a woman in the front row asked. The one who'd been arguing outside. "And I mean *at all*," she added, shooting her co-parent a glare. "What if you argue about how blue the sky is?"

"I couldn't get along with Jim for a good three or four months after we first separated," Jackie said. "And you know who that affected the most? Not Jim. Not me. Our *kids*. When I realized that, that my anger was affecting them in really sad ways, I was determined to change."

"Yeah, but how do you cast that anger aside?" a man wearing a backward baseball cap asked. "My wife cheated on me—she was having an affair with some loser at work for weeks before I found out. I hate the sight of her."

"You try, try, try to remember that when it comes to your children," Jim said, "their feelings, their needs, their existence has to be the most important thing in your life. I'm not saying you're not going to be angry at your wife. But while you're at your son's football game, do you want to scream at the coach for a play gone wrong because you're so riled up over your personal life? Or do you want to cheer on your child who's out there and happy to see you in the stands? We ask our kids to constantly control themselves yet we don't model that for them when we act out because of our problems."

The man took that in, slowly nodding. "I hear you."

Lila leaned over to Jesse. "Platonic is definitely the way to go. At least when we disagree there won't be months or years of anger and resentment built up between us."

This sure was depressing, Jesse thought.

Despite his feelings about marriage, he knew there were beautiful marriages out there. His own parents', for one. Granted, Eddie and Claudia Dawson had been married just three years when his mother died. But they'd loved each other.

Except his father's grief over the loss of his wife had done a number on him. Sent him running. Unable, unwilling to lose again. To the point that he'd had to put emotional distance between himself and his own young son. Which for Eddie had meant *physical* distance.

All adding up to marriage not being anything Jesse wanted to be part of.

"I don't like this class," Jesse whispered. "Let's go find a nice restaurant and I'll treat you to dinner instead."

"But what about learning to co-parent?" Lila asked. "What the students are asking and what the teachers are saying isn't pretty but it's realistic. We might not relate to everything, but the basics are important. Everything *should* be about the kids."

"I'll give the class five more minutes," he said.

Lila glanced at him, eyebrow raised as if surprised by his reaction.

Jim was now talking about different parenting styles. When it came to Wyatt, Jesse seemed to be on the same page as Lila. The baby had a schedule that met all his needs, and they both adhered to it. If something came up and the schedule got a little off, they worked around it. But they'd been co-parenting for what—three days?

"Let's say your co-parent believes in letting your baby cry it out and learn to self-soothe when *you* believe in rushing in to soothe," Jim said to the group. "What can you do?"

Everyone looked around to see if anyone was brave enough to answer.

"It depends on how old," a blonde woman said. "Right? My seven-month-old is being sleep-trained right now. But my ex-husband's mother thinks that's barbaric and I should rush in to comfort my son the minute he cries."

Jesse glanced at the man sitting beside her. He must not be her co-parent because he had absolutely no reaction.

"Ah, yes, the ex–mother-in-law," Jackie said. "When you've got opposition coming from someone close to your ex, that can create even more friction. In that case, I suggest using 'I hear you' language. For example, you can say to your ex, 'I know it's important to you and your mom that little Danny's needs be met. Do you think that waiting, say, one full minute before going in would be reasonable?' And then see what your ex says. He'll likely say okay. It's these little acknowledgments in different parenting styles that can make exes not feel ignored or attacked. It's about compromise."

"But what if the ex is dead wrong?" Jesse asked, surprised it had come out of his mouth. "How do you compromise when you truly believe your ex isn't acting in the child's best interests?"

Was he asking on behalf of himself in case he and Lila discovered they were in opposite corners on an issue in raising Wyatt? Or had he asked from some long-ago question buried deep down in relation to his father? He truly wasn't sure where it had come from.

He felt Lila's gaze on him.

"That's a good question," Jim said. "And it really does come down to compromise. Sleep training isn't a life-and-death thing. That's different, of course. But we once had a divorced couple who were so up in arms over one wanting to let their baby cry it out that they started *screaming* at each other in class—there were a few expletives flung."

"And what happened?" Lila asked.

"We suggested that they try it the other parent's way for three nights," Jackie said. "The wife, who was against sleep training, agreed to follow the plan the husband was following for three nights on her custody days. She found it really hard but in the end, she said she was glad she'd done it because soon enough, the baby was sleeping through the night. Suddenly, she was listening more to her ex's point of view. And because she'd tried, making him feel respected and heard, he was less angry with her and more willing to hear her side of things. They're actually quite friendly now and their baby is in kindergarten. I know this because they take refresher classes from us."

As the students took that in, applying their own situations, there was chatter, and the teachers let them have a couple of minutes to talk.

"I want us always to listen to each other," Jesse said to Lila. "Hear each other. Be willing to try something that doesn't necessarily feel right."

Lila nodded—solemnly, he thought. "It's hard to go against your grain."

"There's nothing I was afraid of more," Jesse said.

"But 'my grain' has been changing. Because my baby son is *everything*."

Lila touched his arm and gave him a beautiful smile that went right inside him.

A few people around them clapped. Jesse felt his cheeks burn. He'd thought they'd been whispering, but maybe not.

Next the teachers covered how to potentially handle holidays and birthdays and new significant others. By the time the class was over, Jesse was exhausted. He'd learned a lot, but nothing he wanted to know or have knocking around his head when he couldn't sleep. The class was a good idea, but he and Lila were simply in a different situation—they weren't contentious exes who had to learn how to put their differences to the side for the sake of their child.

"Headache?" he asked Lila as they headed into the parking lot. He exaggeratedly rubbed his temples.

She smiled. "Nothing a good cheeseburger and fries won't cure. Hungry?"

"Starving," he said, brightening at the thought of a fortifying dinner with Lila after suffering through all that heavy stuff in the class. "And for exactly that too. Know of anywhere good?"

"Yup. Cowboy Pete's Bar and Grill. It's just what we need."

Ten minutes later, seated across from Lila at a table by the window, he wondered how a typical western bar and grill, with a basket of peanuts on the table, could be so damned romantic. The lighting was a bit on the low side and there was a very old country and western song playing softly, but that couldn't explain why he felt like he was suddenly on a date.

Maybe because being here with Lila, out to dinner, had butterflies flapping away in his stomach.

She looked so pretty. Her hair was in a low ponytail and she wore one of her trademark V-necked sweaters, this one green, and jeans with cowboy boots. Had a sexier woman ever existed?

*Platonic*, he reminded himself. Stop noticing how she looks.

But as the waiter came over and took their orders—cheeseburgers and steak fries for them both, he couldn't stop thinking about her lips. How it had felt to kiss her.

"It's a good thing we don't have to worry about becoming exes," she said, sipping her soda. "I certainly wouldn't want to be in any of those scenarios described in the class. I didn't even think about holidays or birthdays and having to split those up."

He nodded and was about to say they'd celebrate all those together. But if they were platonic, then Lila would eventually find that one true love she'd asked the psychic about.

He supposed being platonic meant there wouldn't be jealousy on either side about significant others in their lives.

Not that Jesse planned to get serious about anyone. Possibly ever again. At least that was how he felt now. But beautiful, sexy Lila was looking for love—to the point that it had been her one burning question to ask the psychic.

Jesse tried to picture himself at Lila's farmhouse for Wyatt's first birthday. Her one true love would be there.

And Jesse would be living somewhere else, of course, since the man in her life wouldn't want some guy sharing Lila's home.

Okay, Jesse couldn't see that at all. Didn't want to was more like it.

And what if Jesse didn't like her romantic partner's parenting style? What if that created problems?

He was getting way ahead of himself.

"Are you actively looking for the one true love you asked the psychic about?" he blurted out.

She kind of gaped at him. "That seems random. The question, I mean. What made you bring that up?"

"Just thinking about how your future husband and I might not be on the same page about how we parent," he said.

"Well, any future husband of mine wouldn't be Wyatt's dad," she said.

"Stepfather, then. And sometimes they're right there on the front lines."

She stared at him for a moment. "Jesse, I'm not getting married anytime soon."

"But you are actively looking?" he asked, the butterflies in his stomach suddenly flapping their wings like mad.

"No, of course not," she said. "I'm actively looking only to be the best mother—mother-aunt—I can be to Wyatt. He's my focus. Not my love life."

"Glad to hear it," he said, not quite meaning to say that aloud.

"Why?" she asked.

Why? *Because the thought of you with someone else makes me...unsettled.* Lila kissing someone in the middle of their first date. Spending the night with the guy. Falling in love.

Now he was the one doing the gaping. "Why? For the reason I just said. So there's no issue with a stepfather."

"I see," she said.

He hated it all.

But he had no claim to her in that department. They had to be platonic.

# *Chapter Eleven*

At just after 2:00 a.m., Lila heard Wyatt's cry and hurried into the nursery, wanting Jesse to get some sleep. It was her turn for the middle-of-the-night feeding. And she was happy to have something to do besides lie in bed and think about Jesse Dawson.

What he'd revealed during the class. And during dinner. And afterward, when they'd stopped in a store that was still open so he could get a Christmas present for his aunt and her own significant other. Not only had he gotten Bess something from himself but something from the great-nephew she'd be meeting. The gesture had struck her as so thoughtful that she'd wanted to grab him into a hug, a feeling that kept coming over her.

When she stepped into the nursery, she was surprised to find Jesse already at the crib, taking Wyatt into his arms.

For a moment she was as transfixed by how sexy he looked in his navy Wyoming Cowboys sweats and white T-shirt, his feet bare, his hair tousled, as she was by the sight of him so tender with his baby son. She should be used to both by now.

She cleared her throat to alert him that she was standing there, in the doorway, because she couldn't seem to find her voice.

"He's so sleepy," he said, lifting Wyatt up a bit so he could drop a kiss on the baby's head.

If she had her phone she'd snap another photo. Not just of Jesse's tender expression while holding his son, but of the man himself.

"It's supposed to be my turn to get up with him," she said. "You should be happily snoring away. And how'd you beat me in here anyway? I'd been up for a while and raced in here at his first peep."

"I was actually in here already. I half fell asleep on the rocker."

"Did Wyatt wake earlier and I didn't hear him?" she asked. She never slept through Wyatt's cries. When she first became Wyatt's guardian, she used to be so afraid she wouldn't hear him that her own anxiety over it kept her awake. But these days, she was so used to waking up with him that her body clock seemed to be on his schedule.

"No," Jesse said. "I just couldn't sleep so came in here and hung out on the rocker, watching Wyatt sleep, watching the stars. Thinking."

She waited for him to elaborate. *Please elaborate*, she sent to him telepathically. About the same things she'd been thinking about all night?

Like why he'd suddenly asked her about finding her one true love. How he'd seemed flustered when she wanted to know why.

He didn't seem flustered now. There was something else in his expression, in his eyes—something that sent goosebumps along the back of her neck.

Was he staring at her lips? His eyes were now on hers, so maybe she'd only imagined it. Because she'd been staring at *his* lips. His shoulders in that T-shirt. His biceps.

What she'd give to feel his arms around her right now.

Good thing his arms were occupied.

"Thinking about what?" she dared to ask as they headed out of the nursery and to the kitchen.

He didn't respond, but he did glance at her before heading over to the cabinet where Wyatt's many bottles were kept.

"I've got it," she told him. "Your hands are full."

She was glad to have something to focus on other than how incredibly attracted she was to him. There had to be a way to stop this. To stop wanting him to kiss her again. To stop fantasizing about being in bed with him.

But the attraction was coupled with how emotionally drawn to him she was. How much she liked him as a person. They shared so much.

"Thinking about us," he finally said, his gaze intent on her.

"Us? What about us?" she asked as nonchalantly as she could as she made up Wyatt's bottle.

"Little bit of everything, Lila," he said cryptically. He returned his attention to the baby he held, and she could tell he didn't want to say more.

She wouldn't push, either. There was something crackling in the air between them and she wasn't sure where it would take them. More conversation? More kissing?

They went back to the nursery, Jesse sitting in one of the rockers with a still sleepy Wyatt, Lila in the chair beside him, clutching the squishy stuffed bunny that had been on the seat. She handed him the bottle and watched him feed his son, her heart pinging every second, her nerve endings lighting up.

She was falling hard for this man. There was no stopping that. She would acknowledge it since there was no point denying it. But she didn't have to act on it.

*You don't want to end up one of Jim and Jackie's stories for a class next year. How to co-parent your toddler with the baby's father you weren't supposed to get romantically involved with. But you did and of course it didn't work out because Jesse Dawson isn't looking for love. He's here for his son. He's committed to his son.*

He'd break her heart.

And somehow she'd have to put aside that pain so Wyatt wouldn't suffer for it.

That sounded close to impossible, even if Jackie and Jim said it wasn't, that they themselves were proof.

*The key here is not to get involved in the first place, as you and Jesse have been talking about quite often,* she told herself. *Just stick to the plan.*

No kissing. No touching. No matter how much you want him.

But her gaze was on his strong forearms as he cradled Wyatt between his arm and chest.

"All done," Jesse said, bringing Wyatt up against that chest to burp him. Then he stood and brought him over to the dresser, expertly changing the baby's diaper before cuddling him back in his arms, swaying with him gently and softly humming a lullaby.

Lila might fall asleep herself if she wasn't unable to take her eyes off Jesse's long, tall body.

Wyatt's eyes were half-closed and she knew he'd be asleep in seconds. He was fed and dry and loved. Jesse would put him back in the crib any second now. And it would be just the two of them. Alone. In the middle of the night. The sexual tension between them hot in the air.

Jesse walked a sleeping Wyatt over to the crib and lowered him down. He watched him sleep for a moment, then turned to Lila, his gaze asking something.

What that was she wasn't entirely sure, but there was a question in those blue depths.

And then Jesse held out his hand toward her.

An invitation?

Or was he simply going to lead her from the nursery and back to her own room?

And carry her inside, his lips never leaving hers?

Or wish her a good-night at the door?

Jesse was very aware of the way Lila was looking at his outstretched hand, then at his face, trying to read him. He'd been trying to read her since he'd turned and found her in the doorway of the nursery.

He wasn't interested in a simple hug anymore. A hug would be nice. But it wouldn't come close to touching the deep need he felt for *much* more.

And if he was reading her correctly, she was feeling the same way he was, that one of them was going to make a move, that one of them had to immediately stop it. That both of them had to go to their separate rooms.

But as he looked at her, her beautiful face, her long silky auburn hair, her green eyes, how incredibly sexy she was in her flannel candy-cane pj's and long-sleeved

T-shirt, her full, high breasts making him swallow. He desperately wanted her.

She slipped her hand into his, her eyes on his face.

He gently pulled her to him and kissed her, letting desire and need and want take over. His hand went to either side of her jaw as he deepened the kiss, and when he felt her press closer against him, her arms up around his neck, he knew there'd be no stopping this. Not him, anyway.

He paused to look at her, to make sure she was in like he was. And she was. It was in her expression, her eyes full of desire. He couldn't speak even if he *had* something to say so just took her hand again and led her into her room.

By the bed he lifted up her T-shirt, and the sight of her bare chest had him so rock-hard that he had to still himself for a few seconds.

"You're exquisite," he whispered.

She tilted up her face and kissed him in response, then pulled off his own T-shirt, running her soft, cool hands on his chest, one of them dipping lower into the waistband of his sweatpants, into his boxer briefs until she found his erection. He stilled again, every bit of effort going into keeping his control.

He picked her up, making her laugh, and laid her on the bed, inching down her pajama pants. She helped kick them off, her hands exploring his shoulder, chest and back as she trailed hot kisses along his neck and ear. Her hand disappeared into his waistband again, lower and lower until she found what she sought, her mouth fused to his, her breathy moans driving him wild as she wrapped her hand around him.

In a flurry of movement they were both naked, his mouth now on her breasts, teasing, licking her nipples into taut peaks, both hands on the fullness. He let a hand wander down toward her navel, down farther between her legs until she moaned and arched her back.

She was reaching for something on the table—the drawer knob—while kissing him, her eyes closed. He heard the drawer open and her fumbling around for something inside.

"Thought I had a few of these," she whispered.

He opened his eyes to see a gold-foil-wrapped condom. Good thing she had some in reaching distance because he had one or two in his wallet—all the way in his room.

"Allow me," she whispered, rolling the condom onto his straining erection.

And then there was no waiting anymore. He couldn't. He rolled over and pulled her onto him, her face, her amazing breasts, her long hair falling down her shoulders all on display. He angled himself and slid her down onto him, closing his eyes, again stilling himself for just a moment until he was sure he had control. And then they rocked against each other, her nails in the tops of his shoulders, his mouth fused to hers, until they both exploded in pleasure that had them both making a ton of delicious noise.

She lay against him, her head on his chest, both of them breathing hard, eyes closed.

He could stay like this forever.

A thought that wasn't lost on him.

They didn't have forever; they had only till about

5:10 a.m. when Wyatt would wake for the day. But that was a good three hours.

"That was amazing," she whispered. "My body feels like Jell-O."

He laughed. "Mine too." He leaned over to kiss her on the cheek.

But instead of drifting to sleep, he was wide-awake, a funny feeling settling in his chest. In his head.

Here it comes, he thought. The itch to leave. The discomfort at cuddling for more than two minutes. The raw intimacy.

Just stay here, he ordered himself. Code of the West. Do not leave this woman in bed alone after you just made love. Do not.

It took everything to stay still.

Why? Too much? Too soon? What this could mean? They'd had sex when they'd agreed to be platonic. When they knew what romance could mean for their ability to be good co-parents.

Romance led to inevitable eventual disappointment. Hurt feelings on one or both sides. Arguing. Anger. Disruption of the house.

Now what? How did he go back to his room and hit restart on their platonic relationship without doing damage?

*You could raise the subject*, he thought. *Just talk it out openly and honestly. That you're worried you're going to make a disaster of this relationship.*

A little cry came from down the hall, and they both sat up.

He reached for his sweats. "I've got it," he said.

"Okay," she said a bit awkwardly, clutching the sheet to her chest.

And he was pretty sure she'd been having the same thoughts.

"Maybe it's good we got it out of our system," she said, reaching for clothing. "Let off some tension. We can...just let all that go now."

"Let what go?" he asked, not sure what she meant.

"Us," she said. "There can't be an *us*, right?"

He shook his head. "There can't be. There is, but I don't know what the hell we're going to do about it."

She offered a shaky smile at that. "I think we got the sexual tension out of our system," she repeated. "We should be fine just moving ahead now in being co-parents. Platonic co-parents."

"Right," he said. "Platonic."

She nodded firmly.

Okay, this was good, he thought. They were on the same page. Same line, same word even. *Platonic*.

Neither had hurt the other. Neither was disappointed. Everything was fine. And yes, they'd both let off some much needed steam and tension.

But as he gave her hand a squeeze and took in her beautiful face, her unsure expression, he wanted to crawl back into bed with her and just hold her, assure her, assure himself, that everything would be okay.

Another cry came from the nursery. *Good job, little guy*, he thought. *Just the impetus I need to leave Lila's bedroom.*

He'd have to force himself not to come back.

# *Chapter Twelve*

The morning was awkward, no way around it, Lila thought, as Jesse smiled a little too brightly when he handed her the coffee he'd just poured for her. He'd added cream and sugar, exactly the way she liked it. He'd offered to pop a bagel in the toaster for her—and mentioned they were running low on her veggie cream cheese, her favorite, and that he'd stop into the grocery store for more when he ran some errands later this afternoon.

Oh, and he was picking up Micah from school and then visiting a goat breeding farm to show their young hand what to look for when selecting a new herd for the farm. They'd be back around five or so and Jesse would bring home pizza for the three of them—small Mediterranean for her with extra feta, right?

Right. Sigh.

Jesse Dawson was everything she'd been looking for in a man, in the one true love she'd asked the psychic about. A man who could talk goats all day. Who was thoughtful and kind. Warm and funny. Interested in what she had to say and interesting. Responsible and full of integrity. A man who made her feel *special*. Little things added up, like remembering how she liked her coffee, that she preferred veggie cream cheese to plain, that her favorite pizza had extra feta.

Since she'd become Wyatt's guardian, she'd amended her dream man to include: *someone who'll love Wyatt like I do, a devoted father figure.*

It all added up to Jesse Dawson.

*Great in bed* was a plus she hadn't even had on her list of hopes.

Sex with Jesse had only added a new dimension to her feelings for him. And made those feelings scarier too. Which was why she'd been so quick to get them back to their plan. To be platonic.

*Platonic* felt like protection.

And really stupid at the same time.

*Day by day, minute by minute*, she reminded herself. Only way to go.

The moment Jesse was out the door to care for the goats and do some repair work on the barn, Lila felt the lack of his presence. She both missed him and needed the break from how large that presence loomed.

She'd noted how he'd been just as quick to agree that they should revert back to being platonic. That sex had been just something to get out of their system.

She had to be careful. To stop thinking she was in control here; she wasn't. She simply felt too much for him for that. Lila knew it was why she was all over the place where he was concerned. One minute they were this, the next that.

She finished her coffee, staying away from the window with the view of the barn where Jesse was likely feeding Lulu and Dolly. She had to clear her mind of Jesse Dawson.

She scooped up Wyatt from his baby rocker in the kitchen and took him over to the Christmas tree to show him the ornaments and make a mental list of the gifts she still needed to buy. She glanced at the side of the tree, hoping she'd see that Jesse had moved his two ornaments—the white house with the black cat atop it and the red pickup—but they were still at the very back, out of sight.

*Go into town*, she told herself. She needed a change of scenery to get last night off her mind. And she could shop for Aunt Raina's gifts and the heart locket that had stopped her mom in her tracks a couple of weeks ago while they'd been walking along Main Street and window-shopping with Wyatt in his stroller. The pendant necklace was exactly the kind of thing her mom wouldn't buy herself but coveted—the perfect Christmas present.

A couple of hours later, Lila had Wyatt bundled up on this chilly morning and went into town. She parked by the town square, smiling at the line of children already waiting for Santa on a weekday now that school was out for the holiday break.

As she headed into the coffee shop—open even if the shops weren't yet—she noticed Tania Pickler at the front of the line with her husband, and immediately Lila's heart sank. Where Tania went, so did her identical twin, Terese, and sure enough, when Lila glanced around the large room with tables and couches and overstuffed vintage chairs, she saw Terese and her husband too. Both women had babies a little older than Wyatt and had been in the Lamaze class Kate had taken, Lila her sister's partner. The teacher had constantly mixed up all their names, once even calling Lila *Terese*, which had made the two sets of identicals laugh since it had been a first. Teachers and classmates had mixed up Kate and Lila all the time, but the Lamaze teacher not only had the wrong twin but from a completely different family, at that. She could hear Tania ordering coffee drinks and bagels and treats to stay, which meant the group would be here a while.

And Lila didn't want to see the twins, let alone chat. The reminder that her own twin was gone would be too much.

Lila was pulling the stroller back outside to avoid Tania noticing her when of course she heard her name being called.

"Lila!" Tania was trilling and waving.

Dammit. She'd been spotted. Tania's husband came running over to get the door for her, which actually was helpful and appreciated.

She forced a smile on her face as Tania came over to say hi.

"How *are* you?" Tania asked with that annoying compassionate lilt in her voice. She was sure Tania did feel bad that Lila had lost her sister. But the Mack twins had never really become chummy with the Picklers, despite having a lot in common and going through twelve years of Bear Ridge public schools together. "Gosh, this must be such a hard time of year for you and this darling little man," Tania added, bending down to smile at Wyatt, who was staring at her.

*Yes, it is*, she wanted to snap. Sometimes she liked it when people acknowledged that she'd not only lost her twin but that this was her first Christmas without her sister—and a joyous time for most when she was still grieving. Oftentimes folks didn't know what to say so they said nothing, which was also fine. But the Picklers seemed to relish others' misfortunes.

"Oh, you poor things," Terese said on cue as she came over, the husbands now at the order pickup line at the end of the long counter. "You're getting so big, William!" she added with a little tap on the baby's nose.

"Wyatt," Lila corrected through clenched teeth.

"Oh, of course! Wyatt! I can barely keep anything in my head I'm so busy," Terese added. "What with Christmas and all the planning and shopping and family celebrations."

Lila glanced at the table where the twins' husbands were sitting down with their trays of coffees and food. A pang of jealousy hit her hard. She wished Kate were here so badly that tears sprang to her eyes.

"Aww," Tania said, noticing and patting her hand. "And to be raising Wyatt all on your own. You're like a single mother now."

"Coffee's getting cold," one of the husbands called.

"Well, nice to see you, Lila," Terese said. "You take care."

*Oh, I will,* she wanted to snap as the women walked over to the table. She watched Tania's husband stand and help her off with her long down coat and Terese's husband picking up their son from the stroller beside him and sitting him on his lap. The couples were laughing at something the baby did. *What I would give,* she thought, getting in line for the necessary caffeine despite her wanting to flee, *to have my sister back. The closest of family together at holiday time.*

Instead, she'd never been more alone.

*Hardly true*, she chastised herself. You have Wyatt and your family. You have Jesse, even if you don't have him the way you wish you could.

*I want what the Picklers have. I want love and marriage and family—a husband beside me and Wyatt.*

And the man she was beginning to see this with?

Her platonic partner—because of their deep-seated fear that being together would ruin the great thing they had going.

But wasn't that the risk you took when you married anyone? she asked herself. No one went in thinking their marriage wouldn't work, that the person you loved would one day be signing divorce papers. That you'd feel all the things from Jim and Jackie's class.

So they'd both just be alone for the next eighteen years? That didn't make sense either.

The yearning inside her was so overwhelming she had to grip Wyatt's stroller handle lest she just suddenly fall over from the heavy weight in her chest.

She got a latte and a blueberry muffin for herself and several scones to go for the house, including Micah's favorite flavor, cinnamon chip, then headed to the park just across the road, to the very bench that Jesse had been sitting on before he'd come over and mistaken her for Kate.

She sat there sipping her coffee, Wyatt enjoying looking at the big evergreens flanking the entrance to the park. Her appetite for her muffin had disappeared.

"This is where it all began," she whispered to Wyatt. She thought again how if she'd been five minutes later coming out of the feed shop, if she'd chatted with the owner of the store a bit longer, if anything about the day had been just slightly different, Jesse might have missed her altogether. He might have been long gone to that ranch outside Yellowstone.

*Fate*, psychic Alina would say.

And that meeting, Jesse noticing her, coming over, the pin on Wyatt's snowsuit the telltale sign for him, had changed both their lives in an instant.

"I'm falling in love with your daddy," she blurted out to Wyatt.

And gasped. She *was* falling in love. There was no denying her feelings.

She closed her eyes for a few seconds as memories of last night came over her. How he'd picked her up and laid her down on her bed. Taken off her clothes. Kissed every inch of her body.

But the conversation afterward came back to her too. She frowned.

*Maybe it's good we got it out of our system... Let off some tension. We can...just let all that go now.*

Yeah, right. She wouldn't be able to let anything go.

"We're both so afraid of ruining this good thing we have going," she whispered to Wyatt. "You get it, right? On one hand, it makes total sense. On the other, it makes *no* sense."

She sighed and sipped her coffee. She knew two divorced couples who were once so in love who absolutely despised each other now. Unexpected things happened. Relationships changed. People changed. Like all the fellow students in the co-parenting class.

*But how can we want the best for you if we can't teach you to reach for the moon and stars? That's what love is. Putting your heart out there, putting it on the line.*

*It's risk. For all the reward in the world.*

"What do you think, Wyatt?" she asked.

"Ba!" Wyatt said, his blue eyes so alert.

Lila was so surprised that he actually seemed to be responding that she laughed. "Oh, Wyatt. How I love you. You make me feel so lucky. Those Picklers are right—it *is* hard this time of year. But I'm very grateful to have you."

Still unsure but feeling better nonetheless, Lila got up and tossed her coffee cup in the trash can, then headed for the gift shop, which was just opening, the proprietor turning the sign from Closed to Open. A half hour later, she had the beautiful gold oval locket, which she'd fill with a tiny photo of Wyatt and then wrap up for her mom, and two more little gifts for her aunt Raina— fuzzy wool cat socks and a travel book about day trips and weekend getaways in Wyoming.

When she got back to her car, she saw the Picklers and their husbands and their two baby strollers walking toward the Santa hut.

*If you want that,* she said to herself, *if you want the man you love beside you, pushing the stroller and putting your toddler on his shoulder, and teaching your child about goats and sharing in the beautiful day-to-day of life, you have to make it happen. You have to put yourself out there.*

*And tell Jesse what you want.*

As she settled Wyatt in his car seat, she'd made a decision.

She was going to talk to Jesse tonight.

After putting in a couple of hours on the farm, Jesse had to accept that he was seriously distracted and pulled up a stool in the barn to watch the goats playing on the logs.

He couldn't stop thinking about his night with Lila. And what they talked about afterward. The renewed handshake on being platonic was for the best but made all the harder when he had the kind of thoughts running through his head every second—kissing her, touching her, her nails scraping his back, her hands in his hair, her lips all over him. How was he supposed to forget any of that?

He heard Lila's SUV pulling up, aware that he was a little too excited at seeing her. He was always thrilled to see Wyatt, but his anticipation of being near Lila had goosebumps trailing up his neck. Not good, given their agreement.

He stepped out of the stall to meet her. Wyatt was in his stroller and conked out.

"I come bearing scones," she said, pulling the bakery box from the basket under Wyatt's seat. "Mixed berry, cinnamon chip—though if you take one of those, you'll hear it from Micah—chocolate coconut and apricot."

He plucked out the apricot. "Thanks," he said and then took a bite. "Hits the spot." To force his eyes off Lila he reached for his thermos of coffee for a long sip.

"So I've been thinking," she said—and bit her lip.

"About?"

"The *us* you mentioned yesterday. How I feel, what I want. What Wyatt needs."

Uh-oh. Since they'd agreed to go back to being platonic, this could only mean that she had something else in mind.

Something that struck him as dangerous without even hearing about it yet.

"I'll be honest and open here," she said. "I don't want to be platonic. Not after last night. I feel close to you, Jesse. And the urge to kiss you—all the time. There's clearly something special between us that neither of us expected. That both of us are worried about. But—"

He held up his hand. "Now you can't add that but to those worries, Lila. I can't end up one of Jim and Jackie's awful stories."

"Who says we will? My parents are happily married. Yours were, too. It wasn't fighting and not being on the same page that separated your mom and dad."

"I know," he said. "But losing my mom changed my dad. He was a family man until then. Love someone to that point and lose them and wham—you run hours away to avoid keeping anyone close, including your own little son. You push people away. I don't want that either."

"Jesse, I know what loss feels like. Granted, I didn't lose a spouse. But I did lose my twin. The person closest to me in the world—for twenty-eight years. When I lost Kate, I didn't emotionally retreat from Wyatt."

"We're not the same, Lila," he said before he could stop himself. Sometimes he thought they *were* the same. Their hearts and minds, their goals and dreams. They were all about the baby they shared.

Her face fell, and he wished he hadn't said it.

He stepped closer and took both her hands in his. "I'm scared out of my mind of screwing this up, Lila. And not just because of what it might mean in sharing Wyatt."

"Then what?" she asked.

"Between how I was raised and then getting blindsided by my ex, I'm about as cynical as a person can get about a relationship working out. I hate the thought of doing something, saying something that will hurt you. The arguments and cold wars. I can't bear that between us, Lila."

"So you're going to be alone forever?" she asked. "Is that what you're saying?"

"I'm saying I feel too much for you."

There it was. The big admission. To himself. And to her.

"And I don't want to feel all that," he added.

"Because of what might happen," she said.

"Yes. And what likely will."

"I don't know, Jesse. I have more faith in both of us and what's between us. It feels big. Bigger than anything I've ever felt or experienced. And it's just the start."

He looked at her and just wanted to wrap his arms around her and let that faith of hers carry them both. He wished he could be all in.

But how could he? He had brick walls up that would require a wrecking ball to smash apart.

"I have an idea," she said. "Let's just go with what we feel. Both of us will honor and respect that, whatever it might be. If one of us needs a little space, the other understands." She looked at him hopefully, and he could tell that she meant what she was saying, that she really believed this could work.

Dammit. Everything she said made good sense. Despite being dangerous.

Before he could stop himself, he slid his arms around her and pulled her to him, and she sagged against him, her head against his chest. "I need this," he said. "Us this close. How am I supposed to keep my hands off you anyway?"

She looked up at him and smiled. "Good."

"So we have a new deal," he said.

She nodded. "We do what feels right and good. And this right now feels very good."

It sure did, he thought, wrapping his arms more tightly around her. It was why he was so damned worried. Because good never lasted.

She tilted up her face and kissed him, and it was warm sunshine spreading into his chest.

He did need this. And he was going to run with it.

To make Lila happy. And for Wyatt's sake.

And yes, for his own.

If Jesse wanted to be a good father, he needed to model good behavior.

And not letting fear boss him around was a start.

# *Chapter Thirteen*

"You look really happy," Aunt Raina said with a twinkle in her eyes.

They were in Raina's kitchen, her aunt setting down two cups of eggnog and a tin of sugar cookies on the table.

Lila had needed to talk out everything that had happened with Jesse, and she'd always been able to confide in her aunt. Raina wouldn't blab to Lila's mom either, which made sharing even easier.

Raina sat down and checked on Wyatt, who was napping in his stroller in the corner. "Such a good baby!" she cooed.

"He really is," Lila said, then took a sip of her eggnog—yum. Eggnog was one of the rare things she and her twin hadn't been the same on. Despite loving all things Christmas, Kate had thought eggnog was disgusting whereas Lila could drink an entire carton in one gulp.

"So I'm assuming the happiness radiating off you has something to do with the man staying in your guest room," Raina said, giving her eyebrows a wriggle.

Lila smiled and filled her aunt in on everything that had happened between her and Jesse, ending with the hot kiss he'd given her at her SUV when she'd been about to leave for her aunt's house.

"I get it," Raina said. "Why you two thought being platonic was a good idea *and* why you're giving up on it. But the new plan is definitely the way to go. What's that saying about not being able to stop progress? This is progress."

Lila laughed. "I suppose it is. Scary progress, though." She bit her lip. "I am still worried, though. Not just about how this could affect us as parents, affect Wyatt, but of getting hurt and hurt bad. The way I feel about Jesse— I haven't ever felt like this about a man."

Raina reached over and squeezed her hand. "I totally understand. Believe me, I know all about being afraid, especially with an indispensable relationship."

Jesse was exactly that—indispensable.

Raina took a bite of a cookie. "Did I mention that Errol and I kissed for the first time in the forty years we've known each other?"

Lila gaped at her aunt. "What? You and Errol?" She smiled at the thought as tall, lanky Errol McKinley popped into her head with his curly blond hair and warm brown eyes. Raina and Errol had been best buddies since middle school. They'd been through all of each other's ups and downs, divorces, medical issues, heartbreaking losses, from relatives to relationships. Lila, Kate and their mom had always told Raina she and Errol belonged together, but Raina had insisted they were meant to be friends, that there was no romantic or sexual chemistry at all.

"We were having a casual dinner at the diner," Raina said. "We both got the fish and chips and had been laughing about how we both had a craving for the same thing. Then we were talking about what Errol should get his grandbaby for Christmas, and I suggested that same baby swing that you have, the one that plays the lullabies, and a minute later, when we were leaving, he pointed up and there was a sprig of mistletoe right under the door. And he said, well, now we have to kiss."

Lila was liking where this was going. "And did you?"

"I went to give him a peck on the cheek, and he went to do the same. But one of us turned too fast and we kissed on the lips, and instead of it being a two-second thing, neither of us moved. And we opened our eyes and that was that. Something had changed."

"Wow!" Lila said. "You felt it in the kiss too? Like it wasn't a friendly kiss but a hot kiss?"

"It just suddenly turned into that. Out of the clear blue."

"And then what?" Lila asked. "Are you a couple now?"

"Taking baby steps. We're both scared. Sure, we know each other very, very well. But I've never known him in this context. Suddenly, we're a little shy around each other. And what if it doesn't work out? What if I'm not really what he wants or needs and he's not what I want or need and the romance ends badly and suddenly our forty-year friendship is over? I can't imagine life without Errol."

Lila completely understood. "I know. But you've got to go for it!" She leaned over to give her aunt a hug. "I'm so happy for you—and Errol. I can't imagine not going for it just out of the possibility that the romance might not work out. Surely you can get the friendship back if that happens."

Raina nodded and sipped her eggnog. "Just like you and Jesse will get back to being solid co-parents. But you've got to go for it too. Just like Errol and I are doing."

Lila smiled, a warmth spreading in her chest. She wholeheartedly agreed. And she had a good feeling that Errol and Raina would work out just fine. And maybe there would even be a wedding in the new year. Her aunt had been through hell and back in her divorce and a subsequent relationship that had gone south. She'd been so cynical for so long and had figured that was that—she would just be single. Raina deserved all the happiness in the world.

This felt like an omen. That her aunt was grabbing love instead of letting worry and fear keep her from it.

She and Jesse had come to the right conclusion about their blossoming romance.

Tonight couldn't come soon enough.

Jesse was beginning to understand why his father had specifically mentioned getting a dog in his last wishes for Jesse. Billy, the Border collie mix, was a good pal when Jesse was out on the farm, looking for holes to repair in the fencing, when he was raking the stalls, when he was just taking a break on the porch steps with coffee. The dog would sit beside him and inevitably rest his furry chin on Jesse's thigh, sometimes his shoulder. Billy made him more aware of what was out of sight, since the dog's ears would perk up and he'd stare out into the distance sometimes. And he never jumped up on Jesse when he had the baby in the carrier on his chest. Good dog.

Now, as Jesse double-checked that the goats were settled in their pasture, he liked having Billy trotting at his side. He'd never had a dog—his aunt had been a cat person, and though Jesse liked cats and their mysterious ways, he'd never known just how attuned a dog could be to a person. Man's best friend, indeed.

He talked to Billy a lot, probably a little too much. Same as he did with Wyatt, but with Billy, he allowed himself to talk about Lila. How he was feeling in the minute, since that changed often. Troublesome when they'd shaken on taking their relationship day by day. Just when he'd be thinking they should be led by their feelings and attraction, in the next breath he'd be sure they should go back to being platonic. Where it was safe.

"I don't know what the hell I'm doing, Billy," he said to the sweet dog, whose tail was wagging. "I'm knee-deep with Lila—even with her brother. Suddenly, these people are a big part of my life."

He also liked watching Micah play with Billy, racing around, throwing sticks, which the pooch would fetch and return. Jesse was able to get a sense of Micah through his interaction with the dog; the care he took with Billy, the kind way he spoke to him told him how he'd treat the goats in his care when Jesse wasn't around to watch every second.

Now, it was just past six o'clock and Micah had left. Lila should be returning any minute with Wyatt and then Jesse would bring him over to his aunt's for dinner. He wanted to introduce Bess to Lila, too, but he'd hold off on that for today. For this big surprise, he figured he'd keep it to the two of them. He'd ask Lila about inviting his aunt and her fiancé, Bill, over for dinner in the coming days so that they could meet and get to know each other.

Another reason he wanted it to be just him and Wyatt tonight at Aunt Bess's was so he could ask some questions about his childhood and what Bess thought about Jesse as a parent—questions that might make him feel vulnerable. His aunt knew him better than anyone and he respected her opinion.

He had no idea how his aunt would feel about him suddenly being a dad to a baby. If she'd think he was up to the monumental lifelong task of fatherhood. If he had it in him to be there, every day, *present*, for at least the next eighteen years.

And if she thought he didn't? That he was kidding himself? That he'd always been a fan of novelty and that he'd get the burning desire to leave in a few months. Maybe even a few weeks? If Bess had something to say that was hard to hear, well, he'd just have to counter it.

He felt committed to Wyatt—one hundred percent.

And now he'd agreed with Lila that they should follow their hearts and not their heads with their attraction to each other. He knew it was much more than just lust that drew him to Lila Mack. But he had nothing solid to go on when it came to romantic relationships. He'd sworn off getting emotionally involved after getting betrayed two years ago, and that was a long time to be alone—to get used to being on his own. Not putting someone else first. Not having to consider someone's feelings at all.

He'd have to be careful. He knew he'd be a good father to Wyatt; he felt that in his bones and blood despite how his father had been since Jesse was very young. But romance? A relationship with someone so important in his life? He could screw that up without meaning to, without even realizing he was being a jerk about this or that.

Another reason he was looking forward to talking to his aunt about all this—maybe she'd reassure him.

He headed in the house to take a shower, slough off the farm. He was dressed and ready to go when he heard Lila's SUV pulling in, and he went out to greet her.

"You'll take photos of Wyatt with his new great-aunt, right?" Lila asked as he unbuckled Wyatt from her car seat. He had the baby's bag freshly packed with necessities on his shoulder.

"I promise I will," he said. He looked at her for a moment. "I haven't seen you in a few hours and now I have to rush off. I already miss you."

One hundred percent true. He had missed her.

The sweet smile she gave him told him he'd touched her. "I already miss you too. But I'm glad you're seeing your aunt and introducing Wyatt. That'll be really special."

With Wyatt hoisted in one arm, he tilted up Lila's face with his free hand and kissed her.

"Looking forward to later tonight," she said with a sexy grin.

"Oh, me too." Memories of last night had come into his head all day long.

He kissed her again. "See you in about two hours."

"Can't wait," she said.

He felt that inside his chest. That she meant it. That it was nice, really nice, to have someone waiting for him at home. That he *had* a home.

He was changing before his own eyes.

A few minutes later, with Wyatt resettled in his seat in Lila's SUV, he drove over to his aunt's house. She lived just a few blocks from downtown Bear Ridge in a tidy yellow cape, the very house he'd spent so much time in growing up. When he pulled into her driveway, she and her fiancé came outside to greet him. They were both in their late fifties, tall and wearing sweatshirts that bore the names of places from their travels and jeans. His aunt's dark hair was chin-length with a swish of bangs and she had the Dawson blue eyes. Both had a warm, friendly look.

Jesse liked the fiancé, who he'd met only once, when he'd come home for the engagement party just a few months before his father died. Bess would probably have gotten married this past year but she'd taken the loss of her brother harder than she expected, given that she'd rarely seen him in the last ten years. She hadn't wanted to have a big celebratory event in her life when she was grieving, and Jesse certainly understood that.

Jesse hopped out of the SUV and gave his aunt and Bill hugs.

"New vehicle?" Bess asked.

"Nope," he said, unable to hide his smile. "It's part of the surprise."

His aunt's eyes were brimming with curiosity. "This surprise has to be something major because you're still here in town and normally you'd be halfway across Wyoming."

"We've been trying to guess for the past few hours what it could possibly be," Bill added. "But we've got nothing."

Jesse smiled. "It's both huge and tiny. Take a look in the passenger side rear seat."

His aunt and her fiancé, both clearly trying to figure out the huge and tiny part, walked around his car. Bill looked confused by the rear-facing car seat. His aunt gasped.

She tried to angle herself so she could get a glimpse inside the seat. "Is that a baby?"

"Yup," he said. "Wyatt. He's three months old."

His aunt gasped again. Jesse opened the door and got Wyatt out of the seat. He held him so that the two could get a good look at the baby.

"Oh my God," Bess said. "Are you telling me this is your child?"

Jesse nodded. "Exactly that."

His aunt's hand flew to her mouth and then over her heart, and tears misted her eyes. "Oh, Jesse," she whispered.

"I know," he said with a smile. "This is your great-nephew."

Now tears slid down her cheeks. "He's so precious. Look at those eyes. Just like yours. And your daddy's and grandpa's." She shook her head as if she still couldn't believe what she was hearing and seeing. "Let's get him inside since it's cold. I want to hear everything. And I have to hold him—my great-nephew!"

Jesse followed the pair inside. He got Wyatt out of his snowsuit, the baby's eyes on Bess. She was still teary as she took him in her arms.

"My God, Jesse," Bess said, her gaze so soft on Wyatt. "He really does look just like you."

Bill nodded and ran a gentle finger down the baby's cheeks. "He's your spitting image."

They headed into the living room. Bill excused himself to check on dinner, and Jesse and his aunt sat down on the sofa. He snapped a few photos as he'd promised Lila, and Bill came in to take a few of Bess and Jesse, his aunt holding the baby, before returning to the kitchen.

Jesse looked around. The place hadn't changed much; it rarely had in all the years he'd been spending time here. He'd never liked visiting as an adult, and he'd never been able to pinpoint why. He loved his aunt and the house had always been cozy and inviting. Now he wondered if subconsciously, the house had always reminded him of being *left*.

"I did take a paternity test to make it official," he said—Wyatt's maternal family was adamant about that. "But it was obvious by just looking at him that he was mine."

He took a deep breath and blurted out the whole story—starting a year ago. How beside himself he'd been the night of his father's death. That he'd gone looking for a bar and to drown his sorrows in a couple of beers and that he'd met a woman. He'd even admitted that he'd pulled his usual MO of leaving in the middle of the night and that he'd inexplicably left his pin, the talisman he'd carried around for a while. How it was the pin that made it ironclad that Wyatt was his. The pin that was always on Wyatt's snowsuit.

"And Lila is Wyatt's mother's identical twin," Bess said, looking from Wyatt to Jesse. "Is that an issue at all?"

"It doesn't seem to be. Lila's features are different

enough that when I look at her, I don't see Kate's double. I see Lila. And she seems to see me in a separate way too."

"Good," Bess said. "That tells me you're both focused on the present and the future. Not the past. You're starting in the right place."

He liked the way she put that. Starting in the right place. He thought of Lila's gram telling him to start as he meant to continue—and he supposed he was doing just that. He absolutely meant to continue.

But he knew that *intentions* weren't worth all that much. That was what kept him up nights.

"Speaking of that, Aunt Bess. I'm trying not to let the past get in my way. Which includes Wyatt's way. And my and Lila's way. Now that others are involved, I wonder if..."

He paused and glanced away, hating that he even *had* to wonder, had to ask her thoughts.

His aunt gave him time to finish the question. That had always been her trademark. Her patience. He hoped he'd be half the parent to Wyatt that she'd been to him over the years.

He was grateful when Bill announced from the kitchen that dinner would be ready in ten minutes and that they were having chicken parmigiana and linguini. It gave him a few seconds to collect himself.

"But I wonder if I'm my father's son," he finally finished. "You know what I mean, Aunt Bess. Right now, I feel absolutely committed to Wyatt. But what if I start wanting to leave in a few weeks or a few months? What if it turns out I'm just like my dad?"

He looked at the baby in his aunt's arms, indeed precious. He couldn't imagine ever walking away from this child. His child. But his father had done it. And his father *had* loved him—Jesse would always believe that.

"You won't leave him," his aunt said. "I doubt you'll even leave him *overnight* unless you absolutely had to. And then I can see you calling every half hour to make sure he's okay." She gave him a warm but serious smile. "You don't have to worry about being a good daddy to this baby, Jesse."

It was the answer he wanted. But… "How can you be so sure?" he asked against a lump in his throat.

"Because I know you," she said.

The relief. He could feel his shoulder muscles unbunching.

"And you and Lila…" she prompted.

"We're taking it day by day," he said. Suddenly that didn't sound so good, like they were both unsure of everything.

"That's smart," Bess said. "Takes the pressure off. That you're doing even *that* tells me this Lila must be pretty special."

Jesse felt a weight lift off his chest and shoulders. He'd been so right that Aunt Bess would be full of wisdom. She really did know him so well. And she was positive. She often hadn't been when it came to his father. But with Jesse, she'd always seen potential. And he needed her in his corner.

His aunt knew about the breakup two years ago. How he hadn't been able to commit to anyone or anything since.

"She is," he said. "Very special."

"Oh, Jesse, I'm so happy. For you and for Wyatt and for Lila. And for me." She snuggled Wyatt against her, dropping a kiss on his head. "A great-aunt. I feel so blessed."

He leaned over to give her as much of a hug as he could without smushing his son.

The present and the future—not the past. *That* was his new motto.

## *Chapter Fourteen*

*Tonight was worth the wait*, Lila thought with a satisfied sigh as she collapsed beside Jesse, both of them sated and catching their breath after making love.

When Jesse had returned from his aunt's house, he'd shown her the photos he'd taken and told her about Bess's sweet reaction to her great-nephew and the kind things she'd said about him as a father. His aunt's faith, her belief in him, had buoyed him, and he'd had a sparkle about him that made her feel so hopeful about their future. They'd put Wyatt to bed together, each of them telling the baby a story about themselves, and she'd learned the very funny truth that Jesse loved spinach as a kid— cooked and raw—and hated french fries, that he still loved spinach but maybe loved fries a little bit more.

Then they'd gone to her room and watched a romantic comedy from the '90s on her laptop, consuming a bowl of popcorn. They'd taken a shower together next, the baby monitor on the bathroom counter, and they'd giggled as they'd lathered each other up with soap, washing each other's hair, kissing every few seconds, and then they'd returned to her room and made love. It was magical.

And tonight, there was no talk about being platonic.

A cry came from the nursery, and Jesse woke up immediately, gave her hand a squeeze and was out of bed and into his sweats and a T-shirt before she could blink.

*Oh no*, she thought. *He was out of here without a word. He's not going to come back in here.*

She bit her lip, her heart starting to pound. Was he going to backtrack?

*Day by day, remember?* she reminded herself. There were going to be ups and downs as they both got more comfortable. *Stop reading into every little thing.*

She felt like she held her breath as the seconds ticked away.

But ten minutes later, he was back in her room, getting into bed with her and turning onto his side to face her. "He was barely awake," he said. "Went back to sleep so easily."

"How about you?"

"Oh, I have a much better idea than sleeping right now," he said, trailing kisses along her neck.

She smiled, her heart soaring. He reached for her hand under the blanket and held it.

"I could get used to this," he said.

"Good because me too."

She rested her head on his chest, completely at peace, completely happy. Their hands were still entwined and they chatted a bit, but mostly just snuggled against each other, Jesse seeming to feel as she did: that this felt right.

"My aunt and soon-to-be new uncle would love to meet you," he said. "Next week some time for dinner? I could cook here or we can go out."

"Ooh, I'll cook," she said. "I used to love to cook, even

just fancy meals for myself, but I haven't had any time the past couple of months. Now I get my own nap time, bath time and kitchen time. You even fold laundry. You're okay to have around, Jesse Dawson."

"Ha, you're using me so you can take naps and baths without worrying or pressing a monitor to your ear. I knew it."

She leaned up on one elbow and kissed him on the lips. "I'm so happy you're here. In general and right now—meaning in my bed."

"Me too," he said and kissed her back.

They figured out a date for dinner with Bess and Bill and were talking about their favorite and least favorite foods—Jesse didn't like bananas or shellfish and Lila loved both—when another cry came from the nursery. This was superfussy.

"My turn," she said, popping out of bed and putting on her yoga pants and tunic sweatshirt. She missed Jesse immediately. Billy got out of his plush dog bed by the window and followed her to the nursery.

As she stood over Wyatt's crib and reached for him, the baby continued to cry, which was unusual for him. When he wanted attention for any reason—lonely, hungry, wet, gassy—he let out a fast shrill cry. But now he was practically screaming.

"Wow, what's up, Wyatt?" Jesse said from the doorway. "Miss us that much?"

Lila could feel how hot Wyatt was the moment her hands touched his skin. "He's burning up," she said. "He must have a fever."

Wyatt was red-faced and still crying, kicking out his

feet. She took off his fleece pj's and he still was crying but not as sharply. He must have felt more comfortable.

Jesse came over and touched his forehead. "He's really hot. What do we do?" he asked, concern in his eyes.

"Let's start with baby fever reducer," she said. "Babies get fevers, get sick. So try not to worry, okay?"

He looked very worried.

"Where is it? I'll get it," he said.

"In the bathroom, top shelf."

He hurried out and she changed Wyatt in the meantime, finding a pair of soft cotton pj's for him. Jesse returned in a few seconds with the little bottle. She measured out the dose and gave it to Wyatt, holding the baby vertically against her, gently patting his back. He was still crying a bit and fussy but he clearly felt better being held.

"You're sure he'll be okay?" he asked. "Should we call his doctor? Take him to the ER?"

"He had a fever once before and the doc told me to give him a dose of the medicine and wait a half hour and if he was still very hot with a high fever to bring him to the ER. Raina told me that's what she would advise too."

Jesse nodded but he still looked worried.

"Can I hold him?" he asked.

She transferred Wyatt to Jesse, his expression alarmed at how hot the baby was.

"Poor guy," he cooed, sitting down in one of the rockers and making gentle movements. "It's okay. We're gonna take good care of you."

"We will," she assured both of them as she sat in the rocker beside Jesse.

They were quiet, just listening to Wyatt, his cries subsiding.

Jesse touched the back of his hand to Wyatt's forehead. "He's just as hot."

Lila bolted up and got the forehead thermometer from the basket in Wyatt's dresser.

He was breathing a bit raggedy now.

"This can't be okay," Jesse said, turning to her.

She grabbed her phone and called the pediatrician's office. The answering service assured her the doctor on call would phone back right away. He did within five minutes.

"The doc says we should take him to the clinic's ER— out of an abundance of caution," she told Jesse, pocketing her phone. "Between the breathing and the fever, which doesn't seem to be getting better."

His face fell. She wondered if it was the guidance to seek medical care in the middle of the night or *where*. The Bear Ridge Clinic was where Jesse had lost his dad.

Jesse bolted up, looking paler and upset. They rushed to the front door, getting on their boots and coats, putting Wyatt into his fleece bunting, and then hurrying to Lila's SUV.

In fifteen minutes they were at the clinic. Lila parked and Jesse got Wyatt out of his car seat, and they dashed past the circular snow-covered little green, a huge evergreen lit up with multicolored lights.

"Stupid tree," Jesse muttered. "Maybe no one wants to see some big, dumb, decked-out holiday tree with festive lights when their loved ones are very sick."

Lila didn't respond. She knew where he was coming

from. But some people likely found a decorated Christmas tree very comforting.

Lila checked in at the front desk, and they both paced until a nurse appeared at a door and called Wyatt's name.

"He has to be okay," Jesse said.

"He will be," Lila assured him.

His face was stony, his eyes worried, his jaw hard. "You can't know that."

She didn't respond to that either. The doctor would assure him—she hoped.

Because Wyatt *did* have to be okay.

Lila had been right about what the doctor would say. That Wyatt would be okay.

Jesse, however, wasn't sure he himself would be. He was shaken.

Even after hearing the pediatrician say Wyatt had a common virus that babies easily caught and would be fine with OTC fever reducer, fluids and rest at home for a couple of days, Jesse was unsettled. Babies were vulnerable.

Hell, Jesse was too right now.

"Are you absolutely *sure* Wyatt will be okay?" Jesse had asked the doctor.

"Well, ninety-nine percent," Dr. Merez had said. "You just need to keep a watchful eye. If the fever doesn't go down by morning and/or if he throws up, bring him back here."

"And what would that mean?" Jesse had demanded.

"That he needs a bit stronger medicine, IV fluids. But I really think Wyatt will be okay with rest and his bottle every two and a half hours and the fever reducer you gave him at home earlier."

*I think*... Jesse didn't like *I think*. He would have preferred *Wyatt will*. One hundred percent.

As they'd left the clinic, there was that damned tree
again. Not just the one outside, the majestic evergreen,
but the artificial one in the lobby. He hated that tree.
He'd been in one hell of a mood and the sight of it just
made him feel worse.

Now, as they drove back home, Jesse sat in the back
seat with Wyatt, appreciating the ability to see him in
the rear-facing car seat. To see his chest rising and falling, to see his little bow lips quirk every now and then.
Jesse was quiet, unable to process anything but that his
child was sick.

Lila had tried to assure him when they left the clinic.
He didn't even appreciate it because he'd wanted to remind her of the doctor's ninety-nine percent. She was
trying, he knew, and just as worried about Wyatt as he
was.

When they arrived at the farm, Jesse took Wyatt from
his harness and cuddled him close, hurrying inside to
keep the baby from the biting cold that was Wyoming
in December in the middle of the night. Billy greeted
them at the door, keeping back a bit as if he knew Wyatt
wasn't well right now.

"I'll get him settled in his crib," Jesse said, shrugging
out of his jacket, something he'd quickly learned how to
do with a baby in his arms. Lila took it and hung it beside hers. "I'll sleep in the nursery, keep an eye on him."

Lila seemed about to say something but then didn't.
Finally, she said, "Okay. If you want a break and to
stretch out in bed, just wake me up and I'll sit with him
in the nursery, okay?"

He nodded, but had no doubt he'd want to stay with Wyatt.

She bit her lip and then leaned over to kiss Wyatt on his forehead. She didn't quite look at Jesse, and he could see the tension on her pretty face, the worry in her eyes.

And he knew it was because of him. Because he'd been distant since they'd arrived at the clinic. Because he was shutting her out. He could feel himself doing it, particularly as they'd left the clinic and on the drive back to the farm. But he'd barely been able to make conversation back. He didn't want to talk. Didn't want to do anything but hold Wyatt.

She was heading for her room when he called her name.

As she turned and stopped, he could see she was relieved and he wanted to kick himself for doing anything to add to her worry.

"I'm just..." he started to say but then nothing else came out of his mouth.

"Wyatt's dad," she finished for him with a shaky smile. "And you're upset and worried that he's sick. I get it. You just focus on him, okay?"

He could hug her. Of course she was understanding and kind—that was Lila. He wanted to say something more, something to bring the sparkle back to her eyes, but she gave him another shaky smile, then went into her room.

He moved down the hall to the nursery, Billy padding after him, and carefully sat in the rocker by the window, Wyatt cradled against the length of his arm. Jesse wasn't letting his son out of his sight for a second. Not till morning when the doctor said the fever would break. Wyatt still felt hot, but he wasn't crying and his face wasn't as red.

*What do you* feel? his ex would always ask him, frustrated when he couldn't or wouldn't say. As she'd dumped him—she'd said he might as well have not committed to her since he was always so distant and unreadable.

He knew how he felt right now.

Scared. A bad scared. Chills-up-his-spine scared.

And it was the kind of scared that made him want to just sit here alone with Wyatt. He didn't want to talk to Lila. He didn't want to hug Lila. He didn't want to lie beside Lila in bed.

*You retreat instead of share, instead of give, instead of letting anyone really close to you*, his ex had accused the day she'd told him they were done, that she'd taken up with someone else. *You'll always be alone, Jesse Dawson.*

He'd gone back to being the lone wolf he'd always been. Until now, until Wyatt had come into his life, until Jesse had come into his.

*I will never leave you*, he said silently to his sleeping son. *Never, ever. And that is a promise.*

A promise he'd keep forever. He had no doubt about that.

The promise he couldn't make would be to Lila.

*Then you're not starting as you mean to continue*, he realized with another chill running across the nape of his neck.

Now what the hell was he supposed to do?

Lila was in bed, unable to sleep, tossing and turning, flipping her pillow over. She'd given up on drifting off and looked out the window, surprised to see that it was flurrying. A few snowstorms had come and gone already in the past few weeks but it hadn't snowed in several days. Maybe they'd have a white Christmas. But the thought of the holiday reminded her of his reaction to the tree at the clinic.

Every bit of her heart went out to him.

Something had changed, she knew. Jesse had been spooked bad by Wyatt's illness and he'd taken a big step back. She'd felt it. A sudden chill. Not that he'd been cold to her. Just the absence of warmth from his retreat.

The question was, would he be back in a couple of days once Wyatt's fever had lifted and he was back to his usual happy, well-baby self? Or was the Jesse who'd been in the shower with her earlier and lying beside her with hands entwined as they'd shared popcorn and watched a rom-com, gone for good?

She wished she could ask Alina the psychic. Maybe she'd try to find her. Surely she had a booth set up somewhere.

Now she was pinning her hope on a psychic? *Come on, Lila.* The psychic reading had been in good fun; that was all. Lila did believe that some people had a special kind of intuition. The day after she and Kate had had their reading with Alina, they'd talked a lot about whether a decent human being would "advise" sisters with hope in their eyes to throw all their money into a goat farm and dairy business, quit their jobs and go for their dreams if she didn't see or feel something truly positive for them. She could have just as easily said: *You can try the farm and you should because it's your dream, but who knows if it'll succeed?*

Alina did, actually. Because she was psychic and Lila was running with that.

And right now, even if Alina was just gifted at reading people and making connections quickly, Lila would take it.

Was Jesse lost to her?

Because earlier she believed that he just might be her one true love. And like Alina had said, very unexpectedly.

Jesse Dawson had been one *unexpectedly* after another.

# *Chapter Fifteen*

After a bottle at 3:00 a.m., Jesse had put Wyatt in the crib and had sacked out on the rocking chair. He woke to Wyatt making cooing noises at just before 5:30 a.m. He bolted up and picked him up from the crib, the baby's temperature, from feel alone, at least, back to normal. He took Wyatt's temperature: yup, normal.

He was so relieved. The virus had possibly run its course in just several hours, but as the doc had prescribed, Jesse would keep a close eye on Wyatt. He changed his diaper, put him in fresh pj's and was about to take him downstairs when he almost crashed right into Lila.

"Ah, I should have figured you'd have him," she said with a smile. "I didn't hear him cry but set my alarm for five thirty to get him up for a bottle." She peered at the baby in his arms. "His color looks so much better. How's his temperature?" She felt Wyatt's forehead with the back of her hand.

"Normal. I'm so relieved."

"Me too. I'll take him," she said, holding out her arms. "You probably want to get to the barn now that you can rest assured he's fine. I'll report in an hour with how he's doing."

He stared at her for a moment, then realized she probably wanted to have her time with Wyatt this morning after he'd had last night. "Sounds good," he said. "I'll hit the shower, then."

He leaned over to kiss Wyatt on his head and take a last look at him. He let out a breath, not wanting to leave his son at all, but Lila deserved her time with him and Jesse did have to get to work. Today, he and Lila and Micah would be bringing home the four new goats Lila had decided on after an online search and then a visit to an area dairy. Jesse needed to get the barn ready and the new stalls and pasture prepared.

"Well, I'll get going then," he said awkwardly.

The tight smile she gave him was just as awkward.

And once again she seemed about to say something but then didn't. She left the room, and he felt the absence of both her and Wyatt so acutely. But he also wanted to be alone—and not think about how things between him and Lila had changed. His fault, his doing, he knew.

He was about to hop in the shower when his phone pinged with a text.

His cousin Reed.

Hey, I'm off this morning and on baby duty. I'd love to show Summer the Double Sisters Farm if that works for you.

Perfect timing. Jesse had the kind of questions that only someone who'd also changed his entire life, his entire way of thinking, could answer in a way that would have Jesse listening.

A minute later, he had plans set with Reed, who'd

come by the farm in an hour. Even more perfect timing. Because Jesse had to talk to someone who'd get it—and fast, before he made things worse with Lila.

When he went into the kitchen he saw Lila had made a pot of coffee and he filled up his thermos. She must have taken Wyatt back to the nursery while he was in the shower or getting dressed. He'd been hoping to say goodbye for the next few hours, but it was probably better that he leave Lila be. For his sake and hers.

He was almost done with the new stalls for the goats that were coming this afternoon when he heard a vehicle coming up the drive.

He headed out to see that Reed had parked and was settling Summer in her stroller. The fourteen-month-old was in a yellow snowsuit and wearing a matching wool hat with bear ears. She had big hazel eyes and was impossibly cute.

"I've been telling Summer all about your two goats," Reed said.

Jesse smiled, aware of his cousin's soft gaze on his daughter. Reed had opened up some about how his losses in life had hardened him to the point that even being near babies and children would make his heart clench. And that his own stubbornness had almost cost him the woman and baby he loved so much. But Reed and Aimee had been happily married for over a year now—with Reed a loving, doting father to the baby girl they'd adopted together.

Jesse had so many questions. He figured he'd ask what he wanted to know and Reed could answer or not. He kneeled down in front of Summer. "I have a feeling

you're going to love Dolly and Lulu." He smiled at the little beauty, then stood up. "Why don't I take you two on a short tour since the weather's decent."

"Sounds good," Reed said, glancing toward the barn. "Hey, Summer, there they are," he added, upping his chin at the two goats, who'd come out to the pasture to see the visitors.

The goats got bored quickly and went back inside the barn through their weather flap.

"Well, you've pretty much seen the Double Sisters," Jesse said, waving his arm around. "The two pastures, that field," he added, pointing across the gravel drive. "The barn and the farmhouse. It's a nice property, a good size for the small dairy that Lila and I envision."

"Lila and I," Reed repeated with a curious nod. "That sounds very promising."

"Well," he said, suddenly tongue-tied. "We're partners in business and parenthood."

His cousin tilted his head, and Jesse knew he was waiting for mention of the *romantic* element.

*I don't know anything. Thought I did, for a second there.*

"Enough about me," Jesse said, leading the way into the barn so that Summer could keeping watching the goats. "I wouldn't mind hearing more about *your* path to becoming a family dude."

Reed smiled. "Bumpy, winding path. I stumbled a couple times along the way. But it got me where I truly needed to be—a husband and a father."

As they stopped in front of the pen where Dolly and Lulu were playing on their toddler structure, Jesse thought about what Reed had gone through. A terrible breakup with a woman who'd had a baby daughter—a child he'd helped raised until she was two or maybe three. But then the woman had left Reed for another man and cut off all contact between him and the little girl he'd loved so much. Reed had been crushed.

"I gave up on anything concerning this thing," Reed said, slapping a hand on the region of his heart. "But then a newborn baby named Summer and a patient social worker named Aimee came into my life and changed everything. I was about to lose them if I didn't change my ways by opening up and letting people in. Letting myself *feel*. It was hard, trust me."

"I get it," Jesse said. "My past kept me from getting close to anyone, too. I've been moving from ranch to ranch since I was eighteen. Never able to commit to anything."

"Well, fatherhood has changed you, Jesse. And I'm sure Lila has a big part in this too." He seemed lost in thought for a moment. "I tried so hard not to love Summer and Aimee." Reed laughed and shook his head. "As if I had any control. And thank God I didn't."

"I like being in control, though," Jesse said. "The alternative is pretty uncomfortable."

Reed clapped a hand on Jesse's shoulder. "What's more uncomfortable? Being your own worst enemy by fighting what you feel. Losing battle anyway."

Jesse realized he was doing exactly what Reed described: fighting against his feelings for Lila. "It's like every wall I've ever built up is suddenly getting stronger instead of being chipped at," he said. "I had a scare last night—Wyatt had a really high fever and we took him to the ER. I'd never been that scared of anything in my life. And I don't want to feel like that, you know?"

"Oh, trust me, I know. It's what makes guys like us want to walk away. Run, actually. Never look back. But when there's something to give up, something to walk away from, that changes everything."

"I'd never leave my son," Jesse said. "Ever. I know that."

Reed nodded. "He's got you here," he said, hitting his chest with his fist. "Kids do that very easily. And like you experienced last night, the way you feel is so damned scary that you just want to retreat."

"Exactly," Jesse said. "But that's no good either. I'm hurting Lila. And if things are bad between us and only get worse, it's Wyatt who'll suffer the most. It's why we both tried hard to be platonic in the first place."

"Yeah, I found out real fast that fighting my feelings was pointless. You'll find that out—I have no doubt." Reed's phone pinged with a text. He pulled it out and glanced at the screen. "Ah, gotta head out. Aimee's not feeling well and hopes I'll bring home her favorite ice cream and hot fudge." As they walked toward the door, Reed added, "You want my best advice?"

"Yes. Absolutely."

"Fight against *yourself*," Reed said. "It won't feel good or right. But not only will you get what you really want—even if you don't know it yet—you'll give those you love what they want."

Jesse sucked in a breath. "Damn."

Reed laughed. "Yup. Exactly."

They walked in silence to Reed's SUV.

"Don't worry," his cousin said. "You can't stop progress even if you try. You'll get there."

Did he *want* to, though? That was the question. Jesse didn't get close to people. He didn't commit. That had kept him on an even keel these past couple of years.

He was a hard case. But he supposed Reed had been too. And there he was. Happily married. A family man who was hurrying off to buy ice cream and hot fudge for his under-the-weather wife.

As Jesse watched his cousin drive away, he felt the entire conversation fall to the recesses of his mind. Which was what he always did when he didn't want to think about something.

When he was overwhelmed by the *truth*.

He went back into the barn and started telling the goats all about the four newcomers who'd be sharing their barn. Ranch life, goats, barns—that was Jesse's world, that was where he felt comfortable.

But thoughts of Lila kept barging into his head. Last night. The night before. How he'd almost believed he could try again, give himself to a woman he had feelings for.

Strong feelings.

But he couldn't imagine anything but a tiny baby being able to punch and kick through the brick, the cement wall in his chest.

*You can't stop progress...*

Jesse had a bad feeling he could, though.

At 1:30 p.m., Lila approached the standing signpost for Psychic Readings by Alina at the little silver hut in the Brewer Indoor Holiday Market. Silver velvet curtains parted to reveal two padded silver chairs, a small table between. Lila had checked Alina's website to make an appointment—for a full reading, whatever that would be. She certainly wanted more than just one question and five minutes. Unfortunately, Alina was booked for appointments until the new year, but when Lila saw that she had a booth at this market, she'd decided to use her lunch hour to come here. Appointments were limited to fifteen minutes, but that would be enough time to cover what she wanted to know most.

She supposed she did have just one question. About Jesse.

Things had been awkward between them all morning. Wyatt seemed to be over the mysterious hours-long bug, whatever it had been. He'd been alert and curious and playful since he'd woken up, napped well, ate fine. But when Jesse came in to take over baby duty while she went out to the farm to double-check inventory for the new goats' arrival, his cheer at his son's health didn't extend to their fledgling romance.

It had barely gotten off the ground and now...

And now she was waiting for a reading with Alina, needing to hear a little positive news.

She'd arrived at the holiday market twenty minutes ago, but there'd been someone inside the hut and one person waiting, so Lila had gotten herself a coffee, did a little window-shopping and picked up a gift for Billy, a new chewy ball.

No one was waiting anymore and Lila poked her head in. "Hi, Ms. Alina. Remember me?"

Alina smiled. "Of course! The goat farmer. Please come in."

"I am indeed a goat farmer," Lila said as she stepped inside. "Thanks to your encouraging yes about it."

Alina smiled. "I'm very glad." She pulled the curtains closed. Lila sat down and so did Alina, immediately taking both Lila's hands and studying her face. The scrutiny was both a little uncomfortable and completely welcome. *Study away! Tell me my fortune!*

"I see you've been through sorrow," Alina said. "I'm very sorry."

Lila gasped. "My twin..." She bit her lip, tears stinging her eyes, and couldn't finish the sentence.

"I also see hope and happiness in your expression," Alina said. "Life is a series of ups and downs, from the worst of downs to the most thrilling of ups. Sometimes in the same day."

Lila felt herself brighten. "I felt a bit that way even in the worst of my grief over Kate because of Wyatt— her baby son. My twin named me his legal guardian if anything should happen to her. I'm raising him now."

Alina nodded and gave both her hands a squeeze. "And you have a burning question for me. I can see that in your eyes."

Alina's own eyes struck Lila as full of wisdom. That might have been wishful thinking, but Lila had a good feeling about the psychic, whether she truly had a gift or not.

"Wyatt's father. He's back in Wyatt's life, my life too, and seems truly committed to his son. But..." She bit her lip. "I'm falling hard for him and..."

"And you're worried about where his heart is?"

Lila nodded.

"I can't read another person's heart if he's not here in front of me," Alina said. "But I can tell you I see happiness for you."

"You do?" Lila asked, brightening. "Not heartache and despair?"

Alina smiled gently. "I'm not saying you won't have moments of heartache. We all will. That's life. But this man you're asking about. He is yours."

Lila felt her eyes widen and her heart soar. She knew she shouldn't put so much stock into a psychic. But Alina's pronouncement was what she wanted to hear. And she'd take it.

"That is all," Alina said, letting go of Lila's hands.

Lila got out her phone to transfer the fee. "Thank you."

"Oh, one more thing," the psychic said. "Your one true love's name begins with *S*."

Lila's heart went plummeting to her stomach. "*S*?"

*Don't you mean* J? she wanted to ask.

"*S*," Alina repeated with a firm nod.

Lila frowned and gave the woman a tight smile, then hurried out. Did she know *anyone* whose name started with *S*? At least none of her few exes had *S* names— they were not true love material.

Not even one of her goats had an *S* name.

She sighed.

Either Jesse Dawson wasn't her one true love or Alina wasn't really psychic. Thing was, Lila liked the part about the happiness coming her way and that the man she was asking about was hers. She wanted that part to be true.

But that thing about the *S*...

Lila sighed and tried to smile at the Holiday Market Santa walking around and wishing people Happy Holidays. She didn't feel very merry.

Now she wished she hadn't come to see Alina at all!

# *Chapter Sixteen*

"I think Jesse and I should each get to name one goat," Micah said as they got out of Jesse's pickup at the Wakely Ranch at three thirty that afternoon. They'd come to pick up their new goats for the Double Sisters Farm. Wyatt was with his great-aunt Raina for a couple of hours. Jesse particularly liked that since Wyatt had been so recently sick and she was the nurse in the family. "And Lila," Micah added, "you can name two since it's your farm."

"Oh, thanks," she said, shooting her brother a grin. "But I think you get to name two because you've been doing such a great job."

Micah puffed up a bit at the praise, and Jesse could see how much it had meant to him.

"I agree with Lila," Jesse said, giving Micah a clap on the back.

Micah grinned. "Well, in that case, I'm thinking Voldemort for the buck. And Wonder Woman for the doe."

Lila tilted her head and looked quizzically at her brother. "Really?"

"Uh, *no*," he said in a sing-song voice.

Jesse and Lila laughed. The shared camaraderie lasted

only a couple of seconds before Lila's smile faded. Jesse noticed she'd quickly turned so her brother wouldn't see. Something was bothering her.

And he knew it was him. Them. How things were between them.

They should talk, Jesse knew. About how he was feeling, this inward turn he'd taken and couldn't seem to get rid of. He'd been able to talk to Lila about everything and anything. Maybe they could talk about this.

The problem was that there'd be no resolution, no getting anywhere. It wasn't the kind of thing that could be talked out. Something was still gripping him; that was all he knew.

The proprietor of the Wakely Ranch emerged from an outbuilding with a sign reading Office. "Welcome," John Wakely called as he approached them. "I have four Nubian goats waiting for you all."

That got a smile out of Lila and they headed into one of the barns. The four lop-eared goats, all with sandy-brown faces, white heads, white noses and a darker brown stripe between their eyes, were in a pen, two standing on low tables, one on a tire and the fourth on a raggedy old ottoman.

"I adore them," Lila said beaming now.

Ah, there was that beautiful smile, Jesse thought. Only a true goat lover could get so instantly cheered by looking at one. It truly warmed his heart.

"And look how their ears are pointed toward us," Micah said. "I read that that means they're happy."

Lila smiled at her brother. "I love that you're doing your research and reading."

"They do seem to like the good life of eating, grazing, jumping, playing and sleeping," John said on a laugh.

Jesse looked them over. He'd had a vet check them out this morning and had gotten the report that they were in solid health.

"The buck's name has come to me," Micah said. "Bear. For Bear Ridge. And that small doe," he added, pointing. "Cara, short for Caramel, like her coloring."

"Love both names!" Lila said.

"I'd like to call the one on the tire Sheldon," Jesse said.

"Sheldon?" Micah repeated, wrinkling up his face. "Not very farm-y."

Jesse smiled. "Right? It's actually my given name, but I've always gone by my middle name from the time I was born."

Lila gasped, and Jesse glanced at her. He wondered what her reaction was about.

"It's not that weird to go by your middle name," Micah said to her. "I know two guys at school who do. One would have been Bartholomew and the other one Augustus."

Lila nodded, her eyes suddenly all twinkly. "I was just surprised, that's all. I didn't know."

Jesse studied Lila, whose entire demeanor seemed to have changed. She'd been kind of subdued on the drive over, talking mostly to Micah, and now the sparkle was back in her eyes. He wished he'd had something to do with it since he'd taken the sparkle away with his attitude and own demeanor. But the goats clearly made her very happy.

"Who were you named after?" she asked Jesse.

"My mother's grandfather. But Jesse was her favorite boy name so she decided to just call me that. And my dad thought Jesse was a cowboy's name so he liked that better too."

She was staring at him with a look he couldn't quite pinpoint. What was going on in her head?

"Sheldon Jesse Dawson," she said, tilting her head.

"Birth certificate only," he said.

She was now eyeing the goats. "Okay, we've got Sheldon, Cara, Bear and...let's see." She tilted her head, studying the last goat. "Got it," she said with a snap of her fingers. "April."

Micah laughed. "April? It's December. And now that I think about it, none of them have holiday names."

"Want to change yours to Nutcracker and Garland?" Lila asked. "Tinsel and Holly?"

"Or Santa and Mrs. Claus," Jesse said, the image of him and Lila in their big red suits and wigs popping into his mind.

Lila was looking at him again. As if she was surprised he'd bring up anything personal.

"Nope, mine are definitely Bear and Cara."

Jesse nodded. "And mine is Sheldon."

Lila looked at him with the warmest smile. She definitely seemed to like the name Sheldon. "April, for sure," she said with a nod. "I've just always loved that name."

Twenty minutes later, the paperwork finalized, the goats were loaded into a trailer. Jesse got back behind the wheel. Lila slid into the passenger seat and buckled up.

Was it his imagination or was she definitely...perkier?

"I'm thinking it's taco night," she said. "Micah, want to stay? I even have jalapeños for you."

Micah made a very put-upon face from the back seat. "I wish but ugh, I have a thousand hours of homework to do. Mom said she'd bring me takeout from the diner on her way home if I got two assignments done when she calls to check in. To get my bacon double cheeseburger and steak fries I have to do math and have at least half my history essay done."

"That's a good deal," Jesse said.

Micah raised an eyebrow. "Makes it more bearable, anyway."

Lila glanced at Jesse with a smile. He was very happy to see it on her pretty face.

"So guess what else I did this morning?" Jesse asked.

"What?" Micah asked from the back seat.

"Got *six* tickets to the holiday rodeo in Brewer," Jesse said with a bit of triumph in his voice. The tickets had been sold out for weeks, but he'd done some digging on local community pages on social media and scored six from two different sellers.

"Six?" Lila asked.

"Two for sulky Scotty and his dad—you know, the boy from the Santa hut. And four for us."

"Wyatt's first rodeo!" Lila said with a grin.

Micah pumped a fist. "Awesome! Hey, Jesse—I think Wyatt is gonna really like that you're his dad. You know everything about ranching and the cowboy life—including how to get sold-out tickets to the rodeo."

Jesse was so touched that he couldn't speak for a moment. "I appreciate that, Micah. You have no idea."

He felt Lila looking at him and turned to smile at her. Her expression was soft. Somehow this entire outing had changed things for all of them.

*Wyatt is gonna really like that you're his dad.*

Jesse sure hoped so. He was going to do everything to make Wyatt feel that way.

He was suddenly consumed by the idea of doing something special for Lila. Something more than a ticket to the rodeo. Something to show her that no matter what was going on between them, he cared deeply about her.

Christmas was just a few days away. He could give Lila a gift every day through the twenty-fifth: actions, experiences and physical gifts. He wasn't sure what yet. But he'd think on it. And hope he could make up for him being…*him.*

Lila had a skip in her step as she browned the ground beef for the tacos, the kitchen smelling fragrantly spicy. Hope was back.

Jesse might need time, but her rodeo-side/holiday market psychic had not been wrong yet. Lila had started her farm and walked away from her old life. The man she believed was her one true love *was* very unexpected. And Alina said his name started with *S*—and Jesse's— Sheldon Jesse Dawson's—did. She gave her hips a happy little shake. Hearing that bit of news at the ranch where they'd bought their new goats had been like a Christmas present falling out of the sky.

She heard Jesse's footsteps coming from the nursery and instead of feeling anxious about how things were between them, a warm hope was in her chest.

"Wyatt's asleep," he said. "And he looks great— color in his cheeks and he was alert and happy before he conked out."

She smiled. "Aunt Raina took good care of him."

"I met Errol when I picked up Wyatt," he said, coming into the kitchen and leaning against the counter. "Seems like a really nice guy."

"They were best friends for like forty years and then wham, something changed and now they're a couple."

Jesse raised an eyebrow. "After forty years? Were they always with someone else or something?"

"Pretty much. But Raina said she'd never looked at Errol as anything other than a brother."

"Well, I hope it works out. Could you imagine losing your bestie of forty years because of lust?" He shook his head and turned to the head of lettuce on the cutting board. "Can I cut this up for you? I didn't do a great job on chopping duty last time but hey, it'll be shredded, just not well."

She was still on the first part of what he'd said.

She paused in stirring the meat to look at him. "*First* of all, the odds are highly on their side for their romance to work out just fine. Know why? Because they *know* each other. They have history. They grew up together. Lust is just adding a new component."

"Yeah, but maybe it's just the novelty of it all. Something new and exciting and maybe always 'forbidden' in a *we're just friends* kind of way."

She frowned and eyed the lettuce instead of him, because she was mad at him. "Yes, you can shred the lettuce—and thanks."

"On it," he said, grabbing a knife.

She glared at him, but he was busy cutting and didn't even notice. Humph. "*Second* of all," she said with a little snap in her voice, which had him glancing at her, "they both want this. To be together. So they'll both work through whatever comes up. They'll talk to each other. Communicate."

Suddenly she just felt sad. She wanted what her aunt had. The right man at the right time, for once. But Lila's right man at the right time was himself feeling all kinds of wrong. How did she turn this around the way he'd helped the little boy in the Santa hut? He'd reached Scotty by really listening, by caring. But she didn't know how to reach Jesse where these deep-seated issues were concerned.

He held her gaze and nodded. Then he put down the knife and turned toward her. "I'm sorry about last night, Lila. I pushed you away. It's like I'm taking one step forward, two steps back. And now I feel sort of stuck there."

At this point, she shouldn't be surprised by his candor, by his willingness to open up, to talk about subjects that were hard for him. Maybe it was that very trait of his that would work its own magic on Jesse.

With everything in her she wanted to walk over to him and wrap her arms around him, just hold him, be that physically close to him. But she stayed put. "This is what I know," she said. "We're both going through big changes in our lives. I recently lost my twin. Inherited a baby. Bought a goat farm. Had said baby's father suddenly enter the picture. And in a big way," she added with a soft smile.

"That is *a lot*," he said, pausing in his chopping.

"And you," she added. "You came back to Bear Ridge because there was a letter from your father—with last wishes. Wishes that conflicted with your plans to take off for Yellowstone and a new ranch. You discovered you had a child you didn't know existed. You moved in with me. You were worried about your ability to be a good father. And you've been knocking it out of the park. *That's* also a lot, Jesse. We're gonna have hiccups."

He came over to her and pulled her into his arms. "Thank you, Lila." She slid her arms around his neck and rested her head against his chest. Oh, how she needed exactly this.

She didn't lift her head for a kiss. She didn't want to turn this emotional, tender moment into anything but what it was: a sweet connection between them. An apology, an understanding. *This* was what built relationships.

He went back to badly shredding the lettuce, the sight of which made her smile. No matter what, the man was *trying*. Whether it was chopping vegetables, caring for his son or being with her. He was a good man.

And she was so deep into this, into them, that there was no backing out now.

# *Chapter Seventeen*

Jesse had dried the last of the dinner dishes, his belly happily stuffed with four delicious tacos, when Lila came running in the kitchen with her phone.

"My mom just called me—she's frantic. Micah ran off a half hour ago and hasn't come back," she said, her eyes worried. "He didn't do either homework assignment and so our mom let him have the promised cheeseburger she'd brought him from the diner, but not the fries and they had a bad argument and he took off." She shook her head. "It's really cold out and dark. And he headed in the direction of the park and didn't even take his phone. So we can't even reach him."

He put his hands on both her shoulders. "I'll go, Lila. You stay here with Wyatt. I'll find him."

She bit her lip. "All that good progress and one blip and he's gone," she said, tears misting her eyes.

*Like me*, he thought, shaking his head at himself.

Jesse headed for the front door, stopping to put on his down jacket and a scarf. "What was the big deal about the assignments? Micah sounded fine with them and with the deal when he mentioned them on the way home from the Wakely ranch."

"He couldn't figure out the math, he'd told our mom. And he didn't understand the essay question for history. She said she'd help with both and he got upset, calling himself a stupid idiot who only got Cs even when he tried so what was the point. She tried to calm him down, but he just got angrier and then he left."

"If he headed toward the park, he's likely sitting on a bench or that low bridge wall over the river. He's stewing and sulking, that's all. I'll take Billy to help both find him and calm him down. Try not to worry too much, okay?"

"Billy," she called behind her, and the sweet pooch got up from his dog bed and trotted over.

"Help me find Micah, okay, Billy?" he said to the dog, who wagged his tail.

Lila attached Billy's leash and handed it to Jesse. "You'll text me when you find him?"

"I will." He squeezed her hand and then kissed her fast on the lips, then pushed through the storm door. He hurried to his truck, opening the door for Billy, who jumped up into the passenger seat.

He drove the fifteen minutes as fast as he could without worrying about getting pulled over. The park lot was empty. He jumped out, Billy beside him, and went in the entrance between the two wrought iron benches, one of which he'd sat on when he'd seen Lila Mack for the first time. And his son.

Luckily there were lampposts that gave some illumination to the path. He had a feeling he'd find Micah sitting on the stone wall on the footpath over the river. It was even chillier by the water, flurries starting to come down. He sure hoped Micah had brought gloves.

Billy was pulling a bit—a good sign that Micah was nearby. As they walked on toward the bridge, Billy's tail started wagging like crazy. And at the end of the stone wall sat a lanky figure, hat and gloves on, Jesse was glad to see.

Micah seemed so lost in thought that he either didn't hear Jesse's footsteps or he planned to ignore anyone who might walk by. Though this wasn't exactly a night for a stroll in the park, and he hadn't seen anyone else.

He sent Lila a quick text that he—Billy, really—had found Micah.

She clearly had not put her phone down since he'd left because she responded right away. Thank you! My mom will be so relieved.

Give me about twenty minutes and I'll bring him home.

I don't what I'd do without you, Jesse. You're becoming indispensable.

He swallowed, that last part both touching him deeply and unsettling him.

Something he had no time to think about right now.

"Hey," he called out.

Micah glanced up and only half scowled, another good sign. Meant he was relieved to see Jesse and pissed at the same time.

Billy hurried over to Micah, tail wagging even harder, and Micah jumped down to kneel and bury his face in the dog's soft fur. "Hi, Billy," he said. "You're always a good boy. I, however, am not. I'm the worst." He hopped back up on the wall and hung his head.

*Oh, Micah*, he thought. Jesse knew what it was like to be so down on yourself that you called yourself names. "You're an excellent young man," Jesse said. "Everything I've seen while working with you tells me that. You're hardworking, smart and funny as hell."

"Oh, my mom thinks I'm just hilarious," he said and rolled his eyes. But Jesse could see his praise had gotten through.

He wasn't just placating the kid to get him to go home, either. He'd meant every word. And he was pretty sure at this point that Micah knew Jesse didn't say what he didn't mean.

Micah pulled off his hat to move his mop of dark auburn hair out of his eyes and then stuffed it back on. "Well, since you probably know what the fight was about, you know how stupid I am, so I'm sure you're here to fire me."

"Nope. I'm actually here because, one, I care about you. And two, I want to know why you think you're stupid. Just because you didn't know how to do the math assignment or how to start the essay?"

"Yeah. So I'm stupid," Micah said angrily with a loud and clear tinge of hurt under it. "You said school was important for ranchers. But I'm probably gonna fail out anyway."

"Lila told me a couple days ago that you're doing fine in school. You pulled up grades in two classes—English and science."

Micah shrugged. "Yeah, from an F to a C. Woo-hoo. At best, I'm *average*."

"Nothing wrong with Cs," Jesse said.

Micah didn't respond.

"What was the essay topic, anyway?" Jesse asked.

"Something about the Oregon Trail and wagon trains. I actually find that stuff really interesting. But I didn't understand the question because I'm a moron." He crossed his arms over his chest and stared out at the river.

"Hardly," Jesse said. "Maybe it was worded in a way that was open to interpretation. Some people prefer questions that are more black-and-white. This or that."

Micah brightened a bit. "Yeah, I guess. So if it's open to interpretation, I can write the essay based on what I think the question was? I like the topic."

"I don't have the assignment in front of me, but I'd wager yes. And sometimes, even if your interpretation of the question isn't what the teacher had in mind, an essay that shows you put time and effort and care into it can score serious brownie points."

"Yeah, my history teacher is always saying he cares more about passionate responses than right or wrong— unless we're dead wrong, like if we say the War of 1812 was in 1755 or something."

Jesse laughed. "Yup."

"So is everyone mad at me?" Micah asked.

"I think everyone is worried about your safety. Including me. Lots of black ice in Wyoming in winter at night, for one. I used to run off when I was angry, particularly at myself. My aunt always used to tell me to stay close if I needed to get away and be alone with my thoughts. I found a good tree right on her property and climbed up. She wasn't thrilled that I might break my neck, but she thought it was better than disappearing on her."

Micah nodded. "What do you do now when you want to run off? If you feel like crap about something?"

*Run. Same as you. I just do it mentally now.*

The realization hit him hard. The way he'd emotionally retreated from Lila and shut her out was wrong. He'd hurt her.

If he wanted to be good father to Wyatt and a good role model for Micah, he needed to *do better*.

"I'm going to work hard at saying what's bothering me instead of running away," Jesse told him. "Instead of stewing and being miserable. I'm going to open up— talk—to people I care about, whose opinions matter to me. I've never been great at communicating, but it's something I'm really going to work on."

"Yeah, I guess," Micah said.

"Ready to head home? Tackle that essay? Your mom said she'd help with the math."

"I guess the fries will be really cold by then," he said with a laugh.

Jesse laughed too. Even Billy gave a woof.

Micah jumped off the wall and knelt down again to give Billy some more love.

"Dogs are the best," Jesse said. "I didn't know until I met Billy. He's awesome. He even led me right to you here."

"Yeah, Billy's the best. Did you know he's named Billy because of billy goats?"

Jesse grinned. "Actually, it never occurred to me. But makes total sense."

With Micah talking about how he couldn't wait to see how the new group of goats at the Double Sisters were getting on tomorrow, they walked back to the pickup, Billy at their side.

*You really are a good boy, Billy,* he sent telepathically to the pooch. Billy had found Micah for him in two seconds. Tail wagging, he'd run over to Micah to be a welcome source of comfort for the teen. And he was guiding them safely back to the truck right now, giving an occasional bark at night creatures or a low growl to alert them to something, like a fox.

In fact, the dog made him think about the fact that so far, Jesse had ticked off three wishes on his dad's list—putting down roots, the dog thing and not making Eddie's mistakes as a father. If he did say so himself, he had this father thing down pretty well. And granted, Jesse hadn't bought property in town to put down those roots or adopted a dog of his own. But he was committed to living in Bear Ridge and while he lived at the farm, Billy *was* kind of his too.

He almost stopped in his tracks. *While* he was living at the farm? Meaning what, exactly? That he would leave eventually? Buy his own ranch?

He frowned. He'd live separately from Wyatt? He and Lila would have a custody plan with a visitation schedule? He'd have Wyatt half the week the way he had him half the day when Lila was on farm duty? Jesse didn't want that. He'd hate it, actually. Not seeing his son every day? Or living under the same roof?

Micah was looking at him quizzically, so he resumed walking, trying to keep his expression neutral.

He'd live in the guest room for the next eighteen years while he and Lila were co-parenting? Being platonic and being lovers both weren't working for him. Which meant staying in the guest room indefinitely wasn't going to work either.

Something had to give, and Jesse had a feeling it

wouldn't be his hard head. Or the brick-wall-protected heart in his chest.

But leaving the farmhouse meant leaving Wyatt and he couldn't, wouldn't, do that.

All he knew right now was that the one wish left unfulfilled on his father's list was: Let love—*marriage*—into your life. He couldn't see that one coming true. Reed had said fighting his own feelings would be pointless, that you couldn't stop progress.

But wasn't Jesse a case study in lack of progress when it came to relationships?

*Except when it came to family*, he amended.

He frowned, pausing in his tracks again. Somehow, he'd let in a tiny baby and he'd developed and strengthened relationships with his cousin—and his aunt.

It was just Lila he was keeping out.

"Dude, what's with you?" Micah asked, peering at him.

"Just thinking," Jesse said, walking again.

"About what?"

That surprised Jesse. Though it shouldn't. That Micah liked him, cared what was on his mind, had been most evident twenty minutes ago. He could add Micah to the list of people he'd let in. Who'd *gotten* in.

*Think fast, Jesse*, he told himself. Because he wasn't about to open up to a teenager about his love life— particularly when it involved that teenager's sister. Of whom Micah was very protective.

"I was thinking about what to get you for Christmas," Jesse blurted out. A total lie. But he realized he would need to get something for Micah. *What*, was the question. Something to do with farm life. He'd already scored tickets to the rodeo but that was for the four of them.

*A pin*, he thought. Like the one he'd left behind and now had back—on his baby son's snowsuit.

A bronzed horse like Wyatt's. Or maybe something different, something just for Micah. He'd look into finding one of a bronzed goat. Micah could attach it to his down jacket or his hat.

Buoyed by that idea, he now wondered what to get Lila. It had to be special. He couldn't think of anything meaningful, though. He wanted to do something big for her for Christmas. Something more than helping her get the farm going.

Something to distract him from not giving her what she probably wanted most of all: their *romance* to get going.

Wyatt was asleep in his crib. Billy, knocked out from his adventure in the park, was curled up in his bed by the Christmas tree. And Lila sat on the sofa with Jesse, who'd returned from bringing Micah to their parents' house just a few minutes ago and filled her in.

She'd thanked him profusely, and it took everything she had not to fling herself into his arms to hug him. She had to give him personal space from *them*. And being in his embrace would just make her long for him as hers.

They'd talked a little about how it would be one step forward, two steps back with Micah, and that change always came with hiccups. Just like with the two of them.

Didn't she know it.

Her phone pinged with a text. Her mom.

Please thank Jesse again. Micah let me help with his math homework. And then he disappeared into his room and emerged an hour later to tell me his history essay was done. I asked him if he wanted to go to the diner and get new fries and now we're sharing a large order and each got a milkshake, too. Jesse is magic!

A photo showed her mom and brother in a booth at the Bear Ridge Diner, each holding up a fry.

Lila sent back a heart emoji. She handed Jesse her phone to let him read the text.

His smile was just as touching as the selfie of her mom and brother.

And yes, Jesse was magic. He'd helped bring Micah back to them after he'd almost gotten arrested. And he'd brought him back tonight. Literally and figuratively. He was responsible for that photo, for the two big smiles.

She thought about her reply to him when he'd texted that he'd found Micah. How true it was.

I don't what I'd do without you, Jesse. You're becoming indispensable.

The only part that wasn't true was *becoming*. He *was* indispensable.

"I love that," Jesse said, handing back the phone. "Whodathunk that I, Jesse Dawson, would be any help with family dynamics." He shook his head on a smile. "Must be Christmas working its magic on everyone."

"Nah, it's you," she said and leaned over to kiss him on the cheek before she could stop herself. Because she didn't want to stop herself. The urge was too strong. Plus, it was just a peck on the cheek.

Except at that exact moment, Jesse turned toward her.

And her lips landed on his.

He didn't pull away. Neither did she. He deepened the kiss, his hand going up to her cheek, which made her feel cared for. Wanted. Cherished, even.

"Lila, I want you so bad," he whispered, looking right into her eyes. "But I'm all over the place."

"I know," she said. "*We're* in a hiccup, that's all." She smiled gently and he did too.

"I don't want you to get hurt. *I* don't want to get hurt."

"Day by day," she said. "Right?"

The brief conversation seemed to be all either of them needed. She moved to straddle him, which his expression told her he appreciated.

He kissed her and then stood and picked her up in one motion, kissing her all the way to her bedroom. He laid her down on the bed and leaned over her, trailing his lips and tongue along her collarbone, then peeling off her sweater.

"So sexy," he whispered, his mouth on her breasts as she felt him unhooking her bra and then flinging it off.

She arched her back and moaned, her hands in his hair, then she moved them lower to the buckle of his belt. Then his zipper. He shimmied out of his jeans and soon all that was between them were two scraps of cotton.

He knelt in front of her and inched her underwear down, kissing her stomach and going lower and lower until she writhed and screamed in pleasure.

He quickly removed his sexy boxer briefs and got onto the bed with her, pulling her on top of him. She reached for a condom from the drawer of her bedside table and slid it on him, loving his deep groan.

And then all thought poofed from her head as she felt them become one.

A couple of hours later, when Lila awoke, Jesse was still beside her, fast asleep. Her heart gave a happy leap that he hadn't gone back to his room.

*I love you*, she thought, watching his muscled chest rise and fall. The feeling was as thrilling as it was scary.

Scary because she had no doubt he'd break her heart. And it would be all the worse because he would be in her life on a daily basis for years to come.

*I don't want you to get hurt...*

She inwardly sighed and stared out the window, flurries coming down in the moonlight. She tried to remember all Alina the psychic had said about happiness coming her way. *I see happiness for you. This man you're asking about...he is yours.*

Between that and the fact that Jesse hadn't left her bed for his own room gave her some hope back and she closed her eyes. She felt Jesse stir in his sleep and move even closer to her, his arm sliding over her chest.

*You are mine and I am yours*, she thought. Her own Christmas wish.

*Chapter Eighteen*

"So I have questions," Micah said the next day when he and Jesse and Lila were all in the barn, Wyatt asleep in his stroller in the far corner.

*Me too*, Jesse thought, glancing at Lila, who was spreading out straw on the far side of the new goats' pen. He woke up this morning in Lila's bed to find her gone—she was already downstairs with Wyatt, giving the baby his bottle on the overstuffed chair by the Christmas tree.

It had felt so strange to wake up in a woman's bed—*and* without her there. A first, really, on both counts. He'd always been the one to exit in the middle of the night, to find a reason to leave, to sneak out. When he'd opened his eyes and remembered where he was, he'd turned with anticipation to draw her into his arms only to discover that he was alone.

He'd been disappointed—and now suddenly knew how it felt.

The whole thing had been confusing too. His surprising reaction and then his usual need to get back on his own turf. Seemed like *two* steps forward and just one back. Their mornings were always a little hectic; one of them with the baby, the other needing to get the goats fed and the pen mucked out. Plus, they were both keeping a close eye on how the new goats were adapting. The four were being kept separate from Dolly and Lulu but close by to give them a chance to get used to the others' presence and scents.

Jesse had been busy with the new goats and a feed delivery and working on the separate pen for Sheldon, Cara, Bear and April. He'd barely had time to scarf down lunch. Then John Wakely had come by to check out the barn and make suggestions for where to best set up the milking station. Jesse and Lila had switched duties— he'd gone in the house to care for Wyatt, and she'd taken over on the farm. Then Micah had arrived and Jesse knew he always liked to play with Wyatt for a bit before starting work, so he'd come out to the barn with the baby.

They'd watched the new goats, who were still mostly standing around. Cara was on a low table and seemed to like that. Now, the two sets of goats were outside in separate pastures while the humans cleaned the pens.

"Ask away," Lila said, putting down her rake and turning to her brother.

Right. Micah's questions. Jesse was so caught up in his thoughts that he'd mentally disappeared for a moment.

"I was wondering about after the farm is all set up," Micah said, pausing with his rake. "What's gonna happen then?"

"What do you mean?" Lila asked. "About what?"

Micah resumed raking. "Mom said Jesse is staying in the guest room."

"Right," Jesse said, wondering where this was going. He hoped this wasn't about to get personal and feared it was.

"Well, what happens now?" Micah asked. "Are you going to get your own place, Jesse?"

There it was. Couldn't get more to the point—or more personal—than that.

Except if he'd asked if Jesse and Lila were a couple. Jesse didn't know how he'd begin to answer that.

"I'm set for the time being," he said to Micah. "The farm's just in the beginning stages. Right now, what we have are goats and the basics. Lila and I need to start getting into the nitty gritty of our research into milking equipment and the dairy business she wants to start. There's a lot left to do."

"How long exactly is *the time being*?" Micah asked, looking from Jesse to Lila and back to Jesse.

Oh man.

Jesse slid a fast glance at Lila, who was not looking at either him or Micah and suddenly raking very fast. She was as uncomfortable with this interrogation as he was. "Hard to say." He knew he couldn't leave it at that. Micah seemed to want to know something that the teen wasn't comfortable asking outright. Lila too, he knew.

He'd tell them both what he could say for absolute sure. "The guest room here is perfect for me right now. I can be right there for Wyatt. Lila and I can very easily share caring for him, and I can step right outside to the farm. So I have no plans to go anywhere."

"For the *time being*," Micah repeated. "However long *that* is."

Jesse would like nothing more than to escape inside with Wyatt, who was beginning to stir. It would soon be time for his bottle. But he forced himself to stay, to not make an excuse to leave, to not run from questions he couldn't answer. He'd see this through with Micah.

"Speaking of Wyatt," Micah said, glancing at his nephew, "I think you guys—you two, I mean," he added, wagging a finger between him and Lila, "should just get married."

Lila started coughing.

Jesse froze.

"I mean, you're the legal guardian," Micah said to Lila. "And you're the dad," he added, turning to Jesse. "To keep everything legal for both of you, you should get married."

"Legal for both of us?" Lila repeated, her face a shade paler than it had been a minute ago. "What do you mean?"

"I mean," Micah said, "that Jesse's paternity has been established. He's got the DNA results. So even though you're the legal guardian, that was before Jesse even knew he had a son."

Jesse swallowed, really not liking where this was going. He had a feeling Micah had overheard his mom talking to her own mother or sister. Their questions became his questions all over again. Which was absolutely okay—they had every right to talk about all this and want answers. Jesse just didn't have any—*for the time being*. His new least favorite phrase.

"So to protect you both, you should get married," Micah finished with a smile and a firm nod.

Wyatt, best baby on the planet, began to cry right then. Either because he didn't want them to marry for solely his sake or because he wanted to give Jesse the out he needed at the moment to leave the barn.

Who was he kidding? Wyatt would love to have his two parents married.

Do. Not. Leave. This. Barn.

Do. Not. Run.

See. This. Through.

He owed both Macks that.

Three. Including Wyatt. Who was a Dawson too. A Mack-Dawson.

Jesse looked at brother and sister. He was about to say something, he wasn't sure what exactly yet, when Micah went over to Wyatt, undid his harness and scooped him up.

"Aww, Uncle Micah's got you, little man," the teen said to the baby, giving him a snuggle. Then he looked at Lila and Jesse. "I'll take him to the house and change his diaper and make his bottle so you two can talk."

He left the barn fast, not giving either of them a chance to say a word.

"Wow," Jesse said. "If Micah wants to change Wyatt's diaper, you *know* he's serious."

Lila lifted her chin. "Well, he's also a teenager with out-there ideas, so..." She bit her lip. "I've got things covered here. Why don't you take a break. Go into town or something."

Or something. Meaning: I need space from this entire conversation *and* you.

"I *do* have some Christmas shopping to do," he said. *Your* gifts, as a matter of fact.

"Perfect," she said, and went farther into the pen, rearranging the logs.

She was done talking.

So was he.

But he couldn't get Micah's points out of his head.

Marriage. For legal purposes.

Interesting. The thought never would have occurred to Jesse, of course. But now that the subject had come up, he started thinking about it. He and Lila could marry for Wyatt's sake—and to protect them both.

When he looked at it like that, it didn't seem such an outrageous idea.

Jesse *would* go into town. And think—hard.

The moment Jesse's truck pulled out, Lila felt her shoulders relax.

Then they stiffened right back up again. Because the word *marriage* had gotten her thinking. About a long white gown with beading at the empire waist and a beautiful floaty veil, her hair in a chignon…a venue full of family and friends, and the man she loved at her side, taking vows to love, honor and cherish her forever.

As in love with Jesse Dawson as she was, Lila couldn't imagine marrying him for any reason other than love. Sometimes she thought he did love her. It was in the way he looked at her, spoke to her, treated her. The tenderness in his gaze and the passion in every movement as they made love.

The way he hadn't left her bed last night.

But then she'd think about the walls he had up. Walls she didn't think he wanted anyone blasting through. And until he did, he'd always keep her at a distance, on the outside; she'd never really get inside his heart.

She sighed and left the barn, needing to go talk to her brother. To let him know he couldn't throw around subjects like marriage.

She found Micah standing by the Christmas tree, a burp cloth on his shoulder as he patted Wyatt's back. An empty bottle was on the coffee table.

Wyatt let out a masterful burp.

"There it is," Micah said triumphantly. "I rule at Unclehood."

Even in Lila's mood, she had to laugh. "You absolutely do, Micah. You're wonderful with him." Micah might be emotional, but he knew what he was doing with Wyatt. He'd carefully watched how Lila changed him and made up his bottles and now he could do both himself. He'd asked smart questions. And now she could trust him to babysit for his nephew.

"Thanks for taking care of him," she said.

"Are you mad at me for what I said in the barn?" he asked, peering at her. "I think it's a great idea."

"You want me to marry a man who doesn't love me?" she asked. "That's your dream for your sister?"

"Well, when you put it that way," he said. "But I figure it's win-win."

She raised an eyebrow. "Um, how?"

"Wyatt gets his parents legally bound to each other. That's a good thing. And you'll be marrying a man *you* love." Her face must have expressed her surprise because Micah added, "It's so obvious, Lila."

She wondered if Jesse knew, then. The thought had her cheeks burning a little. Then again, he probably didn't know how she felt. His mind wouldn't go there. And if Jesse did consider that she'd crossed into that level of feeling for him, he'd rationalize his way out of the thought—that he was flattering himself or something. Yup, her secret was safe.

"Micah, have you been eavesdropping on Mom's private conversations with Aunt Raina and Gram?" *Legally bound* wasn't a term her seventeen-year-old brother would be using otherwise.

"Maybe. Just a little. Gram said you and Jesse might as well get married since it's so clear that you love each other and that you guys could figure that out along the way."

So clear we love each other? How was it clear to Gram? Her family knew her so well that she wasn't surprised they were aware she'd fallen hard for Jesse. But that he loved her? Come on.

Lila shook her head. "Our wise grandmother actually thinks we should marry first, ask questions later? Important questions about love?"

"Like I said, she knows you two are like madly in love already. Aunt Raina said you and Jesse might not know it or want to admit it, but they all know it."

Lila had to turn away for a second. She was close to tears. Because it was true for her and she wanted it to be true for Jesse more than anything in the world right now.

And her mom, aunt and grandmother were rarely wrong about anything.

She was about to blurt out to her brother that her one true love's name began with S, and as they knew now, Jesse's first name was Sheldon.

But she wasn't ready to tell her brother that a psychic had given her hope about him. She and Kate hadn't told anyone that it was Alina's *yes* that had given them that extra bit of confidence to make their dream come true to own a goat farm together. It was their sweet little secret. Once the farm was a success, *then* Lila would tell everyone.

Just like once she and Jesse were married and he was madly in love with her, she'd tell them about him being her one true love.

But she didn't see that day ever coming. Jesse was a marvel—as a man, as a father, as a cowboy—but when it came to romance and love…when it came to her…she had to be realistic.

By the time Jesse got to town, the word marriage echoing in his head, he was no closer to proposing to Lila that they marry for Wyatt's sake than he'd been in the barn. One thing he knew about marriage: it didn't last in his family.

His father lost his wife and it changed him to the point that he'd walked away from his own young son, unable to get too close to anyone or anything. His aunt's ex-husband had cheated on her for years and she'd been the last to know, apparently. Thank God Jesse hadn't known; he'd only been two when they'd gotten divorced. As long as he could remember, his father and his aunt had been on their own. His father had girlfriends he referred to over the years, but he'd never brought anyone home when he'd come visit for a week or two. And his aunt had seemed to have sworn off men for a long time. He was happy she'd found her second chance. And he hoped it would last.

He tried to clear his head, not wanting to think about any of this. He looked for a parking spot, but Bear Ridge's Main Street was crowded with holiday shoppers and there were no spots. He drove to the town green and found a spot there way at the end near the woods, but instead of pulling in, he found himself continuing on and making a left on Sycamore Road.

And then a right onto Oak Hill Drive.

Then another right onto Wood Street. He drove slowly to the end, where the woods made the street a dead end. There, the last house on the left, a small white cape. Where he and his father and mother had once lived.

He parked across the street and stared at the house. There was a car in the driveway, and he could see smoke rising from the chimney. The house was in better condition than the last time he'd dared drive over here to take a look. That was years ago and it had been in disrepair. He'd been so disappointed to find it looking that way that he'd vowed never to come back. There'd been a battered For Rent sign up then.

But someone had clearly bought the place and fixed it up. The siding was pristine and there was a nice stone walkway leading to the three steps, a fat green wreath on the door with a bow. The roof and windows twinkled with white lights. The place looked inviting.

He could barely connect the house to himself. But his father had been an entirely different person here. A family man. Happily married with a young child.

"I made most of your wishes for me happen, Dad," he said into the confines of his truck. "But that one about love and marriage—I just can't."

He stared hard at the house, trying to imagine his once-upon-a-time family inside, having dinner, putting him to bed, decorating the Christmas tree.

*You could give your son this*, he thought. Lila and himself. The three of them a family.

*It's the family that's the key,* he realized, his heart lifting a bit. *If you don't believe in love anymore, give Wyatt family.*

Family. The word echoed in his head.

Yes. Family was everything.

He thought about what Micah had said. Marrying for Wyatt's sake.

Marrying with purpose, an important purpose.

Of course. Now it made sense. Marrying for Wyatt's sake was exactly what he and Lila should do. They'd give him his two parents under one roof. They'd be able to easily share in taking care of Wyatt. In raising him. When there were problems, like Wyatt's fever, they could quickly rush him to the clinic together.

They'd be united, he and Lila, as Wyatt's co-parents. As a family.

When he thought of marriage in those terms, the word had an actual nice ring to it.

The marriage would absolutely have to be platonic, though. Or it wouldn't work. The point was to be partners in parenting Wyatt. Not lovers. Not a couple. Marriage for a *purpose.*

So far, they'd failed spectacularly at staying platonic. But marriage was a very big step. For it to work, they had to be platonic.

As partners, they'd be much less likely to disappoint each other. They'd remain on best behavior. No taking each other for granted the way couples did eventually. No big arguments. No cold shoulders.

Divorce was not an option.

Hating each other was not an option.

He took one last look at the house, suddenly not feeling the hurt as much, then drove back to Main Street. The spot at the far end of the town green was still there, and he nabbed it. He wrapped his scarf around his neck and pulled on his gloves and got out. The Santa hut's white lights twinkled in the setting sun. He hurried past it to the gift shop. He had presents to buy.

Including a ring for Lila. An engagement ring.

Knowing they'd be marrying for Wyatt, the thought of purchasing a diamond ring, which would normally represent love and forever, now stood for family.

In the gift shop, which had a large book section, he found a humor book about being a cowboy and a serious one about goat farming for Micah. He looked at all the displays on the counter—bracelets and earrings and—yes, there. Pins. American flags. Initials. WY for Wyoming.

A silver goat with horns.

The fact that he'd found exactly what he'd envisioned told him this whole idea—marriage—was fate. Micah had suggested it. And here was his goat pin.

He added the books to his basket. Lila had the goat farming one on her bedside table with a bookmark about three-quarters of the way through, so it must be a good read. He also got Micah a cowboy hat, a charcoal-colored one that would look great with his black down puffy jacket.

Lila was a little trickier. Nothing in the store fit what he had in mind—not that he even knew what he wanted to get her. He just knew it had to be special. He did see a charm bracelet with baby things on it—a tiny baby carriage, a rattle, a bottle—and he thought she'd like that. There was a circular display of charms to add with names and he spun it around until he found the Ls. There was a vertical Lila and he added that to his basket. He also saw a pair of flannel footie pj's in her favorite color: red. He couldn't resist getting matching plaid Christmas pajamas and wool socks with little bison all over them for his aunt and Bill. Almost done.

Wyatt. Nothing would ever be enough, he knew, but he got his son a few new pairs of pajamas and a baby-sized cowboy hat.

He got everything wrapped in red-and-green-striped gift bags and headed down Main Street for the jewelry shop.

Jesse went inside, the sight of all the bright and shining diamonds overwhelming him.

But as he looked in the case, he saw one that stood out, one he could imagine buying his own one true love if he believed in any of that. It was square, a carat, and had a diamond-studded band. It was a beauty.

He bought it, and watched the saleswoman clean it and put it in a pretty red velvet gift box.

His heart started hammering in his chest. He was going to propose marriage. For the sake of his child. *Their* child.

As he walked out with the ring, the other bags on his wrists, he barely recognized himself. He'd never had anyone to buy gifts for except for his aunt Bess and for the secret Santa grab bags at the ranches he'd worked at over the years. He stopped at the coffee shop and got a large latte to go, then drove over to the feed store parking lot and sat there for a while, thinking about the first time he'd seen Lila in this very spot. The first time he discovered he had a child he hadn't known existed.

On the drive back to the Double Sisters, he went over his proposal in his head, testing out the words on his lips. Nothing sounded right.

But the proposal *was*. That he believed with every bit of his guarded heart.

# Chapter Nineteen

Lila was putting Wyatt to bed when Jesse arrived home. He'd been gone for hours. All that talk of marriage from Micah must have really messed with Jesse. She'd heard the front door open, then his footsteps, then the door to the guest room open and close, and then he appeared in the nursery.

"Lila."

She turned around. He sounded serious.

"Everything okay?" she asked.

"Yes. Now," he said.

"Now?" she repeated.

He walked closer and stood at the edge of the crib, gazing down at his son. Wyatt was asleep, looking particularly baby-elf-like in his red-and-green-striped pj's. He touched a kiss to his fingertips and gently pressed it to Wyatt's forehead. Then he turned to her.

"Sorry for how long I was gone," he said. "I was doing some serious thinking."

"About?" she asked. "I hope you weren't worried about Micah and all that talk of marriage. He's just repeating stuff he heard my mom and aunt and grandmother discussing. You know how relatives can be."

"Actually, I don't," he said. "I *don't* know how big, fun, gabby families are. But I want to. I want that for Wyatt."

"Well, he has that in droves with the Macks. Even Micah contributes. As you know. I mean, telling us he thinks we should get married?" She let out something of a guffaw.

"I think it's a great idea," Jesse said.

She tilted her head. "What is?"

"That we get married. For Wyatt. To give him his family right here in the farmhouse. You, me and Wyatt."

She might have burst into tears if she wasn't so shocked. Right here, in front of her, Jesse Dawson, the man she loved, was telling her they should get married. But not for love. For the sake of their family, for the baby they shared.

She thought of herself as a fourteen-year-old talking with her twin sister about the kind of wedding she wanted. Kate had wanted—even back then—a destination wedding. Italy or France or Spain. Lila had envisioned a church wedding and a reception at a beautiful venue. Neither of their dream weddings had changed over the years either.

Not once in Lila's musings over her big day did she imagine her true love proposing what was basically a *marriage on paper*. For legal purposes, like Micah had been talking about.

"This is for you," he added, pulling something from his pocket.

A ring box. Red velvet.

*Oh no. Please don't let that be what I think it is. I won't be able to handle it.*

He opened the box, and the most beautiful ring she'd

ever seen sparkled back at her. If she could pick a dream ring, it would be this one.

"Let's do this, Lila. For Wyatt."

*If only he could say: Let's do this because I love you.*

She felt tears stinging her eyes and forced her gaze off the ring and onto Jesse. "I think your heart is in the right place." Sort of. "But I won't marry without love."

His face fell a bit. "These are extraordinary circumstances, though. We have a baby to raise. By getting married, we're giving Wyatt his parents, we're forming a family."

If she wasn't madly in love with Jesse, maybe she'd consider it. Because then maybe she would give up on love with her husband for the sake of the family. They'd be like housemates, she supposed, sharing a home, sharing parenthood. They'd be true partners with no potential romantic issues gumming up the works. No dashed expectations in that department. That was how Jesse had always wanted things between them. To protect not only Wyatt from parents who'd possibly be at each other's throats and the inevitable breakup, but to protect themselves from getting hurt.

"Let me ask you something, Jesse. If we got married, how would that work, exactly?"

"Like any marriage, just that we'd be in it more as partners in parenthood."

*Partners in parenthood*—Jackie and Jim's line.

"So, this would be a platonic marriage?" she asked, tilting her head. Waiting. Because she had a feeling he hadn't thought that far ahead. Like after the *I do* at the town hall. She doubted partners in parenthood in platonic marriages had church weddings and fun receptions full of family and friends.

He was silent for a moment. "Yes, definitely. That's the only way to be sure it'll work for the long haul."

"Except staying platonic hasn't worked for us. Wouldn't you agree? It's been pretty much up and down. The famous one step forward, two steps back."

After all, she'd thought him staying the night in her bed was progress. Instead, he'd turned around and proposed a paper marriage.

Though even thinking about marriage was a giant leap for Jesse Dawson.

"Once we're committed to each other in such a profound way," he said, "we can just focus on Wyatt. Being his parents."

"So tell me this, Jesse. Are you planning to step out on your platonic wife? Have discreet one-night stands?" She saw his cheeks flame a bit.

"Of course not."

"So you'll honor your vows," she said flatly. "And we'd have to write our own to fit the needs of the paper marriage. I mean, it's not like we can promise to love and cherish each other. Honor, maybe. We do have a solid base of respect for each other."

"Lila," he said, shifting a bit. Getting more uncomfortable, she could see. Good. "I think marriage is the right step for us."

"You're okay with giving up on love, Jesse. And quite possibly sex for the next eighteen years, which I find very hard to believe. But I'm not. I believe in love. I want it. That's the problem here. You can talk about the benefits of a platonic marriage for our situation. But it comes down to love for me."

He went silent again. "If you could just think about it," he finally said. "Sleep on it."

Ha. As if she'd ever sleep again. She'd be up tossing and turning all night for a long time to come.

She was going to have to tell him the truth—how she felt about him. If she dared hope he felt the same somewhere in that very guarded heart, she'd have to risk telling him she loved him.

"I'm going to be very open here," she said. "Because these *are* extraordinary circumstances. Including your proposal. I think you're the most amazing man, Jesse Dawson. You're such a good person, such a good father. And you're a good friend. You've gone above and beyond with Micah. Even Billy adores you."

"Why do I feel a *but* coming on?"

"*But*," she said. "I love you. Very much. And you don't feel the same."

She paused to give him a chance to tell her she was wrong. That he loved her too.

He didn't. He looked at her with compassion—which meant he didn't return her feelings—and she felt tears sting her eyes.

"Maybe you'll come to love me as a dear friend," she said. "Someone who's become like family—who *is* family. But I can't break my own heart by marrying you when you don't love me back. I'll want more from you as a husband, Jesse. I'll want love. I'll want sex with my husband. I'll want to be *happy*. But I won't be. And a distracted, hurting, longing parent isn't what Wyatt needs."

He looked down, then out the window, then closed

MELISSA SENATE243

his eyes for a moment. "I didn't know you felt that way about me, Lila. I..."

"Please don't say you're sorry."

"I am, though. I told you—the last thing I ever wanted was to hurt you." He closed the ring box, the snap of it echoing in her ears, and put it back in his pocket. "I understand, Lila."

Now she was having trouble controlling the tears. They slipped down her cheeks and she wiped them away.

"I think you should find somewhere else to live, Jesse," she said, her voice cracking—her heart breaking in two. She loved having Jesse here in the house. Living with her. Now she was telling him to leave. "I'm ready to take over the farm. We have a solid plan for going forward for the Double Sisters. So we'll just revamp the schedule of caring for Wyatt. Maybe we can just split the daytime hours, and we'll alternate nights." A sob rose in her throat and she squelched it.

"But I don't want to live somewhere else," he whispered, his own voice breaking. "I don't want to alternate nights. I don't want a custody schedule. I hate this."

"I hate it too. But like Jim and Jackie said, we just have to put Wyatt first and we'll be okay. I know you probably think I'm not putting him first by not accepting your proposal. But I actually am."

Jesse looked so defeated, like he didn't know how to turn this around.

He covered his face with his hands and then dropped back his head. "There has to be another way, Lila."

"We want very different things—fundamental things. What we each need to go forward to be happy is in complete opposition."

"If you could just *consider* the proposal," he began.

She shook her head. "I went to see Alina—the psychic—the other day," she blurted out. "She told me that my one true love's name started with *S*. I thought, well, how can that be when I'm in love with Jesse? And then you went ahead and named the goat after yourself. And I thought we really do have a chance."

"Oh, Lila," he said, reaching for her hand.

But she stepped back. If he touched her, she'd lose it, fall in a heap onto the floor and cry. "We can do right by Wyatt and right by each other by being committed to being the best parents we can be." How she sounded so calm and levelheaded was beyond her when all she wanted was to sob.

He walked over to the crib again and stared down at his son, his expression...anguished. She loved him so much that she wanted to take his pain away. But that would mean taking all that pain on herself and accepting Jesse's proposal. A fake marriage. And she couldn't. Like she'd said, a brokenhearted mess of a parent wasn't what Wyatt needed.

"Can I come over tomorrow to see Wyatt and we'll talk more?"

"Sure, of course. But we'll talk only about a custody schedule." She wondered where he'd go tonight. His cousin Reed's house, most likely.

Jesse closed his eyes for a moment and sucked in a breath, then looked at Wyatt again. He turned and left the nursery, his shoulders bunched, and she heard him go into the guest room.

She moved to the doorway of the nursery and watched him come out of his room with a duffel over his shoulder. At the front door, he stopped to put on his jacket and scarf looking so forlorn that her own heart ached worse.

And then a moment later, he was gone.

That conversation did not go like Jesse had thought it would.

After he left the farm, he drove around for a while, his heart so heavy he was surprised he didn't topple over against the steering wheel.

Custody schedule. Seeing his son every other this or that. This wasn't what he wanted. After his childhood, the thought of being separated from his son made him feel sick.

And love was the answer, apparently. If only he could love Lila, he could have everything he wanted. The family. His child. The woman he cared so much about.

But love—the romantic love Lila was talking about—his heart, mind, soul, everything in him had been long closed to that. He wasn't even sure he'd know what it felt like anymore—to be in love. He was very sexually attracted to Lila. He liked her very much. But the attraction wasn't welcome in a platonic marriage anyway. And Lila didn't want *like*.

As he drove aimlessly, Jesse realized his cousin Reed's house was close by, a small ranch not too far from the Double Sisters Farm. He could ring Reed's doorbell and ask if he could sack out in their guest room until he found a place to rent in town. The most important consideration was being close to the farm, close to Wyatt. Maybe Reed would even know of someone who had an available apartment. But as he drove down Reed's road, planning to stop and text a bit about his situation so that he didn't catch his cousin off guard by just showing up, he found himself driving right past Reed's place.

His aunt Bess's house. That was where he wanted to go. It was in town, so a good fifteen minutes from the farm, but that was nothing. He'd be close enough. Not down-the-hall close, but it would be okay for a few nights until he found a place of his own.

He needed to talk about all this, and no one did know him better than his aunt, except maybe Lila because of the intensity of being together practically 24/7 the past several days.

He pulled up to his aunt's house and parked out front. He sat in the truck for a while and didn't even notice Aunt Bess had come out until she was tapping on his window with a concerned expression.

"Can I crash here for a night or two?" he asked.

"Uh-oh," she said. "You okay?"

He shook his head.

"Come on in. I made loaded potato soup for dinner and have a lot left over. I remember you always loved potato soup."

"Still do," he said, getting out of the truck, the cold late December air almost refreshing on his hot face. He grabbed his duffel from the back and followed his aunt inside.

His soon-to-be uncle was dozing on the recliner in the living room, a book open on his lap.

Bess took off her long down coat and hung it up, then took his jacket. "Let's go into the kitchen."

He waited until she sat down beside him at the round table, a steaming bowl of soup in front of him with a warm roll—pure comfort food—a mug of tea for Bess, and then he launched into the whole story.

Bess had listened without interruption and now sipped her tea. "Well, I guess the question is: Do you love Lila? I suppose if you did, you would have told her so and saved the both of you all this heartache."

He paused, spoonful of soup midway to his mouth. "I know I care about her."

Bess nodded. "I haven't met Lila yet so I can only go on what you've told me—when you brought over Wyatt and tonight. It sounds to me like you're very much in love with the woman."

"I'm not out for love," he said. "I like her, I care about her. But getting involved just destroys relationships. And for Wyatt's sake, we can't afford to end up hating each other, throwing dishes at our heads."

"Why would that happen?" Bess asked. "Why not consider that the two of you might be very happy together?"

"Statistics," he pointed out.

"Or fear. Of finally opening yourself up again."

"There's a lot to lose," he said, taking that sip of soup. Suddenly, he didn't want to talk about his situation anymore. "The soup is delicious." He'd rather talk about the potato soup than about his feelings any day.

"Yes, there's a lot to lose. Either way," she said, leveling a look at him. A look that said, *You do realize that, right?*

Separate homes. Custody schedules. Visitation. His stomach twisted. That was what he had to gain, he thought, his shoulders knotting up.

"I always thought that someone would come along

who'd challenge you, Jesse. Someone who'd make you question the way you live, what you believe about the world. That someone was Wyatt. How you feel about that little baby, your child, dictates how you respond to him. What kind of father you are—"

"You said a minute ago it was fear holding me back from Lila. But I'm not afraid of Wyatt. Or of fatherhood. I love that baby with everything in me."

She reached over and set her hand atop his for a moment. "I know it. Love is very powerful, Jesse. But opening your heart to a baby and opening your heart to a woman are two very different things."

"Maybe I just should finish my soup," he said. "Before it gets cold. No one makes better potato soup than you, Aunt Bess, so I don't want to miss it."

She smiled and nodded. "I have faith in you. Everything will be okay, Jesse."

Faith that the brick walls surrounding his heart would crumble? Even if he decided that love would solve the immediate problems of becoming a part-time father, he couldn't just take a wrecking ball and knock down those walls. They'd have to come down by themselves. And they were fortress-strong.

The words *part-time father* echoed in his head.

What the hell was he going to do?

# *Chapter Twenty*

In the morning, after taking care of all six goats, which Lila was a bit buoyed to discover she could do on her own, she tearfully got Wyatt ready to go meet her family for coffee at the hair salon before it opened. She'd cried on and off for hours last night, letting herself feel what she felt, which was absolute heartache.

And when she'd woken, aware that Jesse wasn't in the guest room, that he wasn't outside with the goats or fixing fencing, she'd cried again. She'd texted her mom, with a broken heart emoji and a crying face, that Jesse had moved out, and her mom responded immediately to come to the salon before the clients poured in at nine thirty. Lila hadn't been sure about telling her family what was going on, but Micah was scheduled to work at the farm after school and he'd catch on that not only was Jesse not there but that he'd left.

All their hard work with her brother would go out the ole window. He'd be upset on both counts—and what it could mean for Wyatt. Lila didn't believe Jesse would leave Bear Ridge, but Micah's faith in what Jesse said and did would be shaken.

She sighed and snuggled Wyatt against her by the

front door. "Ready to go see the Macks?" she asked him. She'd put him in another set of Christmas pajamas, green fleece with red banding, and the cute green booties her parents had given him. Her father and grandfather would be back from their fishing trip late this afternoon, and instead of a joyful meeting between them and Wyatt's dad, that would probably happen without her there. They were all connected and so of course would meet. But everything was changing now. *Had* changed.

And the day after tomorrow was Christmas Eve.

Bah humbug.

She bundled up and got Wyatt into his snowsuit, her gaze latching on the little bronze horse pin. She let out a breath, then then headed out into the chilly morning air, snow flurries coming down from the gray sky. The forecast called for some icy rain late this morning, and she wanted to go see her family and get back before it hit.

She drove the fifteen minutes to town, her heart lifting a bit at the sight of the hair salon, knowing her family was there and waiting with open arms. She needed a hug.

Inside, her mom and grandmother rushed over to give those necessary hugs. Her mom went to the coffee station, which had a Keurig and several kinds of coffee, and made Lila a mug of chocolate mocha just the way she liked it. She pointed to the big covered platter of baked goods next to the sugar assortment. Lila shook her head; she had no appetite but she was desperate for a caffeine boost to help her think straight.

"Raina will be here any minute. She only has a half hour before she's on duty at the clinic, but she'll be here."

Good. Lila could use some of her aunt's wisdom. All the Mack women's wisdom. On how to get through this.

Once her aunt arrived and they were seated in the break room with their coffee, she told them everything, not leaving out any of the more personal details. She wanted them to have the whole story so that they could give her advice based on that.

"Oh, good golly," her aunt said, shaking her head. "That man is so stubborn! He's being his own worst enemy."

"If he doesn't love me, he doesn't love me," Lila said.

Gram stirred her coffee and pointed her spoon at Lila. "That man absolutely loves you."

"I think so too," her mom said. "From everything you just told us, he loves you so much he can't handle it."

"Yup," Raina said. "That's the real roadblock here. It's not whether or not he loves you, Lila. It's that he's so afraid to let himself feel what he feels that he's blocking you."

"I don't know. He really wants this marriage—this paper marriage. He's willing to go that far just so he can have Wyatt full-time, so we can *both* have him full-time. The legal thing is meaningful to Jesse. If he loved me, why would he make himself miserable by moving out and having to talk custody schedules? We might even have to go to court."

She wanted to believe what her relatives were saying. But if becoming a part-time father didn't blast through Jesse's defenses and walls, what would?

Jesse woke up in the very room he'd slept in when he'd stayed with Aunt Bess as a kid. She'd turned it into a guest room and nothing was the same as he remembered, which was probably a good thing.

Most of his world view had formed in his room. He

used to sit on the edge of his bed and look out the window, particularly at night, wondering where his father was exactly and what he was doing, especially when it had been a couple of months since he'd come to see Jesse, since he'd even called. Jesse figured he'd glommed onto his father as a great cowboy-adventurer to protect himself and his image of his father. But the real truth must have slipped inside him all along over the years. That his father had chosen a different life than the one waiting for him at home.

Fatherhood.

Sole parenthood.

Jesse likely reminded him of what he'd lost in his happy marriage to Jesse's mom, so his own brick walls had been erected around his heart and off he went.

Now Jesse was doing the same—but with Lila.

*Don't make my mistakes*...he recalled from the wish list.

About fatherhood. It was easier to keep his focus on that line than to think about the one about letting love into his life. His father hadn't done that either, though. There were always new names whenever his dad mentioned he'd be spending Thanksgiving or Christmas with a girlfriend.

His father had run from love because he was afraid of it. Just like his aunt was saying Jesse was doing now.

He smelled breakfast cooking in the kitchen, bacon and coffee mingling in the air. He forced himself out of bed and took a shower, the hot water and soap and shampoo helping to clear his mind. After breakfast with his aunt and her fiancé, during which Bess thankfully kept to tales of their RV trip, he said his goodbyes, his aunt walking him out.

"Promise you'll think about what we talked about?" she asked as he opened the door of his truck.

"I promise," he said. "I just don't know what will happen next."

She hugged him and made him also promise to call or text with updates. She was deeply invested in this, especially because of her great-nephew. He promised that too, and then headed toward town, planning to park somewhere and do an online search for apartments or houses for rent within fifteen minutes of the Double Sisters Farm. There were often former working ranches that had barns converted into one-bedroom apartments, and that would suit him fine.

But when he found a spot at the town green, crowded with people heading toward the Santa hut and the shops, the thought of finding another home was unbearable.

Part-time father. Two different houses. He couldn't stand it.

He texted Lila about what time he should come over, the connection to her, even over technology, making him feel a little better. He didn't like this separation—*feeling* so separate from her.

How about 2 pm before Micah gets here.

Lila's kid brother weighed heavily on him too. Jesse would just have to talk to Micah, assure him that he wasn't going anywhere, well, anywhere *far*. He'd be staying in town and could absolutely promise that.

See you then, he texted back.

He forced himself to make appointments to see a couple of furnished homes for rent. One a barn apartment and another a cabin on a big ranch, just like what he'd lived in the past twelve years. Just like he'd been used to. But he'd gotten used to something different, even if it was only a short while.

Over the next couple of hours he visited both homes and couldn't see himself in either. All he could think about was bringing Wyatt here for overnights on *his days*. These places would never be Wyatt's home, even temporarily. And he didn't want his son to have a temporary place where he went with his father.

The thought sent acid burning in his gut.

There was one inn in town, where the old boarding house used to be that he'd lived in with his father as a kid when Eddie Dawson had been in Bear Ridge. He could stay there. Or maybe find an Airbnb.

He just wanted to be back in Lila's guest room, in her farmhouse where he belonged.

Finally it was time to go see Lila. At least he'd get to see Wyatt too. She'd basically said they were done talking and all there was left was to discuss the custody schedule.

Maybe she'd given some thought to the marriage proposal.

He doubted it.

As he came up the drive, he saw Lila standing outside with Wyatt in the chest carrier on her red down jacket. They stood in front of the pasture fence, watching Dolly and Lulu, who were eyeing the next pasture where the four newbies were.

He looked at Sheldon. Named for himself. And Lila's one true love.

A chill ran up his spine. He'd never been Sheldon. The *S* was just a formality. So... He shook his head at himself for how he was trying to get around this. He'd thought about it last night. The psychic's pronouncement couldn't be a coincidence. There had been twenty-five other letters to choose from.

He stared at Lila, beautiful, kind, passionate Lila. His heart was thumping at the sight of her. He felt so much for her, cared so deeply. If only she could agree to his proposal.

He walked up to her, his chest feeling tight. "Can I hold him?" What he wanted was to hold Lila too, wrap them both in his embrace, never let them go.

They were his family. Wyatt, of course, but also Lila.

"Sure," she said, taking him from the carrier and handing him over.

*Ahhh*, he thought, once he had Wyatt in his arms. He felt a bit like Popeye having his spinach in those old cartoons and getting a burst of strength.

But he didn't feel *much* better. He didn't want to leave again without Wyatt. And he was sure Lila wouldn't want Wyatt gone today.

He'd hurt her enough.

He didn't want to leave at all.

"I was thinking and talking with my family," she said. "Maybe it's best that we alternate days with Wyatt. I can get a lot done at the farm with him in the carrier or in his stroller. And when it's your day with him, I'll just look at it as having even more time to get the farm ready for the milking equipment and getting the dairy business plan solidified."

His stomach twisted. For a moment he couldn't find

his voice past the lump in his throat. "Every other day with my son." He shook his head. "I hate it, Lila."

"It'll feel awful for me too," she said. "I haven't been away from Wyatt for a night in two months."

He thought of all she'd been through. The loss of her twin. Inheriting a month-old baby to raise on her own. Having Wyatt's father suddenly walk into her life—and going through all the ups and downs since meeting Jesse. And there'd been *a lot*.

She deserved so much more than this.

"You can have Christmas Eve and Christmas morning," he said, his heart cracking. "I can come get him Christmas afternoon, if that's all right." The thought of not seeing his son at all on Christmas was unbearable.

"I appreciate that," she said, her voice breaking some.

God, this was hard. Awful.

Not too long ago, neither of them had wanted anything to do with Christmas and all it brought up for them. Now, he knew it would be hard on Lila to be without Wyatt for just several hours on the holiday. And Jesse would just have to get through Christmas Eve and Christmas morning without his baby son.

"I was wondering," he said, dropping a kiss on Wyatt's head. "Have you thought about the marriage proposal at all?" He could see her eyes get misty and could kick himself for asking. If she had thought of it, she would have said so.

"I'm not open to marriage without love," she said.

He sucked in a breath and nodded, his heart heavy, his shoulders knotted, his gut burning.

She looked at him, her green eyes so sad, then shifted her gaze to Wyatt and ran a finger down his cheek.

"Since I'll have Wyatt tomorrow for Christmas Eve and Christmas morning," she said, "I think you should take him today. I hate the thought of him leaving here at all, but it feels fair."

Relief washed over him. Driving away from the Double Sisters Farm without his son would have done him in.

"His baby bag and stroller are in the barn," she said. "The bag has everything he needs for an overnight, as always." She quickly kissed Wyatt on his cheek, and then she ran inside the house. He could imagine her standing just inside the door, crying.

He felt like absolute hell.

He hoisted Wyatt in his arms and went into the barn and settled him in the stroller. The bag was in the basket. He checked it—bottle, formula, burp cloth, several diapers, a folded baby blanket, two sets of pj's and a couple of toys.

This was it. The start of sharing custody. Of having two places to live, not that Jesse had a home set up.

Exactly not the Christmas he wanted to give his child.

Heart heavy, Jesse headed out to his truck. Time to go.

Where, he had no idea. He had the rest of the day to figure that out. Maybe for tonight they'd stay at Bess's. His aunt would love that, and Jesse would feel like at least he was giving his son family and a real home for the night. Plus he could give Bess and Bill their gifts.

Which reminded him that he needed to drop off the rodeo tickets for Scotty and his dad in the family's mailbox. The thought of the boy's surprised smile was enough to make Jesse smile.

As he settled Wyatt into his car seat, he looked over at the farmhouse and wondered if Lila was watching from a window. He wanted to rush inside and hold her. The urge was overwhelming.

He drove away, his foot light on the gas. He felt like he was taking Wyatt away. Away from his beloved aunt Lila, away from his home.

He forced himself to drive.

He went back to town and dropped off the rodeo tickets. With Wyatt in his stroller he walked around the park for a little while, the overcast skies threatening that forecasted rain. When Wyatt fell asleep, he headed over to the diner and took a table in the back just as the rain started. He got Wyatt out of his snowsuit without waking him—a miracle—and then resettled him in the stroller.

Jesse barely had an appetite but ate half a BLT and stared out the window at the mountain range in the distance, the rain making it hard to see out, which was fine with Jesse. That mountain was the very one he used to look at from his bedroom window at Bess's all the time and wonder about his dad, where he was. As a little kid, he imagined his father was camped out on the summit, having chased a runaway cow or goat.

He thought about Lila at the farm. She'd have brought in the goats before the rain. Normally he would have been there with her, helping with that, making sure all the windows were shut tight.

He sighed.

His phone pinged with a text.

Micah.

Lila slipped and fell on a patch of ice near the barn. She's out cold and Dr isn't sure of anything. She's at the clinic's ER. Hurry!

Jesse's heart seized and he bolted up, hurrying to get Wyatt back in his snowsuit, the silver pin of the horse glinting under the setting sun shining in from the window behind his table. He quickly left a twenty under his water glass.

*The doctor isn't sure...*

No. No, no, no.

This couldn't be happening. Lila was okay. She had to be okay.

*You mean the world to me, Lila. Please be okay.*

He'd been told fear was keeping him from opening his heart to Lila. To love.

But he knew what fear felt like; it felt like this. The terror gripping his heart, his mind.

*I can't lose you. We can't lose you*, he thought desperately, looking at their baby son.

On my way, he texted back. I'm right in town. Be there in a few. What did the doc say?

No response.

She'll be okay, right? Jesse texted.

Micah didn't text back.

His heart hammering in his chest, Jesse rushed out of the diner with Wyatt in his stroller, running the few blocks back to his truck. He could barely think.

She *had* to be okay.

# *Chapter Twenty-One*

When Jesse arrived at the clinic with Wyatt, he rushed past that blasted Christmas tree. He was surprised he didn't see any of the Macks in the waiting room. Were they in her room?

He stopped at the front desk and gave Lila's name. Room 2A. He ran down the hall, the door to 2A slightly ajar.

He sucked in a breath and pushed open the door, his hands trembling.

*Please*, he sent heavenward. *Please, please, please.*

Lila was reclined on the hospital cot, eating a slice of pie and laughing at something Micah just said about Cara, the new goat.

Wait—*what*?

Lila didn't have a mark on her. Not even a bandage.

They both turned as he entered the room, Lila clearly surprised to see him, Micah with a sheepish expression on his face.

Jesse was very confused. "Micah? I thought Lila was unconscious and the doctor wasn't sure of her condition."

"Yeah, about that," Micah said, his green eyes twinkling. "I lied. But lied for good. Bye!" He shot up and ran out of the room before Jesse could blink. Or scream bloody murder at him.

For a moment, Jesse didn't get it. He couldn't quite think straight.

Lila was okay. She wasn't unconscious.

He hadn't lost her.

Micah had made it up.

Jesse's hands had stopped trembling, he realized.

"Oh boy," Lila said, shaking her head. She set down her plate on the swing-out tray over her bed. "Micah didn't mention any of that to me. Sorry."

"I'm just glad you're okay." His heart was just starting to get back to its normal rate. "I mean, you are, right? You're okay?"

"I'm totally fine. Looks like Micah came up with an over-the-top ruse to get you here, to get us talking, I assume. I told Micah what happened between us and he didn't take it well. And a minute later, I slipped on the stupid ice."

He let out one hell of a breath. "I was so scared, Lila. So damned scared."

"Well, I'm fine," she said, that same sadness from earlier in her voice. "Not a scratch on me." Her gaze went to Wyatt in his stroller. "Can you bring him over to me? I need to hold him."

"What happened?" Jesse asked. "You did actually fall on ice by the barn?"

She nodded. "I slipped and Micah was right there and caught me just as I was about to go down. My head knocked against the fence, not hard, but he called Raina and my aunt insisted I come to the clinic to get checked out for a possible concussion in the ole abundance of caution."

"He texted me that you were unconscious. That the doctor didn't know anything yet." He closed his eyes and covered his hands with his face. "I thought the worst."

"Honestly, I'm fine," she said. "Doc said so." She snuggled Wyatt against her, kissing his soft cheek. She was looking everywhere but at Jesse. He couldn't blame her.

"Lila," he began, no idea of what would come out of his mouth.

A rush of memories came over him. Seeing Lila for the first time in the feed store parking lot. Seeing Wyatt. The *pin*.

The moment Lila had confirmed that Wyatt was his child.

The DNA results.

Kissing Lila.

Making love to Lila.

Trimming the Christmas tree, the two ornaments representing his life on the back.

And everything that had happened last night. And then this morning.

And just ten minutes ago, when he thought he'd lost her.

He'd been scared out of his mind.

Because he loved her. So damned much.

*I love you*, a voice said deep inside him.

He gasped, and she looked at him. His heart was thumping, butterflies letting loose in his stomach.

"What's wrong?" she asked.

He tested the words in his head. *I love you. I love you. I love you.*

A rush of warmth overwhelmed him and settled in his chest. A good warmth.

*I love you, Lila*, he thought again.

He loved her. He'd always loved her.

"Jesse?" She was staring at him, concern in her beautiful green eyes.

He walked closer to the bed and sat down in the chair, leaning close to her. "I love you, Lila," he whispered. "So much. I love you."

Now Lila gasped.

"I'm sorry that it took thinking I could lose you to get it into my hard head just how much you mean to me," he said. "How much I love you."

Her eyes misted with tears again. "I wasn't sure I'd hear you say those words."

"I love you. I'll scream it from every rooftop in Bear Ridge."

She laughed. "You can just whisper it in my ear."

He kissed her. "Lila Mack, will you marry me for all the right reasons? Especially the fact that I'm deeply in love with you and want to spend the rest of my life showing you how much."

Her smile lit up her beautiful face. "My answer is yes," she said. "You made my Christmas wish come true."

"And mine," he said. "And we both made my father's last wishes come true. Every one of them."

He couldn't know what number five was going to be since his father hadn't written anything after the five. But he had a good guess: *Choose happy.* It was how his dad used to sign off—from phone calls and texts and the occasional postcard. *Choose happy.*

He'd always hated that because Jesse thought it meant that his father was choosing happiness over his child.

But his father *hadn't* been happy. Not a day since his wife, Jesse's mother, had died.

Eddie Dawson hadn't chosen happy at all.

He was asking his son to, though; Jesse would bet anything that it would have been number five if he could have written it down.

His dad had asked Jesse, in the form of the list of wishes, to live life differently than Eddie had. To choose home, love and a dog.

Jesse had.

*I get it, Dad*, he thought, touching a hand to his heart for a moment. *I understand now.*

*And yes, I'm going to choose happy. And accept that I love Lila Mack with all my heart. And* give *her that heart.*

"I have a little something for you again," he said, pulling the velvet box from his pocket. He opened it to reveal the diamond ring. "Is it my imagination or is it sparkling much brighter now?"

She laughed. "It is for sure."

He slid it on her ring finger. "Merry Christmas," he said.

"Merry Christmas," she whispered, her eyes misty with tears.

Just as they were sharing one hell of a kiss, Micah came back, the entire family behind him.

"Am I in trouble?" Micah asked, looking from Lila to Jesse.

"The opposite," Jesse said. "I owe you, in fact."

Lila held up her ring and there were claps and cheers and hugs. Micah was wolf-whistling and telling everyone this was all his doing. Lila's mom was talking a mile a minute about the big engagement party she'd throw, his aunt and fiancé and all the Dawsons would be receiving fancy invitations.

"You did good, Jesse," Lila's grandmother said, pulling him into a hug.

He smiled and hugged every Mack in the small room.

Suddenly, the man who'd had one relative left in the world now had this huge family—Macks and Dawsons alike.

And this Christmas would be one he'd tell his son about for years to come.

# *Epilogue*

Two weeks later, Lila walked down the aisle to her handsome groom, her father escorting her. The Mack men, her dad and grandfather, had returned the night Lila had accepted Jesse's second marriage proposal, and boy, had they been in for a big surprise. Lila's mom and grandmother had decided to keep the big news—that Wyatt's father had come into their lives—until they'd come home. And given the very happy ending, everyone was glad they had.

Lila was having the wedding she'd always dreamed of. She wore a long white satin gown with beading at the empire waist, her mother's veil and her twin sister's dangling pearl earrings that Kate had bought on a trip they'd taken to Jackson Hole a few years ago. On her wrist was the charm bracelet Jesse had given her for Christmas.

The holiday had been so special—Wyatt's first—and they'd all exchanged way too many gifts with Macks and Dawsons, including Bess and Bill, who Lila had been so happy to meet. They'd welcomed her to the family just as her family had welcomed Jesse to theirs. Bess had even accompanied her and her mother, Aunt Raina and Gram to look for a wedding dress, and when they'd all cried at the very first dress she tried on, her very favorite, she knew without a doubt it was the one.

And Lila had been touched to notice that Jesse had moved his two ornaments to the front of the tree where he could see them. He'd even said that for next year's tree, he'd add many more personal ornaments. They didn't quite need the "hope" tree that Aunt Bess had begun all those years ago, but it had become Mack-Dawson tradition and they would continue it with its special meaning.

Today they'd exchanged wedding rings, and on Jesse's right-hand ring finger was his father's wedding band. She was so moved at how he'd made peace with his father's choices.

Jesse had decided on a tuxedo for himself and Wyatt, and her heart almost couldn't take the adorableness. Wyatt had been part of the ceremony, held by his father as they'd repeated their vows.

The beautiful stone church at the far end of Main Street had been full of her and Jesse's family and friends. He'd surprised her by wanting to invite several cowboys he'd been close to over the years, and they'd all come, happy to witness Jesse Dawson getting hitched and to meet his baby son.

Alina had come too. At the reception, held in the gorgeous ballroom at the Dawson Family Guest Ranch lodge, with its huge arched windows, she'd hugged Lila and told her that life would bring her joy. This time around, Lila hadn't even had to ask. She *knew*. Because she'd married the man she loved, the man who loved her, and because they were raising their beloved Wyatt.

"When we give Wyatt a baby brother or sister," Lila

said as they danced the first dance to a song they both loved, "I think the name should begin with *S*."

Jesse laughed, his blue eyes twinkling. "But we should call the baby by his or her middle name. Keep up the family tradition."

She leaned up to kiss him, so happy her heart might burst.

"Can I cut in?" asked a very squeaky high-pitched voice.

They both turned and smiled.

Standing there was Micah, so grown-up in his charcoal suit—the tiny silver goat pin on the lapel—holding up Wyatt in front of his face.

"What's a baby got to do to dance with his parents around here?" Micah continued in his squeaky voice, still holding Wyatt up.

Jesse laughed and took Wyatt in his arms. Then the three of them swayed to the slow ballad, a family brought together by the miracle of the holiday season and the magic of love.

\* \* \* \* \*

# HARLEQUIN
### Reader Service

# Enjoyed your book?

Try the perfect subscription for Romance readers and get more great books like this delivered right to your door.

See why over 10+ million readers have tried Harlequin Reader Service.

**Start with a Free Welcome Collection with free books and a gift—valued over $20.**

Choose any series in print or ebook. See website for details and order today:

# TryReaderService.com/subscriptions